A TIMELESS Romance ANTHOLOGY

UNDER THE Mistletoe COLLECTION

SIX CONTEMPORARY ROMANCE NOVELLAS

A TIMELESS Romance ANTHOLOGY

UNDER THE Mistletoe COLLECTION

SIX CONTEMPORARY ROMANCE NOVELLAS

Cindy Roland Anderson
Annette Lyon
Julie Coulter Bellon
Sarah M. Eden
Heather B. Moore
Jennifer Griffith

Mirror Press

Copyright © 2015 by Mirror Press, LLC
Print edition, 2016
All rights reserved

No part of this book may be reproduced in any form whatsoever without prior written permission of the publisher, except in the case of brief passages embodied in critical reviews and articles. This is a work of fiction. The characters, names, incidents, places, and dialogue are products of the authors' imaginations and are not to be construed as real.

Interior Design by Rachael Anderson
Edited by Cassidy Wadsworth, Julie Ogborn, Kelsey Down, and Megan Walgren

Cover design by Mirror Press, LLC
ShutterStock Image #167748182
Copyright: Kichigin, used with permission

Published by Mirror Press, LLC
TimelessRomanceAnthologies.blogspot.com

ISBN-10: 1-941145-91-4
ISBN-13: 978-1-941145-91-3

TABLE OF CONTENTS

Forgotten Kisses
by Cindy Roland Anderson

The Last Christmas
by Annette Lyon

Truth or Dare
by Julie Coulter Bellon

Holiday Bucket List
by Sarah M. Eden

Christmas Every Day
by Heather B. Moore

First (and Last) Christmas Date
by Jennifer Griffith

MORE TIMELESS ROMANCE ANTHOLOGIES

Winter Collection
Spring Vacation Collection
Summer Wedding Collection
Autumn Collection
European Collection
Love Letter Collection
Old West Collection
Summer in New York Collection
Silver Bells Collection
All Regency Collection
Annette Lyon Collection
Sarah M. Eden British Isles Collection
Mail Order Bride Collection
Road Trip Collection
Blind Date Collection
Valentine's Day Collection

Forgotten Kisses

Cindy Roland Anderson

OTHER WORKS BY CINDY ROLAND ANDERSON

Fair Catch
Discovering Sophie
Under the Georgia Moon
Just a Kiss in the Moonlight
Christmas in Snow Valley Anthology
Spring in Snow Valley Anthology
Summer in Snow Valley Anthology

One

Madison Taylor didn't like Hollywood. She wasn't particularly fond of Christmas either. Unfortunately, she not only lived in Hollywood, it was also her livelihood. At least the Christmas holiday only came around once a year, which, thankfully, would be over in a week.

Grabbing her double shot latte, she took one last gulp before exiting her car. She needed the jolt of caffeine if she was going to make it through the day. Charlotte, her eight-month-old niece, had kept her up most of the night. Who knew cutting three teeth at one time could be so traumatic?

She hurried onto the set, knowing if she wasn't there before Derrick Jamison, AKA Sir Lancelot, he would threaten to have her fired. Again. She doubted he'd ever go through with it because like it or not, she made him look good week after week, and they both knew it.

Rifling through her purse, she tried to locate her ID badge. It's not like the security guard didn't know who she was. He just liked giving her a hard time since she refused to go out with him.

"Morning, Miss Sunshine," Kevin said with a smirk. "Have a rough night?"

"Nope." She yanked out her badge and held it out for him to inspect. "This is a new look for me."

Kevin eyed her dark hair pulled into a messy ponytail—it wasn't artfully messy, just flat-out the best she could do this morning—and then scanned the rest of her. She had zero makeup on but had moisturized her olive-toned skin lest Beth, the makeup lady, saw her and yelled at her again for being so irresponsible with her skin. His eyes lingered on her T-shirt that was one size too small and emphasized her curves that were not surgically enhanced. Laundry hadn't been a high priority this weekend, and the fitted shirt had been her only clean option.

She snatched her ID badge out of his hand. "May I please go in?"

"I like your new sexy I've-just-gotten-out-of-bed look." The corner of his mouth lifted. "I'd like it even better if I actually got to see—"

"Kevin!" she said, hoping to get his mind out of whatever gutter he'd just ventured into. "Derrick is going to kill me if I don't get in there before he does."

"Derrick?" His eyes flashed with humor. "You haven't heard?"

"Heard what?" She didn't follow the gossip columns on the exploits of the *Forgotten Camelot's* cast. There were too many scandals to keep up with, especially involving Derrick.

"Derrick was caught messing around with a seventeen-year-old fan girl, whose father happens to be an executive with our rivaling network. Our Sir Lancelot is no longer out gallivanting the kingdom, looking for King Arthur. He's in jail and won't be getting out for quite some time." Kevin shook his head. "The network had no choice but to fire him. I mean the guy was stupid enough to send out a Snapchat of him and his jailbait girlfriend skinny dipping in his pool."

Madison splayed a hand across her stomach, feeling sick inside. As much as she detested her job as Sir Lancelot's costume designer, mainly because he was an egotistical jerk, the pay was double what was standard in the industry due to the popularity of the show. She knew she wouldn't be able to find another gig like this one anytime soon. "They just started season two. How can they fire Lancelot?"

"Don't worry," Kevin said irritably. "They found another actor to replace him. I thought I was a shoo-in for the role, but they gave the part to some British guy. They claim he looks similar enough to Derrick that fans won't care. Plus, he's wildly popular with the ladies and will bring in viewers from across the pond."

The nausea gripping her middle ebbed away as the realization that she still had a job sunk in. She was never going to complain about her job again. She loved her job. Actually, there were quite a few aspects about the job she loved.

For one, in the cutthroat industry of film and television, she was Sir Lancelot's costume designer for the weekly TV series *Forgotten Camelot*. The popular show each Saturday night featuring the characters of the once shining city of Camelot who were cursed by Morgan le Fay to live in present-day New York. King Arthur and his court had forgotten who they were. All except Sir Lancelot—also known as Lance Knightly—the star of the show.

"That's fantastic!" She motioned for Kevin to let her in. "I need to get in there so I don't leave a bad impression with the new guy."

Kevin rolled his eyes dramatically. "Don't get too excited." He pressed a button to unlock the gates. "I heard he's already taken."

"I could care less if he's taken or not. I just need my job." Madison slipped through the opening. "Besides, you know I don't date actors."

"You say that now, but once you get a look at the British bad boy you'll change your mind."

Madison froze. British bad boy was a name her one-time fiancé had earned after leaving NYU. Swallowing, she clutched her stomach again. "Um, so what's this guy's name?"

Please don't say it. Please don't say it.

"Caleb Matthews."

Two

HIDDEN BEHIND A PARTITION in the dressing room, Madison peeked at the man sitting in the chair getting his makeup done. She wished she'd taken the time to do her own makeup this morning. At least the free lash extensions Beth had talked her into a couple of weeks ago enhanced her blue eyes, even without applying mascara.

The guy laughed, and she knew this wasn't a bad dream. Caleb Matthews, the one man she'd vowed to never speak to again, sat just yards away in her dressing room . . . er, his dressing room.

He looked good. His dark brown hair still had a slight wave to it, although it was a little shorter now. Beth moved out of the way, and Madison quickly pressed her back against the wall to avoid being seen.

Wasn't her life already hard enough? Just when her parents had finally reconciled their differences and gotten back together a year ago, they had died in a car accident. Madison had been forced to leave her internship with the elite designer India Marcos in New York and return to California to take care of her pregnant younger sister, Jenny.

Ms. Marcos had liked Madison, and had connections in Hollywood. She'd somehow managed to get Madison on as one of the costume consultants right before the pilot of *Forgotten Camelot* aired.

Her nose started to twitch, and she rubbed her finger underneath to prevent the sneeze. Seconds later her anonymity was blown.

"Madison?" Beth asked. "Is that you?"

Tugging on her too-small shirt, she stepped out from behind the partition. "Yeah. Good morning, Beth."

Caleb stared at her, that little smirk she'd once loved hovering on his lips. "Madison Taylor," he said in his sexy British accent. "It's good to see you again, love."

Her heart skittered a little at his term of endearment, but she quickly reminded herself he was British. British people always called people "love."

"You two know each other?" Beth asked.

"Yes, Madison and I were—"

"Acquaintances," Madison said, cutting him off. "At NYU."

Thankfully he didn't correct her. Just gave her that annoying little smirk again.

"Hello, Caleb." She moistened her lips, because her mouth had gone impossibly dry. "I guess we'll be working together."

"Yes." He stood up, removing the plastic cape draped over his shirt. "I'm looking forward to it." His eyes traveled over her, and the smile on his face grew, carving the dimple in his left cheek. "You look good."

She gave a short, sarcastic laugh and rolled her eyes. "Oh, please. I look like I was up all night with a baby, which I was, by the way."

The smile on his face fell, and his eyebrows bunched together. Obviously, no Botox for this guy.

"You . . . you have a baby?" he stammered.

Madison enjoyed the shocked look on his face. *That's right. I haven't been pining away for you the past two years.* It was evil to make him believe she had a baby, but she couldn't help herself.

"Her name is Charlotte, and she's eight months old."

Beth lifted a perfectly plucked eyebrow, and Madison hoped the woman wouldn't clarify her actual relationship with her niece.

"Who is Charlotte's father?" Caleb asked with a slight edge to his voice.

"I'm not really sure."

It was a completely true statement, which, incidentally, made Caleb's face go a pasty white. Madison's sister, Jenny, was a train wreck when it came to men, and she wasn't sure which loser had fathered Charlotte.

"Charlotte is Madison's niece," Beth said, ruining the perfect moment.

Caleb's hazel colored eyes narrowed. "She's your niece, then?"

"Yes." It was her turn to smile. She'd really had him going. "Jenny and Charlotte live with me."

"Jenny's a mum?" he asked, the color coming back. "She can't be. The last time I saw her she was only beginning her secondary school."

"A lot has happened in two years."

"Yes." He cleared his throat and glanced away. "Quite."

"I'll be back to touch up your makeup once you have your costume on, Mr. Matthews," Beth said.

"Beth, please call me Caleb," he said, giving her his trademark smile that revealed his charming dimple.

She grinned. "Okay, Caleb. I'll check back soon."

Beth left, and it was then Madison noticed they had an audience. Several girls working as extras on the set were all making eyes at the new Lancelot. Derrick hooked up regularly with the newbies. She wondered if Caleb would do the same.

Glancing back at Caleb, she found him watching her closely. "We need to talk. Meet me for drinks tonight?"

"Nope." She tried not to smile at the look of shock on his face. "I already have plans."

Her plans involved a cranky baby while Jenny worked the night shift as a CNA at a nearby nursing home. Caleb didn't need to know that.

"Madison . . ."

Before Caleb could say more, Gerard, the director of *Forgotten Camelot,* invaded the dressing room. "Sir Lancelot has never looked better." He winked at Madison. "Right, Mad?"

Ugh. She hated that stupid nickname. She clamped her lips tightly and gave the director a quick nod of her head. Then she picked up her notebook and found a quiet corner to go over her notes.

Gerard laughed at something Caleb said, and she realized he didn't seem too upset about Derrick's sudden departure from the show. Of course, Derrick had been difficult to work with, which probably meant everyone else on the set was also happy with the change.

Everyone except her.

Unable to help herself, her gaze drifted over to the man she'd be forced to work with on such an intimate level. She studied his handsome profile. She knew what it felt like to caress his face, knew the feel of the whiskers shadowing his jaw whenever he'd kissed her. Her fingertips tingled at the memory. So did her lips.

Forgotten Kisses

Gerard slapped Caleb on the back. "We'll be shooting action scenes the next couple of days, so not a whole lot of dialogue for you to memorize."

The director walked away, and Madison dropped her eyes to study the notebook just as Caleb turned to look at her. Her insides quivered like the Jell-O Jenny would sometimes feed Charlotte.

Still sensing his gaze on her, she willed herself not to respond. She did not have feelings for Caleb Matthews. Well, other than loathing him. Annoyance rushed in, and she snapped her eyes over to meet his. "Would you stop staring at me?"

The corner of his mouth twitched. "Sorry, love, but you're even more beautiful than I remembered."

"I threw my hair into a ponytail this morning and neglected to put any makeup on. You're an even bigger liar than I remember."

The humor on his face vanished. "I never meant to lie to you, Madison."

"So you said."

His lips flattened, and she saw the muscle in his jaw tighten. "And it's still true."

An ache inside her chest made it difficult to draw in a breath. Deep down she knew he was right, but a lie of omission was still a lie. And that terrified her. Her father had been an expert at deception, which Madison blamed on his acting skills.

"You have to be ready in fifteen minutes, Caleb." She closed her notebook. "Derrick was a tool and never cared if he delayed production. I hope you're not like that."

Thankfully she got a phone call and walked away to answer it. It reminded her she had a job to do, and working with her ex couldn't possibly be harder than working with

Derrick. She just needed to act like a professional and leave the past in the past.

Three

THIS DAY WAS FINALLY OVER, and Madison was exhausted. Thanks to several wardrobe malfunctions, she'd been able to avoid Caleb for most of the day. She doubted tomorrow she'd be so lucky.

Madison gathered up her belongings, anxious to get home. She just hoped Charlotte was in a better mood. With her sister now working the night shift, Madison took over the care of Charlotte the minute she got home so Jenny could sleep for a few hours without having to wake up to care for her baby.

Finding her keys, she made her way to the parking lot. William, the sweet guy who played the part of Merlin, spotted Madison and hurried to catch up.

"How about I walk you out?" he said, winking at her.

"Thank you."

William was like the father she would've wanted and he frequently escorted her to her car.

"How was it working with Derrick's replacement?"

William asked, holding a door open for her. "He sure seems like a nice guy."

He was a nice guy, and so likeable. Madison didn't want to admit it though for fear she'd find herself hopelessly in love with him again. "It was okay."

"Just okay, huh," William said with a chuckle. "Gossip travels fast, and a little birdie told me you two were once engaged."

"Beth needs to keep her mouth shut." The woman had connected with Caleb and somehow managed to get a whole bunch of information out of him. When Beth had asked why they broke up, Madison overheard Caleb say it had been a big misunderstanding.

"So it's true?" William opened another set of doors.

She glared at him, making his smile widen. "No comment."

"There's a lot of speculation you're still pining away for him and that's why you never date."

Madison snort-laughed. "I never date because I haven't met anyone I want to date. Plus, I'm too busy taking care of Charlotte in the evenings to go out."

"You've heard of getting a babysitter, right?"

"Yes, but babysitters cost money. I don't have a lot of extra money."

"Rita and I have volunteered several times to babysit for free, young lady. You just never let anyone help you."

William's wife was nice, but she frequently lost the family dog. While she trusted William, Rita's absentmindedness scared Madison from ever trusting the woman with a baby.

They stopped next to Madison's seventeen-year-old Honda. William frowned. "You really do need more reliable transportation."

Since the lock was broken on the driver's side, she unlocked the passenger side. "New cars cost money."

"Please let me buy you a car. Some day when you're a famous designer you can pay me back."

This wasn't the first time William had made the offer. He and Rita didn't have any children, and he'd sort of adopted Madison.

"I can't let you do that." She jerked open the door. It made a scraping noise, making William grimace. "I'll get a car when I pay off everything."

Her dad had been a fairly successful actor, but he hadn't been a reliable father or a faithful husband. Her mother had put up with his behavior for years until she finally kicked him out. Then, shortly before the accident, the two of them had gotten back together. They had truly seemed happy.

Unfortunately, they'd been heavily in debt when they died with no life insurance policy on either of them. Madison was left with the staggering debt of the funerals as well as a second mortgage her parents had taken out to pay off their credit cards.

"How much do you owe, Madison?" William asked.

"A lot." She didn't want to tell him, because she knew he would try to give her the money. She had worked hard for everything she had in life, and she couldn't bring herself to take charity.

"Good night, William." She climbed into the car, and crawled over to the driver's side.

"Please come to my Christmas party," William said, ducking down to look at her. "You can bring Jenny and Charlotte with you."

"I can't, but thank you so much for the invitation. You're the best, William."

Madison didn't really do Christmas. Too much stress

and too many painful memories were associated with the holiday. Two years ago she'd almost been a Christmas bride. Now every Christmas decoration and song reminded her why she should've never fallen in love with an actor in the first place.

"I've got to get home so Jenny can sleep. Thank you again for walking me out."

"You're welcome. I'll see you in the morning."

William closed the door and waved as Madison drove away. Traffic was horrible, and it took her a little longer to get home to the small house in Pasadena she and her sister had inherited from her parents.

Pulling into the carport, Madison gathered up her notebook and purse and exited her car. The house was dark except for the glow of the lights on the artificial Christmas tree Jenny had found in the storage closet and set up right after Thanksgiving. The tree was pathetic and not very appealing, especially during the day. But Jenny had fonder memories of Christmas with their parents than Madison did, and wanted to keep up the tradition for her own daughter.

Skimming the darkened room, she spotted her sister in her dad's old recliner. Both Jenny and her daughter were asleep.

Retreating down the hallway, Madison entered her bedroom and changed out of her work clothes into a long-sleeved NYU tee and a comfortable pair of yoga pants. Charlotte started crying just as Madison pulled on a pair of fuzzy socks over her feet.

"Hey," she said, meeting Jenny in the hallway. "Let me take her, and you get some sleep." She held out her arms, and Charlotte dove into them.

"I can't find her pacifier, and it's the last one," Jenny said on a yawn. "I have no idea where they go."

"Okay." Madison tried to hide her dismay. If Charlotte didn't have her pacifier she was in for an even longer night than before. Madison bounced her niece up and down. "When was the last time you gave her Tylenol?"

"An hour ago. Her poor little gums are so swollen. I may have to take her in to the doctor if the teeth don't come through soon."

Jenny kissed her daughter on the forehead and then disappeared inside her room. Madison carried Charlotte back to the living room. The tiny three-bedroom house wasn't much, but it was home. It actually was a miracle they'd been able to keep the house. That probably had more to do with the mortgage being in her mother's name only.

Madison started her search for the missing pacifier. She swept her hand along the crevice of the couch cushions and only found a disgustingly large amount of crumbs and one quarter.

While she rummaged through the diaper bag, Madison's mind conjured up images of Caleb Matthews. He was still so freaking hot and made her heart pound every time she looked at him. He'd always made her feel that way. She remembered the first time she saw him at NYU.

The semester before he'd graduated, Caleb had scored the leading role in an indie film directed by one of the graduate students. Madison had been given a special assignment over the costumes for the production.

Caleb was incredibly sexy with his rugged good looks, a killer dimple, and his British accent. She'd tried to stay immune, but when she'd measured him for his costumes, the instant attraction between the two of them had been unlike anything Madison had experienced before.

Later that night Caleb had asked her out to dinner, and

Madison broke her own rule to never date an actor by saying yes. Over the course of the next few months they fell in love.

Madison had thought she could handle Caleb kissing other women, especially when he'd tell her he imagined he was kissing her during those intimate scenes. Then everything had changed when Ava Sterling starred opposite of him. Just thinking about the conniving woman turned Madison's stomach inside out.

She continued her search but after fifteen minutes of non-stop crying from Charlotte, Madison decided to go buy a pacifier. She changed the baby's wet diaper and put her in warm fleece pajamas.

Once outside, she accessed the passenger side to unlock the back door. She had just clicked the car seat in place when she heard the sound of a car engine. Heart pounding, she straightened up and gripped her keychain armed with pepper spray, watching as Caleb Matthews emerged from the sleek car parked in front of her house.

Four

Poised with her pepper spray, Madison debated about whether or not to go ahead and use the noxious formula on her former fiancé.

"Don't shoot," he teased, holding up his hands.

"What are you doing here?" She winced inwardly at the abrasive tone of her voice. She didn't want to be the stereotypical bitter ex-girlfriend.

He held his ground, but lowered his hands. "I, uh, came to see you."

"Why?"

"Could you please put that away?"

Charlotte's cries pierced her thoughts, and she lowered the keychain. "I don't have time for visitors. As you can hear, my niece is in distress."

"Is everything okay?" Genuine concern flickered across his face.

She stared at him with a blank expression, and he

laughed. "That was a stupid question. What I meant to ask is if I may be of assistance."

"No, thank you." She tossed her purse on the floor of the passenger seat and crawled in, pulling the door shut as she scrambled over to the driver's seat. From the corner of her eye she could see Caleb had moved next to the driver's side window. Ignoring him, she pressed her foot on the clutch and turned the key. A clicking sound met her ears.

"Oh please, don't do this to me now." She tried again, with no luck. Sometimes the car did this, and they'd have to jumpstart it with the booster cables stored in the trunk. She didn't have time to find out if that would work. She had a hysterical baby in the backseat and an ex-fiancé standing by.

A tap on the window made her jump. She glared at Caleb and wanted to shake her head no when he motioned for her to lower her window. Charlotte's wailing made her capitulate.

"Your car won't start," he said.

Again, Madison just stared at him. He smiled, carving the dimple into his cheek. "I know, another stupid observation." He pointed toward the backseat. "Perhaps I can be of service now?"

As much as her pride wanted to refuse his help, her niece's needs were more important.

"She's teething, and we can't find her pacifier. I was going to run to the store to get a new one."

"I'll be glad to take you." He opened her door and grimaced when it scraped against the metal. "Do you need to tell Jenny?"

"She works nights and is sleeping before her shift starts." Of course if the car was dead she had no idea how Jenny would get to work. She glanced at Caleb's beautiful car. "I'll need to strap Charlotte in the backseat."

"Certainly." He didn't even hesitate. Most guys didn't like the possibility of the car seat marring their leather interior. At least the loser Jenny had been dating last month felt that way.

She opened the back door, removing the car seat and its unhappy occupant. Caleb held out his hand. "Let me take her."

She hesitated before making the transfer. "Thank you."

Their fingers touched, and she felt a sizzling heat radiate up her arm. Her eyes met his, and attraction arced between them like a hot jumper cable. Swallowing, she stepped back and rounded the front of the car to retrieve her purse.

Caleb stood by his car, gently rocking the car seat. "It's all right, little love. We'll get you a new dummy."

"Who are you calling a dummy?" Madison asked, reaching out for the car seat.

He smiled. "Forgive me. In England that's what we call a pacifier."

"Seriously?" She stepped back while he opened the car door. "That sounds so demeaning."

Madison placed the car seat rear-facing in the center of the backseat. On her hands and knees, she fumbled with the seatbelt until she found the right receptacle. As she backed out, she looked over her shoulder and caught Caleb staring at her backside.

An unrepentant grin stole across his face. "Ready?"

"Yes." She slid onto the seat. "Thank you."

"My pleasure," he said, closing the door.

The car smelled like Caleb's cologne. He climbed in behind the wheel and pushed a button to start his car. The engine purred to life, hardly making a noise.

"Where to?" he asked, glancing at her over his shoulder.

Charlotte's cries had diminished to a whimper as she

chewed on Madison's finger. "There's a grocery store about five miles south."

He nodded and turned around, easing onto the road.

Madison stared at his handsome profile and felt a twinge of longing. She'd loved this man so much. She blinked, forcing her thoughts elsewhere. "Your car is beautiful."

"Thank you." He looked in the rearview mirror, and the skin around his eyes crinkled. "It's taken a couple of days, but I'm growing accustomed to being on the right side again."

She hadn't thought about that and hoped it was safe to be driving with him. "You've got precious cargo here, so you'd better be more than just accustomed."

He looked in the mirror again, his hazel eyes taking on an intensity that was almost palpable. "Trust me, I know."

He focused his attention back on the road, and Madison let out a shaky breath. Did Caleb deem her as precious cargo as well?

"I've missed you, Madison," he said quietly.

She clamped her lips together before she said how much she'd missed him too. Just being near him stirred up feelings she thought she'd buried.

"How did you know I live at my parents' house?" she asked, changing the subject.

"It was a guess." Caleb stopped at a red light. Their eyes met in the mirror, and she melted at the tenderness reflected there. "I'm sorry about your mum and dad. I wish you would've told me."

Her vision blurred, and her chest constricted. She'd wanted to call him. Needed him so desperately but hadn't been able to bring herself to contact him. "How did you hear about them?"

Forgotten Kisses

"A few months back I ran into an old mate from the university. He told me about your parents and that you worked on the set of *Forgotten Camelot*."

"Oh." Madison looked away, trying to process his words. She didn't want it to mean anything that he'd known she worked on the show he'd just signed onto.

Caleb had been the star of a successful cable network crime series filmed in England. She'd heard the show had recently been canceled, but she'd never expected him to move to Hollywood.

A car honked from behind to alert them of the green light. Caleb proceeded through the intersection and a minute later pulled into the grocery store.

Madison removed her finger from the baby's mouth and reached over to unclick the seatbelt. Charlotte immediately started to whimper. "It's okay, baby girl. In just a few minutes you're going to feel a lot better."

At least, she hoped that was true. Last night had been pretty brutal, and that was without a missing pacifier.

Caleb opened the door for her, and Madison scooted out, bringing the car seat with her. "I've got her," she said, when Caleb reached for the handle of the seat. "You really don't need to come inside with us."

He narrowed his eyes. "It's late. I'm coming with you."

"All right, but don't blame me if people recognize you and someone posts pictures online of you with a woman and a baby. I don't think your girlfriend will appreciate it."

"I don't have a girlfriend."

"Really?" She cut him an icy glare. "Then who is Elizabeth Carmichael?"

Five

"Have you been checking up on me?" Caleb asked with a smile.

"Don't be ridiculous." Madison paused and waited for the automatic doors to open before continuing inside the store. "You're on the cover of almost every tabloid with her."

"And we all know how truthful those are," he said dryly.

Selecting a smaller shopping cart, she placed the baby seat into the basket. Charlotte quieted once she could chew on Madison's finger again.

"I'll bet you ten bucks I can find a picture of you and Elizabeth on the cover of one of the issues right now."

"I'll accept your wager, but only if you agree to spend an evening with me if I win."

Although she could seriously use ten dollars, she said, "Fine, but if I win you have to agree to leave me alone."

He didn't look very happy but nodded his head in agreement. "If that's what you want."

It was what she wanted, right? Not trusting her voice,

Madison steered the cart toward the baby aisle. Caleb walked alongside her—too close for her comfort. The delicious scent of whatever cologne he used permeated the space around her. Occasionally his arm bumped into hers, sending shivers of awareness throughout her body.

"Elizabeth is my best mate's little sister. Her boyfriend, Neil, is on assignment with the Royal Navy and won't be home for another two months."

Madison shot him a disgusted look, and he shook his head. "It's not what you're thinking. Neil is aware our dating is for pretense only. I had a rather tenacious co-star in pursuit of my affection, and she wouldn't take no for an answer. Elizabeth is simply helping me out until Neil comes home."

His explanation annoyed Madison, mostly because it reminded her about Ava Sterling. She had been tenacious as well and had once showed up at Caleb's apartment late one night, wearing nothing but a silky cover up. Caleb had gone out for Chinese takeout. When Madison answered the door, Ava didn't wait to see who had answered and dropped the cover up. Instead of being embarrassed, the conniving woman had put the robe back on and smiled. "Tell Caleb I stopped by, and I'll try again later."

Caleb had denied ever encouraging Ava, and Madison had believed him. Months later, while Madison was in the middle of finals, Caleb got a call from his agent to audition for an original cable based show filmed in England. What he didn't tell Madison was Ava would be auditioning for the part of his love interest. Apparently the casting director thought the two of them had good chemistry onscreen.

"That must be terribly inconvenient to have women throwing themselves at you all the time," Madison said sarcastically.

A flash of pain crossed his features. "It is when I don't desire it and it hurts the people I love most."

Madison's steps faltered, and she averted her gaze. What could she say to that?

She quickened her pace, and Caleb silently kept up with her. Finally they made it to the baby aisle. She had to remove her finger from Charlotte's mouth to search for the correct pacifier. Immediately the baby began crying.

Madison didn't pay any attention to the cute designs and selected a boring package of pink pacifiers. She tore open the package and cleaned the nipple with the pacifier wipes before popping it into Charlotte's mouth. Instantly the little girl visibly relaxed. Madison imagined it felt very similar to when she was highly stressed and would self-medicate with chocolate. She had a feeling she would be going home with chocolate tonight.

"Wow," Caleb said, leaning in so close his breath tickled Madison's ear. "She looks like she just hit Nirvana."

The air around Madison thinned. Feeling the heat of Caleb's body did crazy things to her insides and scrambled her thoughts. Instead of stepping away, she turned to look at him.

Big mistake. His lips were only inches away.

Memories of kisses they'd shared flooded her mind. His cinnamon-scented breath made her long for just one more taste of his mouth. That had been her Nirvana.

Charlotte let out a contented sigh, snapping Madison out of her trance. "I just need to pay for these and then we can go."

He wrinkled his forehead. "Shouldn't you buy more than one package?"

She mentally calculated the amount of cash she had in her wallet. The tight budget she and Jenny lived on didn't leave much room for unnecessary purchases. "No, this will be okay. I'm sure I'll find the other missing pacifiers tomorrow."

"Okay." Caleb smiled and slipped his hands in his pockets. "I need to pick up a few things so I'll meet you at the register."

Before her eyes lingered on his mouth again, Madison quickly left him alone and made her way to the front of the store. Her heart thumped wildly, and she mentally chastised herself for being stupid enough to want to kiss him.

There was only one register open and a line of three other people ahead of her. It would give her plenty of time to peruse the assortment of magazines and tabloids on the endcap, looking for pictures of Caleb and Elizabeth. Even if what he said was true, their bet was still on. She might have to work with him, but spending alone time with him was out of the question.

Madison searched each cover and wasn't surprised to find Derrick on nearly every issue pictured with the seventeen-year-old girl that didn't look the least bit innocent. There were also pictures of Caleb on a few of them, announcing his role as the new Sir Lancelot. Elizabeth wasn't in one photo. She wasn't even mentioned in any of them.

Crap. Now she would have to spend an entire evening with Caleb Matthews.

Feeling more stressed than ever, she picked up a couple of candy bars to add to her purchase. While the cashier slowly scanned the contents of the cart from the person in front of her, another lane opened up. Madison wanted to switch over, but two other people behind her got there first.

The new cashier was twice as fast as the one Madison had. By the time it was her turn, Caleb had apparently made it to the other register.

"Oh my gosh," the cashier there said in a high-pitched voice. "You're Caleb Matthews!"

"Hello," Caleb said.

Madison rolled her eyes at the girl's tittering laugh. Just because the guy's accent made everything he said sound sexy was no excuse to act like an idiot. It would only feed his already-high ego.

"Will you please do a selfie with me? I want to Snapchat my roommates to make them jealous."

Madison's cashier had stopped scanning her items and stared at Caleb with hungry eyes. She looked like she might jump the counter to get to him.

"Excuse me," Madison said. "Could you please scan my things?"

"But that's Caleb Matthews." She fanned her face with the partially empty pacifier package. "He's even hotter in person."

"Yes, well, the sooner you finish with me the sooner you can go talk to him."

Without even scanning the items, the cashier shoved the package into a sack, along with the candy bars. "Here you go, ma'am."

"Don't I need to pay for these?" Madison asked, taking the sack from the girl.

"It's on me." She took off her red apron and smoothed her hair with her fingers. Then she left her post and made a beeline for the next lane over.

Madison glanced behind her and saw it was empty. The person behind her had abandoned her cart and jumped in line to see the British star. Caleb drew everyone to him, making each individual feel like a personal friend. He took selfie after selfie and signed whatever piece of paper was handed to him.

Hoping this didn't last too much longer, Madison took a seat on a bench. At least Charlotte was asleep. Digging her phone out of her purse, she snapped a picture of Charlotte in pacifier heaven and posted it to her private Instagram account, tagging the picture as "Nirvana." Then she sent a Snapchat of the same picture to Jenny to open when she awoke.

After ten more minutes of mindless social media surfing, Madison glanced up at Caleb. She wanted to catch his attention and remind him she and Charlotte were waiting on him.

Finally, Caleb said his goodbyes. "It's been lovely meeting you all," he said in his crisp accent. "Thank you for your kind welcome."

Madison expected Caleb to walk out ahead of her to avoid any rumors, but he stopped in front of her and held out his hand. "Sorry to keep you waiting, love."

She eyed him warily. He'd been in the business long enough to know the rumors about them could be hitting the worldwide web within minutes of them leaving.

She took his hand for only a second to stand up, but in that brief moment several people captured the chivalrous move with their cell phone cameras.

Six

MADISON SNATCHED HER HAND OUT of Caleb's. "It's fine." Her eyes darted to the onlookers. They watched them closely, and Madison could read the speculation in their eyes. "Um, we're only friends, not lovers." She cringed. "I mean, he only called me 'love' because he's British."

Caleb lifted a questioning brow. Madison twisted her hands, hearing the whispers about who she was to Caleb and whether or not the baby belonged to him.

Panicking, she blurted out, "Oh, he's not the father."

Shooting her an annoyed look, Caleb took the cart and said under his breath, "Let's go before you say anything more damaging."

Madison hurried beside him.

"Mr. Matthews!" the cashier said, handing Caleb a plastic grocery sack. "Don't forget these. You can never have enough pacifiers, right?"

"Quite right." He took the bag. "Thank you."

They rushed outside, and Madison didn't dare look to

see if they still had an audience. All she could envision were the tweets going out right now about Caleb Matthews' girlfriend and his questionable paternity to the baby he'd just purchased pacifiers for.

Caleb unlocked the car and opened the back door. Madison avoided looking at him as she loaded Charlotte into the car. She slid in beside the car seat and caught the sack Caleb tossed at her before he closed the door.

Caleb returned the cart before getting into the car. Without saying anything, he put the car in gear and pulled out of the parking lot.

They drove in complete silence. She was forced to speak up when Caleb took the wrong turn.

"You're going the wrong way."

"I know. I'm trying to lose the car following us."

Madison glanced behind her. "How do you know they're following us?"

"Because as they climbed into their vehicle I heard them talk about tailing me to see where I live."

"In that case I'm sure it'll throw them off when you drive through my neighborhood."

"Perhaps, but if they're persistent then they'll discover where you live. Do you want me to chance that?"

"No." Madison glanced at the time. It was nearly nine. Jenny would be getting up in an hour. "But I need to get back soon so I can work on getting the car started for Jenny."

"And how do you propose to do that?"

"There's a portable battery booster in the trunk. It usually works."

Caleb made a right turn and then accelerated down the long stretch of road. He grinned, and Madison glanced out the back window to see the car following them stopped at the red light.

"Turn left up here," Madison said turning back around. "It'll wind through a neighborhood and come out by the park near my house."

"Excellent." He made the turn and pressed a button on the steering wheel to bring up the map display. He pressed another button and gave the voice command to navigate to Madison's home.

She watched the screen display the route to her house. It shouldn't make her feel all warm and fuzzy inside that he'd already programmed her home address into his navigational system, but it did.

With another touch of a button, he made the command to call someone named Franco.

"Hey, boss, what's up?" a man said in an obvious New York accent.

"I need you to bring the Land Rover to me." Caleb then rattled off Madison's address.

"Sure thing. Will you need a tow truck for the Audi?"

"That's not necessary. I'll be loaning it to a friend for a few days."

Madison scowled. "I'd better not be the friend you're talking about."

Caleb ended the call, and his eyes flickered up to the mirror. "Would you have rather I said you were my lover?"

"Ha ha." She leaned forward. "I'm not driving your car."

"Madison, your sister needs a car to get to work and back."

"I'm sure we can jumpstart it."

"And if that doesn't work?"

"Then we'll call a cab."

He sighed. "And what about when she needs to come home or you need to get to work tomorrow? Cabs are expensive."

Biting her lip, Madison sat back and closed her eyes. He was right. She and Jenny didn't get paid for another week, and there wasn't enough money to cover cab fare for the two of them to get to work and back.

"Why are you doing this?" she asked irritably. "It's not like you're some knight in shining armor."

His eyes met hers in the mirror again, and she could tell he was smiling. "Actually, I kind of am. You know, Sir Lancelot?"

Madison rolled her eyes, and he laughed. She wanted to insist he go home and take his beautiful car with him, but she really didn't know what to do. She needed the car, at least until she could scour YouTube for videos about how to fix hers.

She stayed quiet for the remainder of the ride home. Finally, Caleb pulled up behind her car. He cut the engine and came around to open her door.

"Don't forget her new dummies," Caleb said, taking the infant carrier out of her hands.

"Speaking of dummies," she said, retrieving the grocery sacks. "Why did you have to make such a spectacle of yourself by buying more pacifiers?"

"Are you seriously saying I'm the one who made a spectacle?"

Madison felt her cheeks flame, and she wondered if the rumors were already flying about Caleb's possible love child.

"Sorry about that." She reached out and took back the baby seat, careful not to awaken Charlotte. "But, really, why did you buy more pacifiers?"

"Truly?" He narrowed his beautiful eyes. "I assure you I didn't have an ulterior motive. When you purchased one package I only thought to buy a few more since the baby is so attached to them, and they are evidently easily lost."

It really was sweet of him to think of Charlotte. "Thank . . . you. That was very thoughtful of you." The words were easier to say than she'd thought.

"You're welcome."

Madison held his gaze for a moment longer before turning and heading toward the carport. A surge of panic spread through her when she passed by her beat-up car. She hoped it was an easy fix.

Somehow Caleb ended up in front of her. His fingers brushed against hers as he took the keys and opened the door. She murmured her thanks and slipped past him, trying to ignore the tantalizing scent of his cologne.

Caleb came in behind her and followed her across the kitchen floor. When she got to the hall, Madison turned and found him so near she had to tip her head back to look at him. "I'm just going to put her in the crib."

"Need any help?" he asked softly.

"No, thank you." She turned and made her way toward the baby's room. Charlotte squirmed a little when Madison settled her onto the mattress but remained asleep.

She lingered by the crib for a few more moments before tiptoeing out the door. Caleb stood by the pathetic-looking Christmas tree. He turned when he heard her enter the room.

"Hello," he said, watching her closely.

"Hi."

His warm gaze held her captive, and the room seemed to shrink. Madison needed space, or at least something to do other than stare at this gorgeous man. Spying the baby monitor on the coffee table, she picked it up. "I'm going to see if I can jumpstart the car."

"I thought we'd already settled this?" Caleb said.

"As much as I appreciate it, we can't keep your car forever, Caleb."

She hurried outside, flustered when he followed close behind her. She went through the usual ritual to open the driver's side door and found the lever to pop the hood. After propping the hood open, she went around to the trunk and retrieved the battery booster.

Caleb hovered nearby, watching her every move. Her fingers shook as she connected the red and black clamps to the correct battery terminals and then plugged in the booster. Unfortunately, she needed to let the battery charge for a few minutes. Ignoring Caleb was no longer an option.

She turned toward him. The moment their eyes met a current of awareness surged between them. It was so powerful she could probably start the car with a touch of her pinkie finger.

Caleb took a step forward. "Madison, we need to talk."

"Okay." She edged back, stopping when she bumped into the car. "What would you like to talk about?"

"Us."

Seven

STUNNED, MADISON SAID THE FIRST thing that entered her mind. "There is no us."

A frown marred his handsome face. "Madison, when are you going to believe me that there was nothing going on between Ava and me?"

She wasn't sure what to believe. A flashback of the pictures of him and Ava kissing passionately appeared in her mind. "She went to London with you, and you tried to hide it from me."

"She was on my flight, but we weren't together." He ran a hand through his hair. "And it was stupid of me not to tell you, but I knew you'd be upset we were doing a screen test together. I didn't want to distract you from your studies."

"Yeah, well waking up and finding pictures plastered all over Instagram of my fiancé kissing Ava Sterling kind of screwed up my finals. I had to grovel to my professor to let me take another test."

"I'm sorry." He took a step toward her. "But you do

remember the pictures were captured during one of the takes, right?"

That's what he'd said before. At first she'd been too upset to even care. Later, after they'd stopped talking, she'd accepted it as the truth since there weren't any other pictures of them. Ava was devious enough if she had other photographs she would have posted them. In Ava's world there was no such thing as bad press. It was a slight consolation to Madison that her nemesis's efforts had been in vain. Ava's character was killed off after the fourth episode.

Still, because of her parents' struggles, she hadn't been able to bring herself to try and make things right with him.

"Yes. I do realize that." Feeling guilty for not even giving Caleb a chance back then, she shrugged. "It doesn't matter now. It's in the past."

Caleb's eyes looked troubled. Before he could say anything more, she twisted around and opened the car door. "I've already inconvenienced you enough for one night. I'm going to at least check to see if this will work." She climbed in behind the wheel and tried to start the car. It still made a clicking sound.

"Oh, come on," she said, trying a few more times.

Suddenly the passenger door squealed as Caleb opened it and slid onto the seat.

"I haven't been inconvenienced, and I don't care if I have to stay here all night, but we are going to talk about us."

Madison groaned and pressed her forehead against the steering wheel. Why was he being so persistent now? Two years ago he hadn't come home and tried to work things out. Now, too much had been said, or rather, left unsaid, and they had both moved on.

"I should've come after you when you broke off the

engagement, but I was angry and immature," he said, as if reading her thoughts. "I was going to give us a few days to cool off, but then filming started and you ignored all my calls and wouldn't answer any of my messages. I finally stopped trying when you returned your engagement ring."

Listening to him recall the events made her feel like the immature one. She remembered sending him her ring, all the while thinking in the back of her mind if he really loved her and wanted her he would come after her.

Sitting back against the seat, she turned and met his gaze. "I'm sorry I didn't listen to you and that I blamed you for everything."

"Madison, I was never with Ava." He shifted in his seat. "I know now it would have been better to tell you about the audition, but truly I only had your best interest at heart."

Her throat felt too thick to speak. She nodded her head in acknowledgement before she dropped her eyes to look at her lap. Sitting here with him, it was clear she'd allowed her fears that Caleb would turn out to be just like her father taint her judgment.

He leaned forward and lifted her chin with his finger, raising her face. "Do you forgive me?"

With those four words she felt all her anger vanish in a matter of seconds. "Yes," she said, knowing it was true.

Slowly his lips curved up, and it took a great deal of self-control not to press her mouth to his like she'd done so many times in the past when either of them had made an apology. They hadn't argued much when they'd been together, but making up had always been the best part.

"Do you forgive me?" she asked, shifting her gaze to his eyes.

"Always."

His soft answer was familiar and made her long for

Forgotten Kisses

what always followed—a kiss that wiped away all the hurt feelings. Her heart nearly stopped when he lowered his head. He was going to kiss her, and she felt frozen with both fear and desire.

Her breath quickened and she caught the scent of cinnamon as his lips lightly brushed hers. The kiss was so quick she didn't have time to give him a response. And boy did her body want her to respond.

She waited for him to kiss her again, her heart pounding with anticipation. But Caleb remained motionless, his mouth lingering so close to hers their breath mingled. Was he waiting for her to make the next move? Did she want to make the next move?

She curled her fingers into her palms, resisting the urge to grab the front of his shirt. It was obvious he was leaving it up to her to decide if there would be another kiss, but part of her was afraid once she started kissing him she wouldn't be able to stop. Suddenly car lights illuminated the inside of the car.

Caleb sighed and pressed his forehead against hers. "That's my ride."

Madison was still torn. She could easily instigate another kiss. Her decision was taken from her when the monitor crackled to life with Charlotte's whimpers.

All at once Madison was grateful for the reprieve. She had a lot to think about. "I need to go get the baby."

With another sigh, they parted, and Caleb climbed out of the car and came around to open her driver's side. The grinding sound made his forehead crease.

"Don't say it," she said, climbing out. "I will get a new car as soon as I can afford it."

She could tell he wanted to protest, maybe even offer to buy her a car since money wasn't an issue for him. But just because they'd apologized to each other didn't mean they were getting back together or that she would drive his car for longer than necessary.

The lines on his face softened with a smile that was more of a smirk. "By the way, I won the wager, and you owe me an entire evening." He dug the key fob out of his pocket and handed it to her. "Does tomorrow evening work for you?"

The baby's whimpers turned into pitiful cries. "Sure, but be prepared to share it with a cranky but very adorable girl."

"You're not that cranky," he teased.

"Very funny."

Grinning, he backed away. "See you in the morning, Mad."

She stuck her tongue out at him, making him laugh. He winked and then turned and strode purposefully across the yard.

"Caleb?" she said as he opened the passenger side of the SUV.

"Yes?"

"Thank you."

His smile lit her up brighter than the neighbor's obnoxious Santa display.

He waved and slid inside the vehicle. As he drove away, she stared at the tail lights, questioning if everything that had just happened was real. Hope slipped inside her as if the door of emotions she'd locked up had been opened.

Remembering Charlotte, she unplugged the battery booster and went inside to comfort her niece. She met Jenny in the hall.

"You are never going to believe what happened to me tonight," Madison said. "Wait for me in the living room, and I'll tell you all about it."

Eight

THE NEXT MORNING MADISON WAS prepared for the worst. While she waited for her coffee to brew, she searched the Internet for anything about Caleb and her. The only thing she found was several tweets about Caleb shopping at a store late last night and taking the time to sign several autographs and take a few selfies with the customers. There was nothing about Madison or her niece.

Jenny came in from the carport, looking pretty happy for having just worked the entire night. "That is such a sweet ride."

She tossed the key fob at Madison, and she instinctively caught it. "Don't get used to it. Jake is stopping by this morning to check the Honda out."

"Really?" Jenny grabbed a mug and poured herself a cup of the freshly brewed coffee. "So am I supposed to meet him or what?"

Jake owned a local garage not far from their house and had helped them before by taking payment when they got paid. He was a nice guy, not to mention cute if you were into big muscles. He also had a crush on Jenny but was too shy to ever ask her out.

"I told him you didn't sleep until Charlotte's first nap so you would be here."

"Please tell me you did some laundry?"

"I did it all when I couldn't sleep last night."

"Excellent." Jenny grinned. "Do you mind if I wear the J Brand jeans you found at the consignment shop?"

"Not at all, but do Jake a favor and put him out of his misery by asking him out."

"I will if you promise to kiss Caleb tonight."

"I'm not making any promises, Jenny. I told you I'm not sure I can deal with his career. His new role as Lance Knightly has him making out with some girl on almost every episode."

"He's not Dad." She took a sip of her coffee. "Derrick, *he* was like Dad. You know Caleb's not like that."

Madison mulled her sister's words over as she retrieved her travel coffee cup from the dishwasher and filled it up. The baby monitor crackled, and Charlotte started cooing.

Jenny's eyes brightened. "I hope this means we're done with teething."

"Me too." Madison snapped the lid on her mug and grabbed her purse. "Have a good day."

Her sister was right. Caleb's car *was* amazing. Madison especially enjoyed the heated leather seats. The scent of his cologne still lingered, making her stomach flutter with anticipation at seeing him again. She still couldn't believe what had happened last night.

After parking the car, she grabbed her purse and coffee cup and hurried inside the building. Kevin wasn't at his post today. Terrance, his replacement, waved Madison through without making one suggestive comment about the formfitting knit dress she had on. It was awesome.

The set was as crazy as it usually was in the mornings. Gerard was huddled with a few of the actors going over the scene for blocking. Caleb wasn't among them. A sense of relief washed over her when she arrived at his dressing room and no one was there. She needed a few minutes to prepare herself before he showed up.

Storing her purse away, she pulled out her notebook. Most everyone used an iPad, but Madison liked doing things the old-fashioned way with ink and paper. Taking a sip from her coffee mug, she flipped the page to today's scenes and read over her notes.

"Good morning, beautiful," Caleb said in a low voice.

Madison looked up at him through her lashes and gave him a shy smile. Today she felt beautiful, and not just because she had taken extra time on her hair and makeup. Harboring so much anger had really taken its toll, and she felt lighter inside than she had in . . . well, two years. "Good morning to you too."

He picked up her coffee mug. "May I?"

"Sure," she said, feeling a rush of heat surge through her as if she'd swallowed the steaming brew herself.

He held her gaze as he took a long sip.

She bit at her lip and felt her face flush. Knowing his mouth touched the same place hers had been just moments before elicited a heady response. For once the studio didn't feel too cold.

"Something tells me you two have kissed and made up," Beth said wryly.

Madison's blush deepened. She hadn't even heard the stylist come in.

Caleb set the mug down and grinned. "We didn't get

around to the kissing part last night." His smoldering eyes promised kissing would be on the agenda this evening.

"I'll cover for you if you all want to sneak off inside the changing room to get an early start," Beth whispered loudly.

It was wrong to even consider taking Beth up on her offer, but from the look on Caleb's face Madison guessed he was game if she was.

One of the wardrobe guys nixed the crazy idea when he rolled in the rack with Caleb's costumes for the day.

"Later," Caleb mouthed, taking another sip of her coffee.

Gerard sauntered over to speak with Caleb while Madison hung the heavy chainmail costume in the changing room.

After that the rest of the day flew by. She and Caleb didn't get much of a chance to talk, but the nonverbal communication had been sizzling. Every touch or heated look they exchanged hinted at their rediscovered feelings for each other.

Madison still felt her old fears creep up, especially when Sir Lancelot had a kissing scene after rescuing a pretty girl from a dragon. She told herself it was his job, and it didn't mean he was hooking up with the girl after hours.

Like Jenny had pointed out the night before, Caleb's reputation as a bad boy was really only related to his former role as Detective Nick St. James. Some of the articles she'd found even pointed out how different the real Caleb Matthews was from his character. There were multiple pictures of him at children's charity functions, where he donated both money and his time. Funny how her anger had blotted out the good things she remembered about him.

By the end of the day, Madison regretted wearing the three-inch heels. Sure they made her legs look amazing, but her feet were killing her. Since Caleb had to stay and shoot promos for the new season, Madison got off earlier than expected. It would give her time to clean up the house.

Grabbing her purse, she dug her phone out and checked her messages. She opened the one from Jenny and smiled.

> Jake the hottie said it's our starter, which is an easy, inexpensive fix. The part will be here tomorrow and he can fix it then. He also said yes when I asked him out to dinner for Saturday night.

The text ended with a smiley face kissing emoji.

Her sister had every other weekend off, and Madison was glad she would be going out with someone worth dating.

Madison quickly sent a text to offer her babysitting services for the date. She hoped Caleb wouldn't mind coming over to help. Hopefully he would find Charlotte as irresistible as Madison and Jenny did.

Her stomach fluttered with happiness when she saw two messages from Caleb. They had exchanged phone numbers this morning. The first message said the dragon girl kissed like a fish. He couldn't wait to erase the memory and wondered if Madison would be willing to help him out. She refrained from sending him a "yes" in all caps, and settled for a simple smiley face emoji.

The second one was an invitation to accompany him to William's Christmas party on Friday. Attending the party with Caleb would be a big step since their relationship would no longer be a secret. Was she ready for that? She decided not to answer him just yet.

"May I walk you out?" William said, coming up beside Madison.

"Sure, but don't you have to stay longer to shoot promos?"

William flashed his perfect cosmetically enhanced teeth. "Women aren't tuning in every week to see me." He winked at her. "They're all swooning over the new Lance Knightly."

Madison's stomach tightened with insecurity. She didn't want to talk about how hot of a commodity Caleb was.

"I didn't mean to upset you," William said, holding the door open for Madison.

She forced her lips into a smile. "I'm not upset."

"You know, Madison, all men aren't cheaters. Rita and I have been married for thirty-seven years, and I've never strayed."

William was fully aware of Madison's father's indiscretions and how she felt about actors in general.

She glanced over at him. "Why are you telling me this?"

"Because I didn't need Beth to tell me you and Caleb Matthews have reconciled your differences." He gave a low whistle. "The tension between the two of you was as taut as Guinevere's corset."

Madison wanted to laugh it off, but she didn't have her father's acting skills. "The way he makes me feel scares me to death. I don't want to go through what my mother did, always wondering if my husband is staying faithful or not."

They reached the outer doors, and stepped out into a sky painted in rich colors of red and purple. During the winter she rarely got to see a sunset during the weekday, and she took a few moments to now admire it.

"Trusting someone you love isn't easy," William said. "I used to be crazy with jealousy that Rita would find a lover while I was away on assignment. Especially when I came home early to find her eating dinner with an old boyfriend from college."

Madison glanced at him as they proceeded to her parking space. She'd never considered a man feeling that way, since her mother was always the one constantly worrying. "Was she cheating?"

"No. His wife was supposed to accompany him but ended up staying in the hotel with a migraine. Actually, I was supposed to be there too, but I'd completely forgotten about it and had lost my cell phone, so I missed all of Rita's calls." He glanced over at Madison. "Later that night Rita confessed the attraction was still there, and the thought had crossed her mind how easy it would be to have a fling."

Madison was shocked the woman had admitted it. "Didn't that make you mad?"

"I didn't like it, but I chose not to let jealousy determine my response. You see, Rita and I decided early on we would never have any secrets between us." He stopped walking and shoved his hands in his pockets. "Madison, I'm madly in love with my wife, but it doesn't prevent me from ever feeling that kind of chemistry with someone else. Over the years I've been attracted to plenty of women and have even been tempted when they've reciprocated the attraction. But telling my wife about it takes the secrecy out of it and keeps me accountable for my actions."

"So if you're into someone from work you go home and immediately tell Rita?"

"Yes. We've learned to listen to each other without judging or getting jealous."

Madison thought about her relationship with Caleb. He knew how she felt about Ava and hadn't ever discussed any of the love scenes he had to do with her because of that. If he had told her about Ava going to London with him Madison probably would have been upset with him and then worried the entire time, messing up her finals anyway. However, she might not have lost it and broken off the engagement.

Still, looking back, she knew she never fully trusted Caleb and just expected him to one day cheat on her, like it was inevitable. So maybe she would have still gone ahead and broken up with him. "Thank you for sharing all of that with me."

"I need to pass on my wisdom to someone since I don't have any children."

She laughed and pulled the key fob out of her coat pocket to unlock the doors. William's brows shot up. "You got a new car?"

"No, the Honda wouldn't start so Caleb is letting us use his car until we can get it fixed."

William nodded his head, a satisfied smile on his face. "I knew I liked him." He opened the car door for her, and she slipped onto the soft leather seat. "Give him a chance, Madison," he said in a serious tone. "I've been in the business a long time, and I'm a pretty good judge of character. Caleb Matthews is a good man."

Madison knew William was right. Caleb was a good guy, and she was grateful for a second chance with him.

"I will. I promise."

Nine

Madison tiptoed away from Charlotte's room to answer the soft knock at the door. Caleb had texted an hour earlier apologizing for running late and offering to bring Italian takeout for dinner.

Before opening the door she peeked out the window to make sure Caleb was on the other side. He happened to glance her way and smiled when he caught her watching him.

He was really here. It was still hard to believe all that had happened in the last twenty-four hours. A sudden rush of nerves hit her as she unlatched the deadbolt. As hungry as she was for food, all she could think about was Caleb's promise to kiss her.

"Hi," she said, opening the door.

"Hello." He stepped inside and held up the bag he carried. "I hope you're hungry."

"I am." The husky tone of her voice bordered on seductive. She moistened her lips. "For food, that is."

The corner of his mouth lifted as he set the bag onto the coffee table. "Me too." His eyes dipped down to her mouth as he slipped off his leather jacket. "Although I want more than just dinner."

Madison bit at her bottom lip, feeling her cheeks go hot. "Let me hang this up for you," she said, reaching out for his coat.

"Thank you."

She took the coat and walked to the small hall closet, catching a hint of his cologne. She waited until she was hidden behind the closet door before burying her nose in the jacket to inhale the intoxicating scent.

"Mmm," she moaned softly.

"Madison?" Caleb said, startling her.

She jerked her head up to find him watching her with amusement. "Yes?"

"I forgot to get my phone out of my pocket."

"Oh." She nervously cleared her throat and handed over his jacket.

His lips twitched as he dug his hand into the pocket. "Got it." Then, instead of handing her the jacket, he reached around her and hung it up himself.

Pinned against his chest, Madison couldn't help drawing in another deep breath. "You smell so good," she finally confessed as she looked up at him. "What's the name of that cologne?"

"I'm glad you like it." He smiled, and settled his hands on her hips. "It's not on the market yet, and we don't have a name for it, but once I report back to the lab I caught you sniffing my jacket they'll go ahead with production."

She giggled. "You weren't supposed to see that."

"I'm glad I did." His palms slipped around to the curve

of her lower back. "Now I have a secret weapon to lure you with."

"Lure." She wound her arms around his neck. "That's the perfect name for it."

"Yes it is."

They held one another's gaze, and she felt a longing well up inside her. Desire flashed in his eyes just before he lowered his head and covered her mouth with his, kissing her long and slow. She kissed him back, tasting him and breathing him in. Her fingers found their way into the hair at his nape, bringing back a rush of memories of the kisses they'd shared before. His mouth continued to weave magic over her stronger than any of Merlin's spells.

A noise from the baby monitor ended the blissful exchange. With a groan, Caleb ended the kiss. "I forget we're not alone."

"Nope." Madison ducked under his arm. "I'll be right back."

Her legs felt wobbly as she quietly peeked inside Charlotte's room. She expected to find the baby wide awake but instead found her asleep on her tummy with her knees tucked under her and her little bum sticking up. It was adorable.

She stole quietly out of the room and made her way back to Caleb. He sat on the couch, pulling steaming boxes of food out from the takeout bag. Part of her hoped to pick up where they'd left off, but her growling stomach needed nourishment.

"She's still asleep?" Caleb asked.

"Yeah." She sat down close beside him so their thighs touched. "You should see how she's sleeping. It's so cute." She described it for Caleb while they dished up the Italian cuisine.

"This smells wonderful," Madison said. "I wish Jenny was still here so she could've taken some with her to work."

"I thought her shift starts at eleven?"

"It does, but someone went home sick, and they offered Jenny time and a half if she came in four hours earlier."

"Where does she work?" Caleb opened a box filled with fresh breadsticks. "I'm more than happy to take her some of the food."

His genuine offer was so sweet. Madison stared at him, wondering how she'd ever let this man go. "I was an idiot."

One of his brows arched up. "Excuse me?"

All at once the magnitude of what she'd done slammed into her. "I'm so sorry, Caleb. If I could go back and undo things I would."

He watched her intensely, the muscle in his jaw tightening. She swallowed, feeling a lump in her throat like she'd eaten a whole breadstick without chewing.

The hard look on his face softened, his hand coming up to cup her cheek. "Me too, love." He leaned in and gently kissed her.

When he edged back, she wrapped her arms around him and laid her head against his chest. His heart thumped as wildly as hers.

"Can we start over?" she asked.

He tightened his hold. "Yes, please."

The please made her smile and lightened the mood. She pulled back and gave him a quick kiss. "All right, but this time we won't have any secrets between us."

"Except for Christmases and birthdays," he countered.

"Right."

"And don't forget anniversaries."

She desperately wanted to ask if he meant wedding anniversaries but held her tongue. "Deal."

"Seal it with a kiss?"

As if he needed to ask.

She pressed her mouth to his, kissing him without any reservation. The way he kissed her back led her to believe he felt the same freedom. His lips left her mouth, and she made a tiny sound of protest until she felt him trail heated kisses across her jaw. A shiver of pleasure washed over her when he placed a kiss just below her ear.

"You have bewitched me, Madison Taylor."

She laughed softly as he nuzzled her neck. *Pride and Prejudice* was her favorite movie, especially the version with Keira Knightley. Caleb, with his delicious British accent, liked to mimic the line Mr. Darcy said to Elizabeth in the misty early dawn. Although he usually followed up with telling her how ardently he loved her, this time he found her mouth again and gave her one last lingering kiss. Madison wasn't too disappointed and hoped the "I love you" would come soon.

"The food is getting cold." She touched one of the breadsticks. "Correction, the food is cold."

He grinned, making his dimple appear. "Well worth it." He picked up both of their plates. "Let's warm these up in the microwave; then perhaps we should dine at the table. The sofa is too tempting."

Charlotte remained asleep while they ate their dinner. During that time Madison told him all about William's words of wisdom. When she got to the part about immediately telling his spouse if he was attracted to someone, weariness crept back into Caleb's eyes.

"What?" she asked, wondering if he was attracted to the dragon girl after all.

"You know Lady Elaine is coming onto the show, right?"

"Yes." The script had Sir Lancelot's lover starring in the next three episodes.

"Well," Caleb said. "The actress playing her was injured in a skiing accident. Ava Sterling is her replacement."

Madison felt like someone had just sucked the life out of her as if a Dementor from *Harry Potter* had entered the room. "When did this all happen?"

"I'm not sure, but she was there for the promos." He looked at her with a worried expression. "I planned to tell you this evening, I promise."

Madison picked up her glass and took a drink of water. Why did Ava have to show up just when she and Caleb had found each other again? Her hand shook as she placed the glass back onto the table.

"Talk to me." Caleb took her hand, threading their fingers together. "Please."

William's sage advice echoed in her mind. Instead of freaking out, she offered Caleb a smile. "This really sucks."

Relief filled his eyes. "I know, but she's only on for three episodes."

"Unless they decide to write her in for more."

"Madison, even if she's on the show for the rest of the season it doesn't change things between us." He stood up and tugged her to her feet. "I'm going to be completely honest with you. The first time I saw Ava I'll admit I found her attractive, but it only took a couple of days of working with her for that attraction to fizzle out."

She stiffened and wanted to pull away but tried to remember William's counsel. "What about today?"

"My feelings for her haven't changed. Ava is a colleague, nothing more." He brushed a few strands of her hair behind her ear with his fingertips. "She asked me to meet her for drinks, but I told her I was involved with someone else."

"Oh." Madison moistened her lips. "And who is the lucky girl?"

One corner of his mouthed lifted up. "I hope it's you."

A momentary panic engulfed her. "I'm not ready to tell everyone. Are you okay with that?"

His smile faltered for a second, but then he relaxed. "Of course, but if you attend the Christmas party with me I don't think I'm a good enough actor to hide my feelings."

Madison let out a small breath. She didn't think she could hide her feelings either.

A concerned look crossed Caleb's face. "You will go with me, won't you?"

She did want to go with Caleb. Despite her anxiety, it surprised her how the idea of attending the Christmas party didn't bring on a rush of her previous bitterness. Going might be healing, even.

"Yes. I would love to go with you."

Ten

THE NEXT COUPLE OF DAYS at work were tense with Ava working on the set. Madison did her best to hide her insecurities, but it was difficult watching Caleb and Ava's kissing scenes. And there were a lot of them.

So far she'd avoided talking to the woman, but Ava watched Madison closely, a knowing smile always hovering on her lips.

Other than at work, Madison didn't get to see Caleb. He'd had to stay late the last few nights shooting the next two episodes so filming could be on hold during the Christmas break. Since Madison took care of Charlotte, her assistant was the one to stay late.

Caleb texted her as often as he could, and they usually talked while he drove home. She assured him she was okay, but each time she saw him with Ava made it difficult to not fall back into old habits of distrust.

One thing was certain . . . Caleb and Ava did have good onscreen chemistry. Madison wasn't completely surprised when on Friday Gerard announced they were writing Lady Elaine into more episodes.

"I'll expect to see you two at William's party tonight," Gerard said to Ava and Caleb. "*People Magazine, ET*, and *TMZ* are all going to be there, and promoting an off-screen romance should send our ratings soaring."

Madison couldn't watch as Ava clutched onto Caleb and kissed his cheek. She turned away and hurried to get her things. Anxiety gripped her so tightly she could hardly draw a breath. What if in all the craziness the onscreen chemistry between Caleb and Ava had actually morphed into something more?

"Hey," Beth said. "I have time to come by and do your makeup for the party if you want."

"I'm not going to the party." Madison grabbed her jacket and purse. "You have fun, though."

"Seriously?" Beth crossed her arms in front of her. "You're really going to let that vixen go with Caleb?"

Madison felt her lower lip quiver. She couldn't cry. Not yet, anyway. "I can't stand by and watch them play the part of lovers."

"It's called acting."

"Is it?" She sniffed. "I'm not so sure anymore."

Not wanting to argue any longer, she waved at Beth. "Goodnight."

She hurried out of the studio, keeping her head down so she didn't make eye contact with anyone. She found her Honda and dug through her purse for her keys. Caleb's car had been so convenient, but she'd made him have Franco pick it up as soon as Jake had fixed her car.

Just as she backed out of her parking space, she saw Caleb running across the parking lot. She sped up, pretending not to notice him waving his hands at her. Guilt pricked her conscience as she passed through the security gate and onto the street.

Seconds later her phone started playing the ringtone for Caleb. She ignored it, telling herself she'd call him as soon as she was a safe distance from the studio. He continued to call, and after ten minutes had passed she finally answered it.

"Hey," she said, trying to sound cheerful. "What's up?"

"What's up?" he snapped. "You just completely ignored me, and you want to know what's up?"

"I'm driving, Caleb, and I don't have a fancy Bluetooth system to answer my phone."

"We both know you saw me trying to wave you down."

She wished she could deny it. "I'm sorry, but I just had to leave. I was upset."

"I know," he said, his voice softer. "That's why I wanted to talk to you."

"There's nothing to say, Caleb. You and Ava have to pretend to be a couple for the show."

"I'm not doing it. I'm telling Gerard the same thing." He let out a heavy sigh. "You and I are going together. Will you be ready for the party in an hour?"

Her knuckles turned white as her fingers curled around the steering wheel. "I'm not going."

"Don't say that, Madison. Please come."

"I can't do this, Caleb. I thought I could, but I just can't."

"What does that mean?"

Her eyes burned with emotion. "It means I don't want to always wonder if you're acting or if it's real."

"That's not fair. I thought you were going to trust me."

"I know." She sniffed. "But it's harder than I thought."

"Look, I just have to make a showing at the party. It's part of my contract to promote the show, but I'll leave as soon as I can and come over so we can talk."

"Not tonight, Caleb. I just need some time to process everything." She slowed down for the car in front of her. "I need to go so I don't get in a wreck."

She ended the call and tossed her phone onto the passenger seat. As soon as she turned onto her street, the tears started to fall.

"What's wrong?" Jenny asked the minute Madison walked in the door.

"Everything." Madison wanted to hide in her room but knew her sister wouldn't leave her alone until she told her what had happened. She collapsed on the couch.

Jenny listened, but instead of siding with Madison, she defended Caleb.

"He. Is. Not. Dad." She narrowed her eyes. "Think about it . . . you know Caleb is a good guy."

Madison couldn't dispute that. It hadn't taken long for her to remember the man she'd fallen in love with two years earlier.

Jenny reached out and grabbed Madison's hand. "It's time for us to let go of our fears because Dad was an idiot. I seem to date every loser on the planet, and you don't date anyone." She squeezed Madison's hand. "But we both have a shot at being with someone worthwhile. Jake is amazing. He's kind, generous, not to mention totally sexy. Did you know I found out we aren't the only ones he's helped who don't have the money to pay upfront?"

"That doesn't surprise me."

"Give Caleb a chance, Madison."

"What if he doesn't want to give me another chance?"

"There's only one way to find out." Jenny got to her feet and yanked Madison up with her. "You are going to the party to tell him how much you love him, because I know you love him. I don't think you've ever stopped loving him."

"I think you're right."

"I know I'm right." Jenny grinned. "I'm also right about the dress you need to wear." She flung open her bedroom door and pointed to the red evening gown Jenny had found at a consignment shop last year when she'd gone to a Christmas party with one of the doctors she'd met at work.

The dress was a little more daring than the simple black sheath Madison had planned to wear. But she needed to be daring tonight.

"Let's hurry up before Charlotte wakes up."

Thirty minutes later Jenny finished putting the last curl in Madison's hair. Gazing in the mirror, Madison fingered the scooped neckline of the red shimmering dress. "Are you sure this isn't too revealing?" Her sister wasn't as curvy up top as Madison was.

Jenny rolled her eyes. "You're not showing off any more than Elizabeth Bennet did when she went to the ball."

Madison smiled at the reference. She and Jenny had watched both versions of *Pride and Prejudice* multiple times, and they loved the gorgeous dresses from that era.

Jenny practically shoved her out of the door. "Go get your man!"

The drive to William's house went by too quickly. Madison had a hard time relaxing. Her imagination was wild with fear. What if she came into the party and found Caleb and Ava together?

William's mansion came into view. Lit up with tiny white and red lights it looked like a Christmas wonderland. Madison pulled into the circular driveway, and waited as the valet opened her door. It made the horrible grinding noise, but the valet said nothing. After confirming her name on the guest list, he slid in the driver's seat to park her car.

Drawing in a fortifying breath, Madison made her way

inside the house. Over the din of loud voices and laughter, she heard a familiar Christmas melody playing over the intercom system.

The large house was filled with so many people Madison doubted she'd find anyone she knew right away. She was completely surprised when the host of the party greeted her with a hug.

"Madison, you look absolutely lovely."

"Thank you." She glanced around. "I wasn't sure I would find anyone I know."

William's eyes sparkled under the Christmas lights. "I know of one young man who will be very happy to see you."

"Please tell me you're talking about Caleb and not Kevin."

He laughed, and pointed toward the patio. "The last time I saw Caleb he was looking miserable sitting by the pool."

"Thank you." Suddenly her mouth felt dry. "I think I'll visit the powder room first."

William pointed her in the right direction. Before she could enter, a woman dressed in a shiny, silvery gown came out and nearly knocked her over.

"Well, look who decided to finally show up," Ava said.

"Hello." Madison forced her lips into a smile.

"If you're looking for Caleb, don't bother. He's waiting for me by the pool."

For a moment, Madison considered turning around and going home. She dropped her eyes and caught a glimpse of her daring red dress. Tonight she was going to be brave.

She raised her chin and met Ava's gaze. "Thank you."

Ava grabbed onto her arm when Madison tried passing by her. "Where do you think you're going?"

Madison pulled her arm free. "To find Caleb."

"He doesn't want you." Ava leaned in close. "Surely you've seen the way he looks at me after we kiss?"

Doubt crept in again, but then Madison remembered what Beth had said. "Caleb's an incredible actor."

"Yes he is. Don't think for a moment his feelings for you are real." Ava's lips curled into a satisfied smile. "Go home, darling, and save yourself the embarrassment."

She stared at Ava, and contemplated her words. How did Ava know about Caleb's feelings? She wouldn't, unless he'd said something to her.

"What feelings would those be?" Madison asked.

"I don't know that he has any feelings for you." Ava's smile looked strained. "It's just obvious you're smitten with him again." She gave a fake laugh. "It's sad, really, because we both know what happened between Caleb and me in London."

"Actually, nothing happened in London. I misjudged Caleb then and didn't trust him, but I trust him now." Madison straightened her shoulders. "So if you'll excuse me I'm going to find him."

Ava stepped in front of her. "He isn't in love with you."

"You have no idea what my feelings are, Ava." Caleb's voice was cool. "I've asked you to leave me alone several times this evening. I'll not ask you again politely."

At the sound of his voice, both Madison and Ava turned to find Caleb leaning against the wall, the smirk Madison loved so much flickering on his lips.

Ava made an awful gurgling noise and stormed off, leaving the two of them alone.

"Hi," Madison said a little timidly. "I was looking for you."

"So I heard." Caleb slowly walked toward her. "Did I also hear you trust me?"

"I do."

"Truly?" His eyes held hers with a passion that nearly stole her breath.

"Truly."

A sexy smile curved his lips as he settled his hands on her lower back, pulling her to him. "Thank you."

"So." She slid her arms around his neck. "How *do* you feel about me?"

"I love you, Madison Taylor," he said lowering his head. "Most ardently."

"I love you too," she whispered against his mouth.

And then Caleb kissed her . . . most ardently.

ABOUT CINDY ROLAND ANDERSON

CINDY ROLAND ANDERSON is the bestselling author of clean, contemporary romance filled with humor, romantic tension, and some pretty great kissing scenes. Cindy has a degree in nursing and worked in the NICU until she recently retired to write full time. She loves to bake, not cook (there is a difference!) and enjoys spending time with her family. Cindy is lucky to be married to her best friend John. They live in Northern Utah and are parents to five incredible children. Over the past few years their family has expanded by adding a son-in-law, a daughter-in-law, and four adorable grandchildren. Cindy loves to read, almost as much as she loves writing. And she loves chocolate—probably a little too much.

Visit Cindy on-line:
Twitter: @CindyRolandAnde
Facebook: Cindy Roland Anderson - Author
Website: CindyRolandAnderson.weebly.com

The Last Christmas

Annette Lyon

OTHER WORKS BY ANNETTE LYON

Band of Sisters
Coming Home
The Newport Ladies Book Club series
A Portrait for Toni
At the Water's Edge
Lost Without You
A Midwinter Ball
Done & Done
There, Their, They're: A No-Tears Guide to Grammar from the Word Nerd

One

MEREDITH DAVENPORT SLIPPED A SWEET-potato pie into the oven and set the timer, fully intending to keep working on Christmas Eve dinner; she had plenty to do before the family would eat at six o'clock. If she wanted to have downtime to chat with her daughters, Maggie and Becca, and their significant others beforehand, she'd have to hurry. But she couldn't keep her focus on the strawberry-spinach salad, the six cooling pies (in four varieties), or on anything else because Eric hadn't arrived. He absolutely *had* to get his car into the garage, and his luggage into the master bedroom—behind a closed door—before the girls showed up.

She and Eric had yet to decide when or how to break the news of their impending divorce to their grown daughters. The judge would sign the final paperwork next week, and the girls still had no idea. With both girls living hours from the family's Michigan home—Maggie, in a studio apartment in Manhattan, and Becca, finishing her master's in mechanical engineering at MIT—it had been easy to pretend that nothing had happened since they'd left home. The long distances made for wonderfully vague texts and emails. Eric could have taken off to Milan, and Meredith to Johannesburg, and their daughters would have never been any the wiser, so long as she and Eric remembered which time zone they were supposed to be communicating from.

Meredith washed the strawberries and checked the clock above the stove again, then shook her head. Eric should have been here an hour ago. After twenty-five years of marriage, she should have known better than to give him the actual time he needed to show up. She should have told him to come an hour earlier. Then he still would have shown up late, in his mind, but really have plenty of time to settle in without the girls having a clue. If he didn't get here soon, Maggie or Becca would see their dad, bringing a suitcase into the house, and what good explanation could they give? Yes, he traveled a lot for work, but never on holidays.

Eric had his faults—loads of them—but he wouldn't overtly lie to the kids. Any direct questions from their grown children would mean telling them the full truth. And the truth wasn't an option until *after* Christmas.

Meredith quickly finished the salad, then tried to distract herself by checking the ham in the oven. She brushed it with another coat of honey glaze before closing the door and wiping her hands on a dish towel. She faced the kitchen entry, where the living room was barely visible beyond, and bit her lip. In spite of herself, she hurried in that direction, ending up in the living room's bay window, looking onto the street.

She searched the darkness both ways for cars—specifically, for Eric's gray Pathfinder—knowing that his headlights would show up first because his car was essentially camouflaged in the dark. She had no idea what

The Last Christmas

cars to expect the girls to be driving; they'd likely rented sedans at the airport. Soon, a set of headlights shone through the snowfall, approaching the house. She stood stiffly, holding her breath until the car passed.

Not Eric, she thought, *and neither of the girls, either.*

She looked across the street at Edith Carson's house and the freshly shoveled walk Meredith had provided for the old widow, who would be spending the holiday alone. If the snow didn't let up, the walk would need to be cleared again. Edith's door opened, spilling warm light onto her porch. By the glow of the outside lights, Meredith made out Edith's sudden grin at seeing her cleared walk—and then an even brighter one, after her eyes landed on the gift basket. She bent down and brought it inside with the slow shuffle of the elderly. Meredith now felt warmer than she had in some time, knowing that she'd anonymously put a smile on the sweet lady's face.

But then Meredith's phone dinged. She fished it out of her pocket and found a text from Edith, who continued to surprise Meredith with how well she kept up with technology, compared to others of her generation.

Thank you for clearing my walk. And thank you for the wonderful basket. You are a gem. God bless. Merry Christmas.

Meredith smiled again as she tucked the phone into her pocket. *So much for staying anonymous.* She stood at the window another minute, but no other cars appeared. The warmth Edith had given her gave way to the nerves she'd been fighting all day.

Eric's Pathfinder did well on the slippery, steep streets of their neighborhood even in the worst of winters, and this wasn't the Armageddon of storm after storm from a few years ago, when the snowbanks grew taller than she was. That winter, just walking next door made her feel like a mouse winding through in a maze, unable to see above the walls.

Turning from the window, Meredith closed her eyes, holding her mouth in a small O, and let out a breath to the count of eight. The technique usually helped, but today, the attempt at being Zen-like didn't work. So she opened her eyes, and her gaze found the trimmed tree, flocked white and covered with silver and pink decorations. She'd decorated it yesterday, a good three weeks later than it usually went up.

Then she'd put up all the holiday decorations by herself: the olivewood nativity on the bookcase, the cheery wreaths on both sides of the door. She made the wreaths when the kids were little, using a glue gun and wired ribbon and accenting them with fake berries and leaves. The wreaths no longer looked new, but she still loved them.

She'd wound the garland around the banister leading from the entry to the second floor. Decorating that had always been the girls' job, so doing it herself had felt odd. When they were little, the girls' efforts turned out adorably uneven. She'd tried to help even it out once, but that hurt their feelings. After that, she always let them do whatever they wanted to the banister. She'd spent years loving the askew garland and their original touches, like the year Barbie dolls and stuffed animals hung from the garland.

This year, the garland was even—ropes of silver and pink beads that matched the tree. It all looked *too* even, though even if had Maggie and Becca been here, it still wouldn't have had the askew Barbie touch of years past.

She'd also laid a layer of fake snow across the mantel and arranged on it decorations that the girls had made in grade school, intermingled with ones she'd collected on family trips. Each figurine represented a time together filled with happy memories. Not wanting to muss her makeup

The Last Christmas

right before everyone arrived, Meredith used one finger to dab a budding tear from the corner of each eye. That's when she looked at the arch leading from the living room to the kitchen, where she'd hung—per tradition—the plastic sprig of mistletoe. How many times had the girls purposely "tricked" one of their parents into walking right under it to get a kiss on one of their soft cheeks? Hundreds, if once.

Somewhere around the girls' twelfth year, they finagled a way to get Eric and Meredith under the mistletoe together, thinking it would be hilarious to make them kiss. Of course, the joke was on them; Eric dipped her and planted a long kiss on Meredith, which she happily returned.

The girls covered their faces and ran upstairs, saying, "Oh, gross!"

Meredith deliberately looked away and headed to the coffee table, where she lit two scented candles—one cinnamon, the other pine—then dimmed the lights to make the room feel warm and homey and everything else it no longer was. Deliberately avoiding the decorations—especially the mistletoe, which she wanted to tear off the arch and hide—she returned to the kitchen.

The first thing she saw was the basket beside the telephone base. She hadn't sent out Christmas cards this year. What picture would she have used? What could she have written in a card—to all of their high school and college friends, colleagues, relatives, and past neighbors—that wasn't a lie? Any of their friends' cards had been quietly slipped into the basket. She couldn't make herself display them on the pantry door as she once had.

The sound of the garage door, chunking its way up, came through the door. It had to be Eric; the girls would have parked in the driveway and come in the front door. Even though she'd been preparing to see him again, preparing to spend the weekend pretending to be a happy couple, Meredith felt exposed, wholly unready to see him. They hadn't laid eyes on each other since he'd been served divorce papers several weeks ago. She walked over to the adjoining dining room and reached for the back of a chair to steady herself.

No finishing dinner preparations, she thought, *until we get the awkward hello out of the way.* She eyed a pint of cream on the counter. She wanted to whip it right now—and not with the KitchenAid, either—with the hand mixer, which would mean expending some of her nervous energy as she moved the bowl and the mixer herself.

After what felt like far too long, the handle on the kitchen door turned, and there he was. Eric's blonde hair had started thinning on top but was still thicker than most of his friends'. His broad shoulders and narrow waist made people assume that he was a swimmer. It was a build many of her friends said they wished their husbands had, hinting, it seemed, that they would have traded in their helpful, attentive husbands for one with such a build.

They had no idea what they were saying, of course. Physical features could change. Eric had done well in the genetic lottery, but no matter how often even he went to the gym, his physique would eventually soften with age. If he didn't go bald, he'd turn gray. He, too, would wrinkle.

But character didn't change, and behavior could poison a life.

He'd never been abusive, which is why she'd stayed as long as she had. He'd also been unaware of her needs and never seemed to care about them anyway. He'd been happy to take everything she gave, with no indication that he should return the love and service in kind. The result? Meredith had been sucked dry, until she had nothing left to give.

The Last Christmas

She watched Eric lift his ugly yellow suitcase over the threshold. He extended the handle before looking up and seeing her.

I would have taken him at twice the weight, with three chins, she thought, *if it had meant feeling valued and loved.*

With her emotions threatening to bubble to the surface, Meredith turned to the table, where she smoothed a nonexistent wrinkle in the cloth.

"You're late," she said, staring at the threads in the linen. She steeled herself then lifted her gaze to meet his, one hand still gripping the chair back so that he wouldn't see her tremble. Maybe the stance would help her look stronger than she felt.

"Nice to see you too," Eric said dryly—and with a humorous half smile.

She gritted her teeth and looked away. After everything that had happened between them, he seriously had to make a joke *now*, of all times? He pulled the suitcase behind him, moseying across the kitchen tile, seemingly content to move no faster than a tortoise. Meredith's eyes darted over her shoulder in the direction of the living room. Maggie and Becca could be driving up at that very moment. The girls *couldn't* find them like this.

"Eric, please hurry." She made every effort to sound calm and unruffled as she hurried after him. "The girls will be here any minute. The last thing they need to see is *that*." She pointed at the suitcase and immediately regretted letting go of the chair. "Hide it in the closet or something."

His mouth quirked a bit more to the left, but he didn't move any faster. In fact, he paused as he smirked, raising an eyebrow now too.

Damn man, she thought, *always laughing at my expense.*

Sure, twenty-six years ago, while they were dating, she'd

laughed at his jokes. Eventually, she grew tired of them and wanted to carry on a semiserious conversation with her husband without any wisecracks thrown in. Tonight, his maddening, oh-so-familiar half smile felt like a jab. Didn't he understand that tonight, the stakes were too high for jokes?

Christmas had always meant more to her and the girls than it had to him, but he'd agreed to maintain the charade until after the holiday, when they could figure out a good way to break the news.

One last merry Christmas as a family—was *that* really too much to ask? Three days of pretending to be a happy family before a lifetime of the girls' having to take turns, seeing their parents separately on holidays, before Meredith could plan on spending some Christmases alone, even when she would have grandchildren but wouldn't get to snuggle them by the crackling Christmas fire?

It probably *was* too much to ask. After all, if at thirty seconds in the house, Eric had already come close to ruining the whole thing, what chance was there of Eric's *not* ruining Christmas?

"What's so funny?" she demanded—and ordered her eyes to stay dry.

"*You* are," Eric said, heading for the stairs.

"I'm funny? What's that supposed to mean?"

Eric sighed and turned around. "Just that you're worrying too much. Take a breath. It's going to be *fine*."

Meredith wanted to punch him in the nose. She'd always been the one who had to nurture and protect the girls. Eric had been the goof-off, the parent who didn't give any consequences when they broke rules. In many ways, the girls had come to see him as a hero simply because he never took anything seriously, unlike their mother, who committed such sins as insisting that homework got done and that the girls planned for college.

The Last Christmas

Meredith silently hoped that one day, they'd remember which parent had done the lion's share of raising them, which parent had come to every play, game, concert, competition, spelling bee, graduation, book report, and everything else—usually alone. Which parent had been home when they needed a shoulder to cry on, whether the tears were over not being asked to the prom, not getting cast in the school play, or something else—a million moments.

In other circumstances, Meredith would have marched back to the kitchen and gone to work whipping the cream, but not now, when her daughters' hearts were at stake. She pictured her spine being as strong as a steel rod.

"We had an agreement—the girls can't know about us yet," she said. "Make this last Christmas a good one for them. You promised."

"I will," he said, and though his tone wasn't as serious as she would have liked, it no longer had the teasing edge to it.

"Thank you," Meredith said, breathing out a sigh of relief. She reached up with both hands to smooth back a few wisps of hair, and Eric pointed at her left hand.

"But if you're serious about fooling them, I suggest you put your ring back on." He chuckled in that maddening way of his—the jokester was back—and shot her a grin as if he'd noticed something particularly funny.

This isn't humorous, she thought, *not remotely.*

Her increased independence had given Meredith a lot of things, among them, a greater sense of self. She'd relearned who she'd once been. She'd gotten to know the real Meredith again. Solitude had proven to be a wonderful schoolteacher, a way to meditate and re-center. But those lessons had yet to teach her to think of witty comebacks off the top of her head.

One lesson she hadn't expected, however, was that there's a fine line between solitude and loneliness. She'd hoped against hope that Christmas would be a happy time for the family, even with the unspoken lie quietly being carried out.

She hurried up the stairs behind him while keeping an ear tuned to the front door for any footsteps. On the way up, she glanced at her left hand. It looked oddly bare, with a slight indentation from where the ring used to be. She shook her head at her foolishness. How had she managed to plan a Christmas with every tradition exactly like old times, yet forget one of the most crucial aspects of the ruse?

As soon as Eric had crossed the threshold into the room they'd once shared, Meredith flew past him, wordlessly dropping to her knees before her dresser and yanking the bottom drawer open.

"Looking for something?" Eric asked on his way to the walk-in closet.

"Yes," she said, knowing full well that he knew what she was looking for. She gave him a shooing motion with one hand. "Go on. Put your things away. I don't want you to be unpacking when they get here." She found the ring box under a stack of old sweatshirts and slipped the ring on. After closing the drawer, she stood and found Eric exactly where he'd been before.

"What?" she asked, her hands searching her person from hair to ring to clothing. "Did I forget something else?"

He shook his head but didn't speak at first—rather unlike him. "It's just that—" His voice cut off, and he tried again. "You look great." His tone didn't seem to have an underlying joke or caveat.

Meredith raised one eyebrow. Was he teasing again? "I don't understand . . ."

Eric cleared his throat and jabbed a thumb over his shoulder, where the suitcase sat in the closet behind him.

"Should I leave my stuff packed? It's only for a few days." He shrugged. "I don't suppose the girls will look inside our closet, but I can hang up the few clothes I brought if you think it's necessary . . ."

His voice trailed off, and his eyes sought hers. For a moment, as they gazed at each other, his face shifted, looking vulnerable and young—an expression she hadn't seen in years. It was a side he didn't show easily or often, but he'd worn it the night he proposed.

Over the years, he'd hidden that part of himself behind layers and layers of masks until she could hardly recognize the man she called her husband. The man she was divorcing bore little to no resemblance to the man she'd married.

That man—the one who used to show his heart and tenderness and caring—somehow stood before her again for a brief moment. The sight was enough to make her eyes burn; she had to blink several times to prevent tears from betraying her.

She had a temptation to tell him to unpack everything—use hangers and the still-empty drawers of his dresser—and to stay longer than three days. To move back home and be hers again.

But he isn't the man I fell in love with—if he ever really was. He isn't the man I think I'm looking at now.

Instead of believing this face was the real one beneath the masks, as she'd long believed, she'd come to believe that this face was simply another mask, one Eric knew could melt a woman's heart and trap her in a relationship until she no longer knew which way was up.

What was real? Who was Eric? Who did he used to be? Who was he today? And was she the same person who'd married him so long ago?

Definitely not. I've changed, become stronger. He can't

stay, or I'll cave to his whims all over again. I won't be a doormat for another day.

She tried to answer his question but couldn't remember what he'd asked. To buy herself a moment, she swallowed, smoothed her apron, and stepped toward the door.

"You don't need to unpack if you'd rather not," she said. "Just be sure to shut the closet door, so neither of the girls wanders in and sees the suitcase." That puke-yellow atrocity *would* be noticed otherwise.

"Will do," Eric said, and disappeared into the closet again.

As Meredith headed out of the room, she caught sight of headlights flashing through the living room window as a car pulled into the driveway, followed by another. At any moment, the girls would tumble into the house with cheerful laughs and excitement. Eric had arrived without a moment to spare. She was halfway down the stairs when his voice floated out of their room.

"It'll be nice to have a decent mattress again after the motel one I've been on."

She froze mid-step. She'd hidden a twin-size blow-up mattress and pump under the bed to avoid the issue of sleeping side by side. But before she could answer—or figure out what to say—voices came from the other side of the door. Meredith adjusted her ring, put on a smile, and turned the doorknob.

Two

MEREDITH OPENED THE DOOR WIDE just as Becca and Maggie picked their way up the frozen walk with their bags and boyfriends in tow.

No need to pretend for this part. Meredith felt genuinely thrilled to have her chicks back in the nest even for a few days and had wanted to meet their boyfriends for a long time now. The couples might start working on wedding plans over the holiday—if either had such news to announce. Of course, by the time any wedding could take place, the truth would be out.

Will Eric have a new wife by the time the girls get married? Will I sit alone at their weddings?

"Mom!" Becca hurried over, dropped a duffel bag at Meredith's feet, and gave her a big hug, her cheeks cool from the winter air.

"Oh, it's so good to see you," Meredith said, squeezing her firstborn. She gave her cheek a peck before pulling away, cupping Becca's face with both hands. "You're getting prettier all the time, and I'm not saying that just because I'm your mother."

"Couldn't agree more," a handsome, athletic-looking man behind Becca said. He smiled at Meredith, though his feet seemed unable to decide where to stand, constantly shifting. Meredith opted for easing his nerves.

"You must be Brandon," she said.

"Yes, ma'am," he said with a dip of his head. He held out one hand, but Meredith ignored it and stepped around Becca to give him a hug.

"It's so good to meet you, Brandon," she said. "I've heard so many good things about you." She pulled back then added, "Please, call me Meredith."

Maggie came up the walk next. "Mama!"

A similar reunion occurred, with Meredith hugging both Maggie and her boyfriend, Spencer. Then she invited them all in.

"Dinner's almost ready," she said as they stomped off snow and took off coats. "Make yourselves comfortable. I'll finish up a few things in the kitchen. Your father should be down soon." She'd scarcely made it to the kitchen before Eric's voice boomed from the staircase.

"There's my girls!"

In the kitchen, Meredith finally poured cream into a mixing bowl. She jammed the beaters into it and flipped the switch. The sound drowned out the reunion in the living room. For the moment, everything was fine. The girls had no reason to suspect a thing. The first real challenge would be getting through dinner.

All too soon, the cream had turned into fluffy goodness. Meredith reluctantly turned off the beaters; she couldn't justify mixing until she had her emotions in check. That would mean turning the cream into butter, and for

The Last Christmas

Christmas Eve dinner, that was tantamount to disaster. She added a little vanilla extract and a tablespoon of confectioner's sugar, mixed them into the cream on low, then covered the whipped cream with plastic wrap.

After she slipped it into the fridge, she looked at the six handmade pies in the corner. She'd gone back and forth about whether to make a pecan one—Eric was the only member of the family who liked it. By the time New Year's came around, she always threw away more than half of his uneaten pie. Not making his favorite would have saved her time, but the girls would have noted the absence and would have pestered her with questions about why she didn't make Dad's favorite.

Because I didn't want to, she thought. *Because I'm tired of doing what everybody else wants.*

In spite of such thoughts, she'd made the pie. Now, sitting in the upper right corner of the two rows, the pie seemed almost like a reminder of the years she'd ignored her own desires. Then again, to the left of the pecan pie sat a chocolate mousse one, *her* favorite flavor. This was the first year she'd made one for Christmas since their first together, when Eric insisted that chocolate wasn't a holiday flavor. This year, he got his pecan, and she finally got her chocolate.

She brought the ham and various side dishes to the dining room then looked over the spread: Flickering votive candles floated in shallow glass bowls. The maroon linen was perfectly pressed, and the dark green napkins were folded just so. China and silver and crystal goblets were in place. Her renowned mashed potatoes, the girls' favorite salad, her grandmother's rolls, and more were all ready. It looked perfect. She untied her apron and went back to the kitchen to hang it on the hook in the pantry.

"Dinner's ready," she called.

A murmur erupted from the living room as the five of them made their way to the dining room. Meredith gave a commanding performance as the unfazed happy hostess. Becca and Brandon sat on one side of the table, with Maggie and Spencer on the other. That left the ends of the table for Eric and Meredith, which was fine with her; she wouldn't have to worry about holding hands or giving him a peck on the lips or having to act natural if Eric slipped his arm around her shoulders.

Eric said grace, and then everyone served themselves, passing dishes around the table. As they ate, Brandon gushed over the sweet potato casserole, and Spencer declared her rolls to be even better than his mother's. *High praise indeed,* she thought, assuming he meant the sentiment and wasn't just buttering up his girlfriend's mother.

Conversation flowed easily; the girls had so much to say about what their lives were like in big cities states away from home, about the things they loved out there and the things they missed. Any time the talk seemed to inch toward an uncomfortable pause, Meredith asked the young men something about themselves. At one point, she asked them to tell the stories of how they met Becca and Maggie—she'd heard about it from her girls, of course, but a man's perspective was always different.

"It was about a week into the new semester," Brandon began, "when I noticed this utterly gorgeous woman walking into my nuclear thermal hydraulics class." Brandon squeezed Becca's hand on the table and smiled at her. She smiled back, practically radiating joy.

Meredith had no idea what *nuclear thermal hydraulics* meant, but she wasn't about to interrupt to ask—the important part of the story was coming up.

"More and more women are going into STEM programs

than ever, of course," Brandon said. "But men still make up the vast majority of the graduate program. So the moment I laid eyes on her, I knew that if I didn't act soon, someone else would steal her from me." He slipped his arm around her shoulders. Becca leaned in and looked up at him as he went on, with a love and light in her eyes that Meredith had never seen in her daughter.

I remember wearing that very expression, she thought, *a long, long time ago.* She met Eric in a similar way, too. He'd slipped into their undergraduate stats class a few minutes late, sitting right by her. After that, they'd both gone out of their way to sit near each other, and by the end of the semester, they were inseparable. She'd hated the class, but she would have taken it again every semester if it had meant spending an hour with the handsome boy in the next seat.

"From that day on," Brandon continued, "I made a point of getting to class early, staking out a spot close to the door, and saving Becca a seat with my backpack."

Brandon's words returned Meredith to the present. She'd probably missed part of the story. *No matter; I'll ask Maggie to tell it again later.*

Becca gazed lovingly at Brandon. "He was pretty slick about it too—he took one seat in from the aisle and put his backpack on the aisle seat. I always had to hurry across campus because I taught an undergrad class right before, so I was always two minutes late. By that point, the room was full, but by some stroke of luck—or so I thought—one seat by the door was always available." She nudged him playfully with her elbow. "Somehow he slipped his backpack to the floor without my noticing, so I kept thinking how I'd lucked out by getting such a good seat."

She leaned her head against his shoulder—a sweet action, yet one that twisted Meredith's insides. She remembered the fluttery sensation of early love, the bubble of romantic fantasy that protected young loves from the cares of the world, making them believe that they'd live in blissful happiness forever.

Of course, all bubbles eventually burst. Most couples adjust, finding a new, deeper love and connection after the twitterpated type fade. Instead, Meredith and Eric had lapsed into an unhealthy give-and-take: she gave, he took.

"I pulled that seat-saving trick over and over again," Brandon said with a grin. He leaned in to kiss Becca's temple then looked up. "Took me a few weeks to ask her out—I wanted to be sure she got to know me as something other than a creepy stalker guy."

"And I had no clue," Becca said. "Three months after our first date, he finally told me how he'd orchestrated it all." She gave a one-shouldered shrug. "Not that I objected to the truth in the least."

Maggie leaned back in her chair and sighed. "That is *so* sweet," she said with an almost dreamy tone. "Not a lot of guys will put in that kind of effort these days." She gave Brandon an approving nod. "I knew I'd like you."

Now it was Brandon's turn to blush slightly, but he looked pleased.

"Mom, Dad," Maggie said. "Isn't their story just like yours?" She motioned between her parents.

"A little, but not really," Meredith started, even though she'd had the same thought. She found herself pushing creamed peas around her plate with a fork. "I wouldn't say it's exactly like—"

"Close enough," Eric chimed in. Everyone looked at him, including Meredith, who instinctively held her breath.

What would he say next?

"I used to be quite the romantic," Eric said. "Sat with

your mom every day in stats, although sometimes she saved a seat for me. I always walked her to her next class. At the end of the day, I walked her to her apartment. Sometimes, I even brought along a rose . . ."

"Daddy, I had no idea," Maggie said, clearly impressed. She gestured to her mother with her left hand. "No wonder he swept you off your feet."

Something caught Meredith's eye. Instead of answering, she reached for Maggie's left hand and drew it nearer. Her ring finger bore a gorgeous solitaire.

Meredith looked at her daughter's face then over to Spencer's and back to Maggie's. "This—are you—you're—"

A huge grin broke out across Maggie face. She looked at Spencer, who was also grinning. He slipped his arm around her shoulders and squeezed her closer.

"Wh—when?" Meredith managed. She wasn't sure whether she meant when did they get engaged or when did they plan to be married.

"He popped the question two days ago," Maggie said, but she apparently had eyes only for Spencer. "We wanted it to be a surprise."

Eric cheerfully slapped the table with an open palm. "And what a delightful surprise it is." He stood and held out a hand to Spencer, who rose as well and shook hands.

"I—uh, I'm sorry I didn't ask you for your blessing first," Spencer said.

"No worries," Eric said. "I didn't ask Meredith's father either." He pulled Spencer into a man hug, thumping his back twice before releasing him.

"Mom and Dad," Maggie said, her eyes brimming with tears. "If Spencer and I can be half as happy as you two have been, it'll be more than I could have dreamed of."

With that, a floodgate of excitement opened between

sisters. They talked and laughed and swapped dating stories, with Spencer and Brandon getting few words in edgewise. Eric had taken his seat again and now gazed across the table at Meredith. He seemed to be trying to say something across the seemingly vast expanse. But what?

Did his look mean that after the girls had inferred that their parents were still living happily ever after, that it was time to tell the truth? She gave him a tiny shake of her head. *Not yet.* Not on Christmas Eve. Not until after Christmas Day had come and gone. Preferably not until after the New Year.

Preferably not ever, she couldn't help adding, as if that were possible.

Conversation continued to buzz across the table between the two young couples, but Eric never took his eyes off her. Finally, unable to take it any longer, Meredith scooted her chair out and stood. "Anyone up for some pie?" she asked. "I made apple, pumpkin, chocolate mousse, and pecan."

"I'll help," Eric said, scooting out and rising too.

Meredith had turned to head back into the kitchen but stopped her in her tracks, eyebrows up. She widened her eyes forcefully as if to say, *What are you doing? Sit down.*

She wouldn't mind having help, if that's what he intended. But he didn't do that kind of thing. Did he want to talk privately in the kitchen—only feet away from the dining room? That would have to wait.

Eric turned to those at the table. "I'll have the pecan, of course. What about the rest of you?"

"Pumpkin," Brandon said.

As Eric took pie requests, Meredith ducked into the kitchen, feeling heat climbing up her neck and dreading the fact that Eric would soon be walking in behind her. He really did seem to be planning to help.

The Last Christmas

She tried to feel incensed that he was intruding on her territory in some twisted way, but instead, a mixture of emotions came over her—sadness that this was the first time in memory he'd ever offered to help in the kitchen with anything, and gratitude, maybe, though she didn't want to admit it.

I don't want to appreciate him.

He appeared, carrying a stack of dirty plates, and she couldn't help but mutter a thank you. He hadn't scraped the food onto the top plate or gathered the silverware like she would have, so the pile tilted skiwampus, like a Dr. Seuss drawing. First efforts weren't always perfect, though. He'd never helped clear the table. Too bad he didn't think of doing little things like that years ago.

She grabbed a knife, slid the pecan pie over, and practically stabbed the life out of it. *If he thinks that carrying a few plates will change anything, he's lost his mind.*

Three

LATER, MEREDITH LAY AT THE far edge of the king-size bed, the comforter pulled high, her arms crossed on top. Normally she fell asleep on her left side. Tonight, she didn't dare move from lying on her back, staring straight up at the ceiling. The last thing either of them needed was accidental spooning or their feet intertwining like they used to, when he sought out her ice-cold toes to warm them up against his always-warm calves.

Staring into the darkness, she had to admit that she'd missed sleeping near someone who willingly warmed her toes. It was one of a few things she missed, and that one thing felt large and important now, with Eric only inches away. She had to remind herself of the many things she didn't miss the slightest bit and remind herself of the many things she'd finally been able to experience and enjoy since reclaiming her life.

If the price for independence was cold toes, she'd pay it.

"I don't bite, you know," Eric said.

The Last Christmas

Her gaze slid his direction, but she didn't move her head a fraction of an inch. By the light of the porch lamp, spilling through the window, he looked positively relaxed, spread out on his half of the bed, with his hands interlocked behind his head.

Of course he's relaxed, she thought, looking at the ceiling again. He'd always remained maddeningly calm, no matter what—no matter how hurt she was or how frazzled or how much in need of his help. No, Eric had never let anything worry him. Not even his family. And *that* bothered Meredith.

"Did I *say* that you bite?" Meredith countered.

"You might as well have. You look ready to grab a baseball bat and go to town on me." He rolled to his side, facing her. Though she didn't look his way again, she could tell from the corner of her eye that he was propped on one arm, as if expecting a conversation. Of course he wanted to talk—now that it was nearly midnight and she needed rest.

"For the record," Eric said, "I'm *not* an intruder."

She crooked an eyebrow at that and turned her face ever so slightly in his direction. The dim light reflected off his toothy grin. She looked away. "That's debatable."

"My name is on the house."

"Not for much longer."

She certainly felt intruded upon. Before going to bed, she'd pulled the blow-up mattress out. He'd laughed at it and toed it back under the bed skirt, saying that Maggie and Becca would notice if he didn't sleep in the same bed. Like a fool, she'd acquiesced.

Just as I folded on everything else for twenty-five years.

No more being a doormat. No more letting someone else make the decisions and staying silent to avoid making ripples or creating contention. The price of such counterfeit "peace" had been inner turmoil as she'd given up her voice and opinions on every topic, no matter the significance.

"I won't attack you, I swear," Eric said. He raised a hand as if in surrender. "I won't even touch you all night if I can help it—if my foot grazes your pinkie toe while I'm unconscious, don't hold it against me."

"Noted," Meredith said with a lighter tone. "Are we done talking? Because I have a big day tomorrow. I need my sleep." She mentally patted herself on the back for saying even that much. After so many years of never standing up for herself even in small ways, speaking like this felt strange—almost rebellious.

She couldn't count the times she'd lost precious hours of shut-eye because predictable Eric had insisted on talking—just as she'd been on the verge of sleep—and not about anything that mattered, either. Usually he'd watched TV for an hour as she tried to sleep. He nudged her shoulder and commented on the lame writing of a sitcom. Or he shook her harder, until she turned around, and then pointed to the television and ask where he recognized that actor from. A thousand times, if once, she'd reminded him that he could look it up on IMDB.

Ideally, she would have gotten the television out of their bedroom altogether, but that would have required sticking up for herself, and, well, she couldn't do that. At least, she couldn't before the divorce. The fancy flat-screen TV *was* gone now. She'd happily handed it over then spackled and painted over the holes.

Tonight, without the TV to distract him, he'd be even more likely to talk. She deliberately rolled away so he'd get the hint, but instead of trying to sleep, she stared into the darkness and imagined how their lives might have turned out if Eric had ever wanted to talk about something that mattered—a concern, a hurt, or a worry—or even if he'd asked for her opinion—her genuine opinion, not just what he wanted to hear—about something more important than who she would root for in the Super Bowl.

We did talk like that, she thought, eyes blurring with tears. *A long, long time ago, when we were love-struck young things.*

Neither of those people existed anymore. In the weeks since he'd moved out, she'd come to like herself again. She'd enjoyed getting ready for bed with only light music playing— pieces she'd chosen herself. She loved crawling into bed, reading a chapter or two of a good book, then turning off her lamp, and falling straight to sleep. She hadn't missed the television or his constant trivial questions.

Why hadn't he ever asked about things that mattered to her? Eric had been nothing if not predictable—happy to talk about a colleague, a work lunch, or golf—but never asking about her day caring for their young children.

Granted, she'd always gotten the generic question, "Doing good?" She hated questions that presumed an affirmative answer. The very same question, or a variation of it, came out regularly, rolling off his tongue with no more thought than he gave to a "thank you" tossed at the drive-thru window as he took his food.

He'd never wanted to know how she was doing. His "questions" contained no genuine interest or caring—no love that she could see. Actions speak so much louder than words, and "Doing good?" came out so that he could check off an item from the list of things a good husband was supposed to do: Walk in the door from work. Ask her "Doing good, hon?" *Check.*

Meredith closed her eyes tightly. *Marriage should be more than a list of things you're proud of having checked off.*

On their wedding day, she'd taken her pastor's counsel seriously and had fully believed that by being the perfect wife—which Pastor Jeffrey defined as "always putting your spouse's needs and desires above your own"—that their marriage would be happy. It turned out that the advice didn't work if only one person applied it.

She couldn't fault Eric entirely; she knew that now. Hundreds of years ago, Newton had explained inertia. He applied the law to physical objects, but it applied to people, too. If a person gets and gets and gets, it's only natural to take and take and take. If someone willing hands over everything they possess—even their very identity—without demanding anything in return, why would you demand more of yourself?

That summed up their marriage in a sad, painful nutshell. She'd given him so much that she'd lost herself piece by piece, until she was nothing but an empty, hollow version of the woman she used to be. Yet somehow, people thought that *she* was the bad one for wanting a divorce—the girls would, too, when they found out—while Eric was the hero. Even though he'd never worked on the marriage.

No, it was more that. She'd come to hate a lot more than his inaction. She resented Eric for not being there for her and for the kids. She'd been the one to attend unending soccer games, play practices, and piano lessons. She'd cheered from the stands and applauded—almost always alone. She'd attended every piano recital, done all of the housework. She'd done all of the yard work. She'd even taught herself how to take apart and fix the garbage disposal because Eric always claimed to be too busy or too tired to be bothered.

If he'd ever cheated or laid a hand on her, calling it quits would have been easier. The neighbor families could have understood the divorce then. They'd be in her corner. But this? *This* kind of divorce they didn't understand, and it couldn't be explained in a single tidy sentence. Twenty-five years held a multitude of subtle, yet complicated things combined into a Gordian knot of a noose. Her choices had come down to two options: suffocate or slice the knot to set herself free.

Two more weeks, and the divorce would be final; the journey was nearly over. And somehow, she lay beside Eric again. It almost felt normal. The mattress moved as he shifted positions. She closed her eyes and prayed that he was close to sleep. Tears leaked from her eyes and landed on her pillow with a soft taps. Her nose grew stuffy, so she breathed through her mouth and hoped Eric wouldn't know she was crying. She tried to sleep, but thoughts of the last few months kept resurfacing.

He's changed since moving out. Or has he?

He did mow the lawn the last few times of the season, and he'd started exercising more. She knew that last one less because of any overt evidence, like seeing him after a workout, covered in sweat, and more because his arms and chest were toned more than they'd been in a long time. He certainly seemed to have found an increased interest in taking care of himself.

Must be a midlife crisis, a way to pick up some young thing whose body is still perky, with everything pointing up. Just watch: he'll buy himself a red convertible.

Meredith could see it now—Eric, with salon highlights in his hair, a tight T-shirt across his newly muscular chest, driving a shiny new Corvette with the top down. Beside him, a fake blonde, with more silicon in her body than Meredith owned in bakeware.

The tramp better be older than our girls.

She couldn't help but tear up more at the thought.

Maggie and Becca needed to find out soon—and from their parents, not from social media. In her mind's eye, Meredith could see a Facebook post of their dad doing Jell-O shots with a bimbo the girls went to high school with. Meredith reached up and surreptitiously wiped both cheeks, then chastised herself for crying over something that hadn't even happened.

The mattress shifted again; this time, the comforter moved too. She braced herself, breathing deliberately through her mouth so she wouldn't sniffle. A hand rested on her shoulder. Its weight felt warm, familiar, comforting. She wanted to shrug it off, to tell him to keep his distance, but she didn't—couldn't.

She also couldn't roll over and slip into Eric's embrace. If she tried, he'd probably let her. But then something more might happen—something they'd both regret. And *that* would mess with her mind and heart too soon after she'd worked so hard to find peace. So she did nothing. She let his hand stay there, the warmth seeping into her and, oddly, calming her.

After a moment, his thumb moved back and forth in a gentle arc. In spite of herself, Meredith couldn't help but focus on it—and be glad of it.

"It'll be okay," Eric whispered. He gave her shoulder a squeeze then rolled over, facing away from her—surely giving her the space she'd asked for, making sure she knew that he would ask nothing of her tonight.

After a few minutes of trying to sort through her emotions, she rolled over too, facing his back. This time, she reached into the darkness, wanting to touch him, to scoot close and slip her arm over his waist or better yet, to have him roll onto his back, so she could curl into the space under his arm, where her shoulder fit perfectly beneath his, her head fitting in the slight dip between his chest and shoulder. But she didn't touch him.

No going down that road again. No losing myself again, no turning back into a doormat. No more being the one sucked dry.

She and Eric knew no other dynamic. If she reached out and crossed the chasm now, she'd wind up in the same miserable boat again.

And yet . . . his hand on her shoulder had felt *good*. She'd wanted it to stay.

For months now, she'd been in search of the whole person she used to be instead of the half a person she'd been in half a marriage. She'd worked on herself, on finding out who Meredith Davenport, née Jones, really was.

She still didn't know completely, but needed to. Figuring that out was important to her in ways she was only starting to grasp. She'd spent years burying wants, needs, and interests of her own, instead letting her identity be consumed by the labels of *wife* and *mother*. She had no regrets about becoming either of those things. Being a mother, especially, had brought her more joy and had shown her how deep her capacity was to love than any other role she'd ever possessed.

Yet she was the one eating the leftover mint chocolate chip ice cream, when she secretly preferred pralines and cream. She ate the burnt toast, let the family choose which movie to watch, even though she was sick to death of both superheroes and Nicholas Sparks.

When she stood by herself, without her children or her husband, who was Meredith Davenport? She didn't know.

She could almost still feel Eric's touch, and again fought the urge to reach out, reminding herself about why she'd filed for divorce.

Do I have to be alone to figure out who I am? Maybe. Maybe not.

The man beside her was technically still her husband. She could easily sidle close to him. He probably would roll over and hold her, kiss her brow . . .

No. Down that path lay danger.

She pressed one hand into her eyes to get rid of the images and the desire they brought with them, wiping a few lingering tears at the same time. Slowly, she rolled to her back and pulled the comforter up to her chin again. If she slept at all tonight, it would be a miracle.

Four

MEREDITH DIDN'T KNOW HOW LONG she lay in the darkness, unable to sleep. She assumed that Eric slumbered away without a care in the world, until he shifted onto his back and spoke.

"Can I ask a question?" he said.

She stiffened. After a hard swallow, she hoped her voice would sound unruffled. "Of course."

She immediately wanted to take back those two words; she didn't want to hear whatever was pinging around his brain—something painful, no doubt. The comforter suddenly felt like a weight, trapping her in the bed. She wanted to pace the room or at least grab her stress ball from the bathroom counter, but she didn't move a muscle. Eric didn't ask his question for some time.

Might as well get it over with, she thought, so she finally prompted him.

"What's the question?" she asked.

After a pause, he said, "Why?"

The single word carried the weight of a life together, of burdens larger than Meredith could vocalize. She knew what he meant, of course. But what did he really want to know? Why she'd filed for divorce? Why she'd been miserable for so long? Or how she'd reached the end of her rope? She opted to answer with another question.

"Why do you think?"

She heard a slight ruffling of his pillowcase, which indicated a shake of his head.

"I don't know," he said. "Is there . . . someone else?"

"What? No. Of course not," she said. "How could you think that?"

Meredith wasn't capable of such a betrayal. She'd been obsessively devoted to Eric, always waiting for the day he'd respond in kind. Wasn't that what Dr. Phil always said? *Marriage isn't 50/50—it's 100/100.* She'd given it her all, while he'd sailed along, seeming to care nothing for the wake of pain he left behind.

"I couldn't come up with another reason," Eric said. "I thought we were doing okay."

Angry now, blood pumped through her as she sat up and threw off the covers. "You thought we were doing okay?" she demanded. "*We* weren't doing anything. *I* was, and *you* got all the credit, until I had nothing left."

She clamped her mouth shut, suddenly scared. That was the most blunt she'd been with him, ever. Dozens of times over the years, she'd tried to explain her hurt, frustration, and weariness. He'd never listened. When all of your attempts to communicate don't stick—when your partner might as well be emotional Teflon—eventually you stop trying. Same with expecting him to carry burdens with her. He had to be asked to "help" with his own house and his own kids, and even then, he rarely followed through.

On the other hand, she'd never confronted him in the middle of the night like this. Maybe if she had—fifteen years ago—things would be different now.

"Oh," was all he said.

Meredith licked her lips and pulled the top of the comforter into her lap with both hands. For several minutes, neither of them spoke, but the tension grew as the silence stretched between them.

She looked over to the window. Through the rounded top, she watched as snow fell. By morning, the streets would look like no cars had driven on them, and the world would look fresh, clean, untouched. There had been a time when Meredith could feel the magic of fresh snow. Now, it meant having to blow and shovel it by herself, getting freezing cold. It would take several mugs of hot cocoa to warm her back up.

But hot cocoa can't warm a heart. Her chest constantly felt like something hard had gotten lodged inside it—an eternal block of ice. She wanted the block to melt but didn't know how to make that happen.

"Then . . . why?" he asked again.

She looked down at the shape of the comforter on her lap. "I *tried* telling you that I needed a partner, that I was miserable," she said. "I did, over and over, but you didn't listen. Turns out that a person can speak to a brick wall only so many times before realizing that they're really banging their head against it. I guess you could say that I got too many emotional concussions."

Eric sat up too. "I don't remember you trying to explain anything."

She lifted her face to the ceiling, wanting to yell and scream but knowing that this might be her only chance to make him see, so she had to stay calm. "I hate my car. I said the Element is ugly and boxy. We agreed to a new car, not an ugly used one. You bought it anyway."

"No," he said countered. "We agreed to a car that was both safe and a good deal. That's what we got. You joked about the shape. You never said you hated it."

"Yes, I—" She cut off, suddenly unsure. Had she actually said the word *hate*? Or had she only joked about the car, assuming he'd figure it out? Sixty seconds ago, she'd been so sure. Now . . . she couldn't say with any certainty how the stupid Element had come to be hers.

She shook her head and tried to make her point a different way. "It's not just about the car. What about quitting your job at the firm without finding a new one first—without telling me?"

"I was miserable there," he said. "I told *you* that over and over. Maybe *you* didn't hear *me*."

She wouldn't let her own words used against her. "You still shouldn't have quit without telling me first—without discussing it with me first."

"You're right," Eric said. "I shouldn't have."

"What?" Meredith's stared at him. She hadn't expected that reaction.

"I should have discussed it with you," Eric went on. "But that day, I had to make a snap decision. Pete was assigning me to the Frankfurt branch for eight months. He didn't ask. It was either leave for Germany that Monday or quit. I knew you'd never travel that far for so long away from the girls, and I wasn't about to go away for eight months without you. So, I quit."

Why hadn't he told her that at the time? *Maybe because I was so mad at him for quitting that he didn't think I'd listen.*

Would I have?

"What about raising the girls? That wasn't a one-time thing. You didn't exactly do your share of parenting. You brushed off my requests and concerns. You never offered to help. It was all on me." Then she gave him specifics—the games and recitals and more that she'd gone to alone.

"I traveled for work a lot," Eric said. "I couldn't be in two places at once."

"You could have found a way to travel less."

"Yeah. I guess," he admitted.

"And you could have at least texted the girls to congratulate them or wish them luck."

"You're right," he said. But she could sense a lingering argument hanging in the air.

"But?" she said, knowing that's what he was thinking.

"But I didn't say no to work trips because they meant bigger bonuses, more stock options, and better promotions. It's thanks to those trips I could pay for things like a top-of-the-line car that wouldn't break down when I was away, even though no, it technically wasn't brand new. I went on those trips so that when I did have time off, the family could travel—I guess I thought that all the time we spent together on those trips was worth the sacrifice."

Meredith wasn't sure what to say. She'd never considered that his workaholic ways might be an intentional gift to the family in his eyes. She thought of the ornaments they'd gathered from around the world and saw them in a new light. She'd come close to not putting them up this year but was suddenly glad, for Eric's sake, that she had. They probably represented family to him more than anything else.

"The trips *were* wonderful," she said, her voice softening. "We all have memories from them that we'll never forget."

"And the girls were able to do any extracurricular things they wanted to do, no matter how much they cost. They both got to attend expensive universities, and we have this big, beautiful home, and—"

"I know," Meredith interrupted, putting a hand on his leg to stop him. They looked at each other in the darkness for a silent moment. "As wonderful as all of that was—and is— we wanted *you* more. But you weren't here."

"I was here when it counted," he said, defensive again. "I never missed a graduation or a big holiday—"

"Oh, yes," Meredith said. "The holidays."

He sighed. "What about them?"

"Every year, I slave and slave in the kitchen—"

"You don't have to make everything from scratch, you know."

She let out a frustrated laugh. "Yes, I *do*."

"I have no idea what you mean."

"When the girls were little," she said. "They helped me make pies, form rolls, and peel potatoes. Preparing the meals was as close to a family affair as I could make it." Hopefully Eric would realize that someone had been missing from the early family traditions. Sure, he'd been under the same roof, but he was usually sleeping or watching TV.

"When the girls reached high school," she continued, "you took them out on Christmas while I cooked. You went sledding or ice-skating or to a movie. Christmas became a time for the three of you—I wasn't invited. But the food was still expected to be ready when you returned."

"You could have joined us," Eric said.

"No, I couldn't," she said. "I tried once. I ordered Christmas dinner from a restaurant. When we got home from skating, suddenly *I* was a traitor because their food didn't taste like mine, and they'd forgotten the pecan pie. According to all of you, I *ruined* Christmas."

"I—" To his credit, he cut off there. He tried to object again, but managed only, "I don't remember that."

"I do," she said simply. "If I didn't bust my butt to serve

the family, I was the bad guy. And you didn't lift a finger." She swiped at her tears angrily as the old feelings resurfaced.

"We haven't gone out on Christmas for a long time," he offered. "The last few years, we've stayed in." Was that a defense or a statement of fact?

"Even then," she continued. "You and the girls did some activity while I cooked. None of you helped me. Last year, it was a *Doctor Who* marathon; the year before that, *Lord of the Rings*."

"And before that, *Back to the Future*," Eric said, seeming to understand, if only a little.

"The only time I saw any of you was when you sent Becca to ask me when dinner would be ready." She snatched a tissue from her nightstand and blew her nose.

"So I used to screw up holidays." Eric's voice was monotone. Did the man *feel* anything?

"It happened again tonight," she pointed out. "After dinner, you took everyone into the living room to chat, while I stayed in the kitchen."

"You didn't have to do the dishes right then," Eric countered.

"I didn't. They're still in the sink. I got the leftovers put away and decided to join you, but by then, you'd already heard stories that I know nothing about."

"Okay, so on Brandon and Becca's first date—"

"Stop," Meredith interrupted. "The point is that I missed out again. *You* got to know Brandon and Spencer and it sounds like you three already have inside jokes. *Five minutes* of help in the kitchen from you, and I could have been there too. You have no idea how many parts of the kids' lives you've cut me out of. I showed up when it mattered," she continued. "You showed up for the fun."

"That's not true," he said.

"No? You brought treats and games. I made them do homework. After a long day, I got them to bed, only to have you sneak them out of their rooms to chase you and climb over 'Grumpy Bear.'"

"They loved Grumpy Bear," Eric said quietly.

"And hated me for sending them back to bed."

"I didn't think it was a big deal."

"You never did," Meredith said. "Every time you let them out of their rooms, I wanted to cry. I needed a little time without being the mom. Then you riled them up, and *I* ended up spending two more hours trying to calm them down while you went to bed. And you wondered why I was crabby the next day. For twenty-five years, you made life harder for me." She shook her head. "That's not what a partner is supposed to do."

The courage—or foolishness—she'd pulled out to say all of that had drained her. It had abandoned her now.

Eric has never listened like this. He still doesn't get it, but at least he hasn't quipped about how I'm overreacting and need to relax.

"I thought I was making your life easier," he said. "You never had to work. You got to be with the girls at home when they were little . . ."

His voice trailed off, but she knew what he was probably thinking—she got new cars and a pretty house and trips. Even her ring, she suddenly realized, was probably something he assumed would make her happy, even though it was far bigger than anything she would have picked out. Providing gifts and trips and possessions—maybe that was Eric's way of being a good partner.

But those weren't the things she'd needed. *Maybe that was his way of giving 100 percent.* The thought made her feel as if the bed had been tilted off-kilter.

"Does that answer your question?" she said quietly.

"I—I think so." He rubbed his thumb across the opposite palm, an old nervous habit. "Is it safe to say that you haven't felt important?"

"Partly," she said. "Not so much needing to feel important and more needing to be acknowledged and appreciated, helped as an equal."

"I've always said thank you." He sounded genuinely confused.

Meredith sighed. "Most people say those two words to total strangers every day."

Eric turned to look at her. In the dim light, his eyes looked much like they had twenty-five years ago. They were the first thing about him that she'd fallen in love with. As she gazed into them, her heart thumped in a way it hadn't in a very, very long time. He reached over and brushed back a lock of hair that had fallen into her eyes—the most intimate touch they'd shared in months.

"I'm so sorry," he said. "I'm sorry that I didn't make you feel how amazing you are, sorry that I took you for granted, that I didn't say how much I love you—how much I've always loved you. I was dumb enough to think that providing for you said it for me."

"It's too late for apologies." Traitorous tears welled in her eyes. "You had thousands of chances to change, and you blew every one. Actions speak much louder than words."

Eric cupped her cheek in his hand, and with his thumb, wiped a tear. She didn't pull away; the touch felt oh, so familiar. She'd missed the intimacy of small moments like this. He leaned closer, his lips brushing hers once, twice. The third time, she kissed him back, and his mouth pressed against hers.

She couldn't help but close her eyes and feel, for a

moment, as if she'd been transported back to when they'd been innocently in love, when neither could imagine a time that their love couldn't conquer all.

She threaded her fingers through his hair. He slipped her nightgown off one shoulder. As his fingers trailed down her neck to her collarbone, his kisses followed the same path. Meredith wanted to revel in his touch, to feel close to him again, but she forced herself to push away.

"No." She pulled her sleeve up.

"But we're still married," Eric said, his voice quiet and tender. "It's okay."

She wanted to yield, to belong—to *matter* to him—but this wasn't right. They were married in name only now; spending a night like this felt *wrong*. Before she could change her mind, Meredith swung her legs off the bed and stood, facing Eric.

"That would only open a can of worms," she said.

A wave of mixed emotions came over her, and a big part felt like regret. She knew full well that it would have felt wonderful to be with him. She also knew that by morning, she would have felt hollow.

"Mer," he said.

She grabbed her phone from the nightstand as if it were a security blanket and headed for the door. She'd pace the house to calm down then find a place to sleep where the girls wouldn't see her.

"What . . ." Eric's voice stopped her. When he didn't finish, she waited but didn't turn around. "What do you need?" He sounded serious and sincere. He hadn't asked what he could do to make her take him back. He'd asked what she needed.

She clutched her phone, tears streaking both cheeks. "I need change," she managed. "Genuine, permanent change—no bandages for covering gaping wounds—and not *things*."

The Last Christmas

She hurried out and walked to the stairs. Halfway down, she heard whispers. Being careful to make no noise, she peered over the banister. In the archway, lit only by the lights of the Christmas tree, were Becca and Brandon. Meredith watched him slip a ring onto Becca's left hand. It sparkled, reflecting light from the tree.

"I love you so much, Becca," he murmured.

"I love you too," she said. "More than I ever thought I could love anyone."

They kissed, sealing their apparent engagement beneath the mistletoe. Meredith had to lower herself to the stairs, covering her face with both hands to hold back any sound that might betray her because she cried even harder than before.

I'm happy for her, Meredith thought. *So happy.*

Five

Meredith opened her eyes and tried to orient herself. She blinked to clear the blurriness of sleep. She was in her bed, and it was morning. How had she gotten there? She remembered seeing Becca, newly engaged, kissing her sweetheart. She remembered crying on the stairs.

Her eyes widened, and she covered her eyes with her hands, praying that her actions hadn't let out their secret. Did Eric have to tell them? She looked over to his side of the bed—empty. Where was he?

More memories tumbled through her mind: the things she'd said to him, his explanations—which made more sense than she'd wanted to admit—the way he'd touched her. She'd laid everything on the table. She'd been blunt—maybe a little mean. He'd asked, and she'd given him an honest answer.

Eric hadn't gotten mad, though he had to be hurting. Instead, he'd kissed her tenderly, sweetly. If she hadn't pulled away, things would have turned out very differently. She touched the slight hollow where Eric had slept.

The Last Christmas

Should I have stayed?

She'd stopped something that would have led to confusing, tangled emotions at a time when she needed clarity. *Saying no was the right thing to do.*

Even if that meant crying on the stairs, embarrassing her daughter, and ruining Christmas? She wasn't sure anymore. She sat up again and noticed that Eric's dirty socks weren't on the floor where he'd left them last night—a first.

She went into the master bathroom. The mirror had no splatter dots. Eric was incapable of washing his hands or brushing his teeth without leaving them. He must have wiped them off.

He remembered how much I hate that, she marveled. She hadn't mentioned mirror spots last night.

She left the bathroom and noticed her cell on the nightstand—plugged in—and hurried over to it. Last night, she'd left with her phone, so Eric must have plugged it in. He'd done several little thoughtful things—the socks, the mirror, the phone. She sat on the bed and sighed.

Nice of him to make an effort, she thought. *Too little, too late.*

She clicked her phone on and, with dismay, read 9:00 on the display. She should have served a big breakfast by now. She should be well on the way toward getting the turkey in the oven.

He turned off my alarm, she thought. *How is that thoughtful for Christmas morning?*

Trying not to panic, she grabbed a notepad and pen from the nightstand and began making a new plan. A shower would have to wait until after making and cleaning up breakfast and putting the turkey in the oven—and until after exchanging gifts.

She hated the idea of beginning the holiday looking like

an orphan from *Oliver Twist*, but what else could she do? With no time for vanity, she focused on the list. Her famous cinnamon rolls took hours to make from start to finish, so she'd have to make something else.

I'll salvage the day, she thought. Homemade blueberry muffins would suffice. She scribbled in a time line for making parts of dinner, noting items she'd have to skip or simplify, all the while praying that this last Christmas as a complete family would still be good.

The smell of something baking wafted into her room from the kitchen. Her pen stopped mid-word, and her head came up. What was baking? And *who* was baking it?

She hurried to the closet and unhooked her flannel robe. She tied it about her waist while hurrying downstairs. The scent of baked goods was eclipsed by the sounds of voices and laughter—and dishes clanking. Everyone else who'd slept under this roof, all five of them, were in the kitchen, having a grand old time—without her.

At the base of the stairs, she clutched the newel post. Her heart felt pinched. She needed to start on Christmas dinner. She needed to make an appearance—and offer an explanation for missing breakfast. But she stood there, unsure of how to join the group without having a spotlight trained right on her—in her bathrobe, her hair a mess, wearing no makeup.

"These are great, Dad," Maggie said.

"Yeah, thanks for breakfast, Mr. Davenport," she heard Brandon say.

"Call me Eric," he said. "And, you're welcome. I have a knack for preheating an oven and following the directions on a can." He laughed then added, "You're all lucky I found three cans of orange rolls in the deep freeze. As for how long they've been there . . ."

"Don't tell us!" Becca said, giggling. "We'll pretend they're fresh."

"Okay," Eric said in a mock-serious tone. "Don't complain if you end up in the ER with food poisoning."

"I'll take the risk," Spencer said.

Meredith stood there, staring blankly. They were eating Pillsbury orange rolls? She supposed they were in the same category as cinnamon rolls, loosely speaking.

They don't need me. She took a step backward. She'd take that shower now, then march into the kitchen as if nothing were wrong, as if she and Eric hadn't fought last night, as if he hadn't tucked her into bed, plugged in her phone, and turned off her alarm.

Had Becca announced her engagement without her mother there? Probably. She felt pushed outside the circle even further.

She took another step backward and bumped into the wreath on the front door. Its bells jangled. Startled, she whirled around to look at the bells, then turned, ready to bolt upstairs. But the noise made several curious faces poke out from the kitchen—Eric's and the girls'.

"Mom!" Maggie said. "Come eat. Are you feeling better? Dad said you were sick."

Meredith found herself walking into the kitchen, eying Eric questioningly.

"I'll clean up," he said. "Promise." He held up three fingers, like a Boy Scout, then began unloading the dishwasher. Had he loaded it last night?

"Th—thanks," Meredith said from the archway. She self-consciously felt her hair.

Brandon stood from the nearest barstool and offered it to her. She thanked him and slid onto it. He stood behind Becca, his arms around her. Meredith poured herself a glass of orange juice.

Everyone wore pajamas, and the lively conversation continued while Eric worked. Meredith relaxed and noted with a smile that Becca kept her left hand in her lap. That likely meant that she hadn't announced anything.

Feeling hungry, Meredith took an orange roll after all—it was a bit overdone, and the flavor was clearly factory-made, but not horrible. A few times, Eric needed help finding the home for a dish or pot, but he told her to stay put and eat. He was probably trying to show that he understood what she'd tried telling him last night.

Sweet sentiment. But canned rolls and an empty dishwasher don't show an understanding of what I've gone through or what the underlying problems were. Are.

With the dishwasher loaded and started, and the counter wiped down, the younger folk migrated to the front room—Meredith's cue to work. She headed for the turkey in the outside fridge. As she opened the door to the garage, Eric reached out and closed the door.

"Nope."

She pointed at the door. "But—I need to get started on—"

"Last night, I *did* get to know Spencer and Brandon in a way you didn't," Eric interrupted. "I heard stuff from the girls that you didn't get to. I don't know why I didn't see this stuff before." He held up a hand to stop her from speaking. "Yes, I know you probably told me a thousand times, but I didn't hear it before."

Meredith furrowed her brow. "But—"

"Go," Eric said gently. "Really."

This time he took her by the shoulders and looked her in the eyes. "You have a lot of years of conversations to catch up on—something I took for granted." He looked into her eyes in a way she hadn't seen in she didn't know how long.

The tenderness she saw there created a bittersweet ache in her chest. Eric gently turned her around and nudged her forward.

"Go," he said. "I'll take care of dinner."

"They'll blame me for breaking tradition and—"

"I'll take the blame," he said.

"Or the credit," Meredith countered.

"No, you get all that for the years and years you've already worked."

Meredith looked at Eric as if he'd grown horns. The day's menu required a level of skill way beyond preheating an oven.

"Go," he said again. "I'm serious."

"But you don't know the first thing about—"

"I'll wing it," he said, interrupting her. "It'll be me, your recipe box, and Google. Between the three of us, we'll figure it out."

"Okay," she said, then she slowly left the kitchen and joined the group in the front room.

The next several hours were filled with laughter as Meredith sat with the kids. They reminisced about childhood memories. The girls told her about their courtships. The young men asked Meredith about herself, something that gave them serious points in her book. After an hour or so, she wondered if they should take a break to shower and get dressed. She couldn't deny that sitting on a sofa by the fireplace and twinkling tree lights felt remarkably comfortable.

Eric appeared around the corner.

"Need help?" she asked, moving to stand.

"Nope." He entered with a tray of steaming mugs. He lowered it to the coffee table, revealing the fixings for hot cocoa—three varieties, mini marshmallows in a little bowl, a pressurized can of whipped cream, a bottle of cinnamon, and a piece of chocolate beside a vegetable peeler for adding garnish—just how she used to make hot cocoa trays.

He paid attention.

"Enjoy," Eric said. "I'll be starting the rolls if you need anything."

Spencer and Brandon dug into the tray, but Maggie and Becca watched him leave, wearing expressions of worry.

"Uh, Mom?" Maggie gestured toward the kitchen.

"Yeah," Becca added, turning to their mother. "Is Dad having a midlife crisis or something?"

"No." Meredith chuckled silently and shook her head. She almost went on to say that he was making Christmas dinner so she could be out here with them, but she couldn't form the words. Saying that much would lead to questions, which might lead to talking about the divorce. Even if it didn't, Meredith couldn't bear it if her girls thought that their mother had given up on a marriage that their dad had gone above and beyond for.

One morning doesn't equate heroic measures.

A loud clank came from the kitchen, followed by a gasp and a curse, repeated several times, followed by, "I'm fine."

Had Eric dropped an empty pot or done something messier, like splatter melted butter all over? In spite of her curiosity, Meredith casually mixed amaretto cocoa powder into a mug of steaming water. She added whipped cream and chocolate curls, followed by a sprinkling of cinnamon. Perfect. Meredith sat back, inhaling the wonderful scent, and sipped. Her daughters followed her example by making their own mugs.

The rest of the day followed a similar pattern: wonderful conversation interspersed with sounds that portended doom followed by Eric's yelled assurances that all was well. They always continued their conversation. Meredith heard how Maggie and Spencer once got lost at the Metropolitan Museum of Art, how Becca had solved a supposedly unsolvable equation, and how that had clinched Brandon's admiration for her. The stories included funny situations, embarrassing moments, hard times. In a few hours, Meredith felt like she knew her children better than she had since they were in grade school.

Eventually, they parted to shower and get dressed, and then they gathered again in the front room, where they played card games and talked some more. Meredith couldn't remember a more enjoyable Christmas, although a tiny part of her had to admit that the fact that Eric was struggling in the kitchen brought a little bit of joy all by itself.

Around three o'clock—a full hour later than Meredith traditionally served dinner—Eric appeared, a dirty apron covering his pajamas, his hair disheveled, and his face sweaty.

"Dinner's ready," he said. He turned around and walked toward the dining room, his shoulders rounded.

Meredith tried to find some sense of satisfaction in the sight. After all, he'd gone into the adventure, thinking he could conquer it the way he'd conquered the business world—and had gotten quite an overdue, eye-opening experience. But she felt no sense of justice or triumph.

The others reached the dining room first and quickly found seats. Meredith followed behind, eying Eric, who stood in the dining room entry, looking exhausted and spent. Becca took a roll from the basket and tapped it against her plate, showing how hard it was. The girls chuckled quietly. The rolls did look a bit dark.

The table's spread didn't include either of the salads she'd planned or the creamed peas, a recipe handed down from Eric's mother. A small bowl looked like it might hold gravy, but even from six feet away, she could see lumps in it. There were the mashed potatoes, and something that was probably dressing, but the most important item was missing.

Maggie turned to her father. "Where's the turkey?"

"It's raw," Eric said flatly. "I thought I gave it plenty of time, but I've never cooked a bird before, and it's not even close to being done. Maybe the oven wasn't on high enough. I don't know." Eric ran a hand through his hair and left traces of flour behind. "Sorry I ruined Christmas. We still have some leftovers from yesterday, and more of Mom's pies."

"It's fine," Becca said. "We'll just have to be careful not to break any teeth on the rolls." She grinned, and Eric cracked a slight smile.

Maggie took her spoon and snitched a taste of dressing. One eye closed entirely, and her mouth puckered. She drank an entire goblet of water to get rid of the taste. At Eric's dejected face, she set her glass down and said, "Dad, it's okay. Christmas isn't only about the food. It's been a great day." She looked at Meredith, who'd just taken her seat. "We haven't had a chance to talk to Mom like this in a long time. It's been awesome."

"It *has* been pretty great," Meredith said.

Becca set the roll on her plate with a clunk. "Remember how we used to help you in the kitchen? Those are some of my happiest Christmas memories."

"Really?" Meredith's eyes burned slightly with happy tears. She blinked to clear them.

"It was fun making the food," Maggie agree. "But we loved spending time with you, too. That's why I'm kind of glad you got sick or whatever last night, so Dad got stuck in the kitchen. I've missed *you*."

What had happened to the teens who'd declared Christmas ruined by an imperfect meal? *Maybe that was just their teen alter egos speaking.*

She caught Eric's eye. His eyebrows were slightly raised, and he swallowed deliberately. He seemed to be asking a silent question. Almost pleading.

Maggie and Spencer leaned toward each other. He slipped an arm around her shoulders.

"I think it's great that you two negotiate roles so far into marriage," Maggie said. "Trying new things, filling in for each other, seeing what the other person needs, and making sure they get it—*that* right there is why you have a successful marriage."

At that, Meredith had to clear her throat. She hoped her face wasn't turning red, but it sure felt hot. Eric's gaze never faltered; he still looked right at her with the same expression showing equal parts hope and dread, as if she were an executioner about to decide his fate.

"Is that what this is?" Meredith asked him in a voice barely louder than a whisper. She hoped he understood what she meant. Was he, at long last, trying to understand what she needed—and give it to her? Had she finally expressed her needs in a way that he understood?

A meal that was partly burned, partly raw didn't necessarily mean any of that. It promised no permanent change, and it didn't mean that Eric understood anything she'd said on a core level. But it could mean that he was trying to understand her needs for the first time, trying to make things better, if only for today.

He did this for me because he knows I wanted a good Christmas, even though we're over.

In spite of herself, Meredith's pulse picked up its pace, and she let herself really look into her husband's eyes.

Neither spoke. No one else did, either. Even the walls seemed to be holding their breath.

Suddenly, in spite of his crow's feet and a little gray hair, Meredith felt as if she were seeing the young Eric. In that moment, she imagined that they were their younger selves, and she remembered why she'd fallen in love with him so long ago. Her eyes began to well up with tears. She fought them back but still had to dab her eyes. She turned in her seat to face him.

"Are you going to keep ruining dinners for me?" she asked.

Eric took a tentative step closer. "If you'll let me, I'll cook every meal for the rest of your life. I'll try my best, but they might still end up raw or burned to a crisp."

One side of her mouth twitched; she bit her lips to restrain the smile. "What about Valentine's Day?"

"Dinner? Yes," he said. "But I'll leave truffles to the experts. I wouldn't want to ruin chocolate for you on top of everything else." He took another step closer and held out a hand. "Will you let me bring you truffles on Valentine's Day?" he asked.

He had rings under his eyes; he probably hadn't slept last night. Then there was the stained apron and the disheveled hair. In spite of all that—or perhaps because of it all—he'd never looked more attractive.

He'd spent last night and the whole day trying to make this Christmas a good one—for her. He'd done it in spite of knowing it would be embarrassing to fail in front of the girls' boyfriends. Grasping his hand, she stood, then walked out of the dining room, pulling him behind her. The others looked at one another and followed.

When they reached the archway, Meredith glanced up to be sure they stood directly under the mistletoe. She took

Eric's face between her hands, pulling him close, and she kissed him long and thoroughly. He seemed tense at first—shocked, no doubt—but soon relaxed and wrapped his arms around her waist in a way she knew so well. The girls clapped and sighed with a sweet sound, and the boys whistled their approval.

Eric and Meredith pulled apart slightly, both blushing. Even so, she reached up and pressed another kiss to his stubbled cheek—she'd always loved him with a little scruff.

"Make me dinner for New Year's Eve—here, at home?" she asked.

She and Eric were the only ones with any idea of what she meant. He took her left hand and admired her ring, then met her gaze again.

"Only if you're sure that's what you want," he said.

"Dad," Becca piped in. "Of course she'd love a romantic dinner."

Maggie agreed. "Of course she would."

But Meredith knew that Eric wasn't referring to cooking again next week. He was asking if they could try again. He wanted to change; she could feel it. In that moment, she felt that she could learn to forgive the hurts from years past and admit where she'd gone wrong. She could change too. And if they both wanted to change, they might have a shot at working things out after all.

If they could find their old selves—really find them—if she could voice her needs, and he remained willing to listen, then maybe this wouldn't be their last Christmas as a family. Trying again would be a big risk, but something told her it would be worth it.

"I'd like a New Year's dinner very much," she said.

"Are you sure?" Eric asked again.

"I'm sure that I want to teach you to cook," she said

slowly. She knew he'd understand; she couldn't be more specific in front of the girls.

"Really?" he asked.

"Yeah." She grinned. "I think you really want to learn how."

The pleading, pained look softened, replaced by the most genuine smile she'd seen from him in a long time. She lifted a finger and gently jabbed his chest.

"But I expect an amazing barbecue for the Fourth of July," she said, "and the perfect turkey for Thanksgiving. Don't worry about the gravy; I'll handle that."

"Deal." He kissed her again.

Even though she was oh-so aware of their grown children watching, Meredith didn't care about anything but the fact that she'd found her love for this man again.

And to think I almost threw it away.

Eric pulled back. "One more question. Before we see if anything on the table is edible."

"What's that?" she asked.

"What do you think about investing in a paper shredder?" he said. The girls looked at each other with utter confusion, but Meredith imagined destroying their divorce papers.

"Excellent idea," she said. "Let's buy one first thing in the morning and break it in right away." Tears finally spilled down her cheeks. Eric pinched an index finger and thumb across his eyes, wiping tears of his own. He held her close, and she hugged him back, breathing him in, listening to the thumping of his heart.

"I'm so, so sorry, Mer," he whispered, so only she could hear. More tears leaked onto his pajama top.

"I know," she said. "So am I." As they returned to the dining room and took their seats, Meredith laughed through her tears at the others' expressions.

The Last Christmas

"Everything is great," she assured them.

"Let's say grace," Eric suggested. "I don't think the mashed potatoes will kill anyone, but it can't hurt to cover our bases."

ABOUT ANNETTE LYON

ANNETTE LYON is a *USA Today* bestselling author, a four-time recipient of Utah's Best of State medal for fiction, a Whitney Award winner, and a five-time publication award winner from the League of Utah Writers. She's the author of more than a dozen novels, even more novellas, and several nonfiction books. When she's not writing, knitting, or eating chocolate, she can be found mothering and avoiding housework. Annette is a member of the Women's Fiction Writers Association and is represented by Heather Karpas at ICM Partners.

Find her online:
Blog: http://blog.AnnetteLyon.com
Twitter: @AnnetteLyon
Facebook: http://Facebook.com/AnnetteLyon
Instagram: https://www.instagram.com/annette.lyon/
Pinterest: http://Pinterest.com/AnnetteLyon
Newsletter: http://bit.ly/1n3I87y

Truth or Dare

Julie Coulter Bellon

OTHER WORKS BY JULIE COULTER BELLON

Ashes Ashes
Ring Around the Rosie
Through Loves Trials
Love's Broken Road
All Fall Down
Ribbon of Darkness
Time Will Tell
All's Fair
Dangerous Connections
Griffin Force Series
Hostage Negotiation Series

One

THE SPOT WHERE JONAH'S FOOT should have been—had been until a year ago—was hurting again. The phantom pains from the amputation came mostly in the evenings now, which always made it hard to sleep. Jonah sat in the darkness of the family room, enjoying its black comfort, how it hid the display of track and field medals and trophies he'd won in high school. With the snowstorm that had been threatening all day finally unleashing itself, it was as if Mother Nature was commiserating with him. The howling wind outside perfectly matched his mood.

Good thing his parents weren't home to see this. His mother would frown and turn the lights on and offer to watch TV with him. Or she'd bustle around getting him something to eat or wanting to know how he was feeling. That was the most dreaded question of all. He didn't know how he was feeling, but he did know he needed some peace and quiet. Since coming home from rehab three days ago, this was the first evening he'd been alone. His friends and neighbors meant well, but there had been a steady stream of visitors to the house, coming to tell him how sorry they were for his "accident." Like losing his foot to a roadside bomb in Afghanistan was equivalent to a fender bender or something. But it was the pity in their eyes that bothered him the most. He didn't want anyone to pity him.

He leaned back in his father's recliner. His mother had instilled manners in him, so he'd smiled at everyone who came and tried to make it okay for them, but he'd never felt more alone. No one would ever understand what it was like to try to buy one shoe or have to put your pants on sitting down.

He flexed his good leg, careful not to hit the dog sleeping at his feet. Or really, just his foot. Jonah grimaced. Would he ever get used to only having one foot? Even after a year of rehab it didn't feel natural. Maybe it never would. His thoughts turned to the wine in the fridge. It would be so easy to numb himself, but going down that road never led anywhere good. He'd tried. It was time to get up and turn the lights on. Stop feeling sorry for himself and read a book or grab a movie to watch. Anything except more sitting in the dark.

Bending down to get his prosthetic foot, he pulled up the pant leg on his sweatpants, put the liner and sock over his stump, then strapped the prosthetic foot on and ratcheted it tight. "Wake up, Magnus." The golden retriever didn't even move. Jonah poked him gently in the side. "Hey."

Magnus's ears perked up and he turned his face toward the door as if someone were there. "Just the wind, boy," Jonah assured him. "It's getting bad out there." But then he heard it, too. Something or someone was scratching at the back door.

Glad now that the lights were off, Jonah stood. If

someone thought they could break into his house, they could think again. His military training kicked in and he crept to the window. With the barest movement of the blinds, Jonah squinted to see the back porch through the swirling snow. It wasn't a human trying to break in, but a dog that wanted to come in.

He let out a breath, trying to calm the adrenaline running through his veins. "It's for you, Mag," he said, before he turned to flip on the lights.

His dog was standing in front of the door, pawing it. He obviously knew his visitor. Jonah walked over and opened it, letting in some snow and a smaller golden retriever who was obviously happy to see Magnus. She shook out the ice and snow from her fur and Jonah watched, amused, as they greeted each other. "You've been holding out on me, buddy." He bent down to scratch her behind her ears. "And who do you belong to?"

She gave him a cursory glance before turning her attention back to Magnus. Jonah watched the dogs for a moment longer and then headed back to the recliner. They followed him and flopped down next to his chair when he sat down. The pair got comfortable lying next to each other. "A girl who likes a quiet evening at home? You're a lucky dog, Magnus."

The quiet didn't last long before the doorbell echoed through the house. Since he knew his parents had a key and he didn't expect them for another hour or so, Jonah thought about not answering it. But with the storm raging outside, he knew he had to let them in. "Probably someone looking for your girlfriend," he said to Magnus as he got up from the chair. "At least I hope it is. Please don't let it be Ms. Davis." His mother's friend meant well, but when she'd come by earlier today she couldn't stop saying "you poor boy." It was enough to make any soldier want to go AWOL.

He walked down the hall, grateful his parents didn't have stairs, or the person at the door would be waiting a lot longer. He opened it with both dogs at his heels. A woman stood in front of him, bundled in a parka, hat, and scarf so only her eyes were visible. She pulled her scarf down. "Hey, Jonah, I'm looking for my dog, Lola. Did she come over here?" She craned her neck, trying to get a look at the dogs that were hiding behind him.

Jonah was battling to hold the door with the wind and snow slamming into them so hard he could barely see the porch stairs. He motioned her inside. Once she was in, she pulled off her hat and scarf. Her short brown hair was sticking up at odd angles, but she didn't seem to care about anything except her dog.

"Lola, honey! You scared me! Never do that again." She hugged her dog while she scolded her. Magnus was trying to nose in on the hugging action, too, and got a scratch behind the ears for his trouble.

Jonah looked down at the reunion. She'd started to peel off her coat and gloves, while her dog danced around her. The woman's heart-shaped face dredged up memories from a lifetime ago.

Cami Jackson. A little zing of awareness skittered up his spine. Her smile was intertwined with so many of his happiest high school memories. Being on the track team together. Star-gazing. Best friends for life. Or so he'd promised. She'd matched him in humor, goals, and ambition, but after graduation, he'd joined the service, she'd fallen off the grid, and he'd let her go. "Hey, Cami."

She managed to look up at him while her dog finished bathing Cami's chin. "We haven't seen each other in nearly six years and all I get is a *hey, Cami*? Come on, you can do better than that."

He gave her an impassive stare. He just didn't have the energy to entertain one more person. And besides, what did she want him to say? "Okay. How about, it looks like you need to get a leash for your dog."

She frowned up at him and he saw the shadows under her eyes. She looked exhausted and in that moment, he wished he'd said something to make her smile.

"I can see we're bothering you. I'll just take Lola and head home." She stood and both dogs zigzagged around her legs, begging for more attention. "Just give me a second."

She tried to bend down and grab her gloves and got some more wet doggie kisses for her trouble. Magnus was totally focused on her, but looked back at Jonah every now and then. Would he even come to Jonah's side if he called? He wasn't sure. His dog was giving Lola and Cami some pretty adoring looks and Jonah hadn't been a part of Magnus's life for a while.

He folded his arms, feeling silly standing there watching her try to put her things back on and keep her balance with two dogs jumping on her. Not that he didn't have a nice view. Now that he could see her clearly, he was surprised at how different she looked. The thin girl he remembered from high school was still trim, but her jeans and sweater now had curves in all the right places. Yet, her eyes that had always been laughing in high school, weren't laughing anymore. She had a hollow look in her face, like the people he'd seen visiting their loved ones at the rehab center. Did that have to do with losing her dog? Or seeing him? Probably the latter. Who wouldn't look like that, seeing him now? He opened the door. "I'm glad you found your dog."

Cami didn't say a word to Jonah, just snapped a leash on Lola's collar. The dog immediately sat down on her haunches in the doorway and began to whine. It did look pretty bad out there. The frigid wind effortlessly pushed the snow into drifts, blasting it sideways across the yard. Jonah turned in time to see Cami square her shoulders, her mouth pulled into a tight line. He sighed inwardly. Okay, his mom had raised him better than this. He was out of line and that wasn't like him. The old him, anyway. "Hey, that storm's really picked up. Do you want to wait a bit and warm up at least?"

Even to him, his voice didn't sound very welcoming and Cami's look of misgiving confirmed it. He was out of practice. Magnus stared up at him, clearly unimpressed at his attempt. The dog darted a glance at Cami as if to say, *yeah, my human's a little rusty at this. Sorry.* Jonah straightened. His dog was not going to be embarrassed by his lack of manners. He could fix this.

Cami pulled on the leash. "No, thanks. We've bothered you enough. Come on, girl." She ducked her head, but not before he saw the hurt in her eyes. Guilt welled in him.

Jonah grabbed her arm as she squeezed by. "Hey, I'm sorry about what I said. Give me a chance to make it up to you." He bent down so she'd be forced to look at him. "I was just about to eat some of my mom's stew and that would definitely warm you up. Are you hungry?"

She hesitated, pinning him with her gaze as if to gauge his sincerity before she finally relented. "Okay, that would be great, actually." She didn't look exactly convinced as she took off her coat and gloves for the second time, but at least she'd agreed to stay.

When she turned, he could see her jeans were soaking wet. *How long was she looking for her dog?* "You know, I have some sweatpants you could borrow and we could throw your jeans in the dryer."

She shivered and looked down. "Thanks. I'm freezing."

He was about to turn down the hall to his room, but his prosthetic foot caught on the rug in the entryway and he stumbled. Biting back a curse, he put his hand on the wall to anchor himself and find his balance. He stood there for a moment, unwilling to meet her gaze. How could he walk in front of the girl who remembered him as a confident track star? He didn't want her to see what he was now.

When he didn't move, she stepped forward. "Jonah?" Her cold fingers on his arm jolted him out of his thoughts.

He forced his feet to step forward, hoping all that gait training he'd suffered through to make his walk look normal had worked. "I'll be right back. You can wait in the kitchen. It's right through there."

"I know." Cami's voice was warmer now and it helped Jonah to relax a bit. "It felt like we were either here or at the track all through high school." She looked around and for just a second the exhaustion on her face melted away. "Don't you wish you could go back sometimes? Everything was simpler then."

Every day. Jonah still struggled to accept his new reality sometimes. It was too easy to wish for his life before the pain and rehab and managing a prosthetic. "We had some good times."

The brightness in her eyes faded. "Yeah, we did."

He waited until she'd started toward the kitchen before he walked down the hall to get the dry clothing for her. Magnus stood beside him and licked his hand as if to ask him if he was okay. That dog still read him like a book. Jonah touched his silky head. "I'm okay."

When he walked into the kitchen, Cami was hunched over the island, her head in her hands. She looked small and defeated, something he'd never seen on her before. "You okay?" he asked as he joined her.

"Just tired." She tried to muster up a smile, but it looked more like a grimace.

"You still staying up late star-gazing?" He wanted to see a real smile on her face, one that reached her eyes.

"I wish." She looked down at her hands, folded in front of her. "Remember how hard I tried to teach you the constellations? You claimed you could never see them, but I always thought you could."

"I just wanted an excuse to stay out late." And to be near her. Even with her struggles in her home life she was light and fun, intelligent and driven, and that had drawn him to her. So many times he'd thought about taking it further, but he didn't want to ruin the friendship. His reaction when he first saw her tonight was telling, though. Those old feelings were still there, but what could he offer her now? His tried and true friend-zone tactics kicked in and he stood to put some distance between them. "I'll warm up the stew and get the sugar cookies for dessert." He put his lead foot down carefully and walked slowly to the fridge.

"I love your mom's cookies. Did you decorate them?"

"She tried to get me to." It was a Christmas tradition at their house and he'd put a damper on it for his mom. His conscience twinged with guilt. He should have humored her.

"You were just trying to make sure they all stayed edible, I'm sure." Cami barely held back a grin. "You always did use way too much icing."

He could feel one of their old debates coming on. Carefully setting down the container of stew, he rested his palms on the counter, facing her. "Hey, I'm an expert at decorating those. And you can never have too much icing."

"When you can't tell if the cookie is supposed to be Santa or a stocking, there's too much icing." She quirked an eyebrow in challenge.

He shook his head. This was too easy. "Who cares what it's supposed to be as long as it tastes good?"

She didn't admit defeat gracefully and merely rolled her eyes. "Because it's a sugar cookie, and decorating it to look like something is part of the fun."

"Mine look like something. Something good to eat." He leaned toward her. "You have to admit, I've got you there. I mean, what can you say to that? You know it's true because you finished off every cookie I ever brought you."

"How do you know I didn't give them to my dog?" Cami laughed and Lola pricked up her ears at her mistress, as if she was hoping for that very thing.

Jonah narrowed his eyes and pointed his finger toward her. "My cookies are a work of art. You just don't want to admit it."

She held up her hands in mock surrender. "Okay, okay, I'll plead the Fifth." She looked up at him and, for a moment, it was like they were back in high school again with nothing more to worry about than next week's math test or tomorrow's track meet. But Cami dropped her eyes quickly and the moment was gone. She picked up the folded sweatpants from the counter. "Thanks again for letting me borrow these. I'll just go change out of my wet clothes before I say something that might incriminate me."

He chuckled as she disappeared into the guest bathroom. He couldn't remember the last time he'd joked around like that with someone. He'd missed it.

Turning toward the task at hand, he got things ready for their meal, getting out bowls and spoons. Before long, Jonah heard the bathroom door open and the dryer next to the mudroom start running.

When she came back into the kitchen, he noticed she'd smoothed her hair. It was strange not seeing her in the ponytail she'd worn through high school, but he could definitely get used to her short hair and how it drew attention to her eyes. As his gaze traveled downward to the sweatpants she'd borrowed, though, he could hardly smother a laugh. The pants were pulled above her waist and she'd rolled up the pant leg bottoms until it looked like she was wearing fat ankle weights. "Let me guess. The pants didn't fit?"

She gave him her best are-you-kidding-me look. "Yeah, you're a bit taller than me." She turned her ankle to model the uneven rolls for him. "I might start a new fashion, though. Winter Storm Chic. What do you think?"

"It could work." He gestured to the rolls. "And it has the extra feature of being able to pull them down over your cold feet, which could be a selling point."

She shook her head. "I think someone already invented something for that. Called socks." She wiggled her bare toes.

"Do you need some socks? I've got extra." He inwardly winced. Of course with only one foot he'd have lots of extra socks, but he didn't want to call any attention to his injury if he could help it. Cami didn't even glance at his feet, though.

"I think I'm good, thanks." She moved past him and sat down on a stool at the kitchen island. "So, is it weird being home?"

Here it comes. He'd wanted her to be different, but no one could resist fishing for gossip on how the town's newest amputee was doing. He glanced over at her, disappointed. "Not really."

But her face was still open and smiling. "It's all your dad was able to talk about. He's so glad you're here."

Jonah resisted the urge to stare at her. She wasn't looking for gossip; she was just happy for him and his family. *When did I get so suspicious of people's motives?* "My dad loves to talk. Probably because his patients are captive audiences."

She laughed. "The perk of being a dentist, I guess."

"Is that where you saw my dad? At his office?" He rubbed his hand over his jaw. He wasn't surprised his dad had talked about him. His parents had been there for him through every step of his recovery, spending as much time with him as they could while he was at Walter Reed in Bethesda. When they'd asked him to come home for Christmas, he couldn't say no.

"No." She shifted in her stool. "He came by the school the other day with his sponsorship banner and we got to talk a bit." Then, as if she couldn't sit still, she slid off the stool and came to help him dish up the stew.

"He's sponsoring something?"

"Harrison Dental proudly supports the Morgan Huskies." She took the smaller bowl and headed for the microwave.

"Are you a sponsor, too?" He was trying to connect the dots, but something wasn't clicking. She'd always wanted to be an Olympic runner. What was she doing back in Morgan, anyway?

"I'm the new track coach at Morgan High." She leaned in and he caught the faint, flowery scent of her shampoo. "I finally replaced Coach Stubbs. After thirty years of coaching, though, he can't leave it alone and still comes out to watch my practices."

"You replaced Coach Stubbs?" he repeated. Jonah had never thought that man would retire. Coach Stubbs lived and breathed the track team. He was the most intense man Jonah had ever met before he joined the Marines. Even then, he could only think of one or two drill sergeants that were more intense than Coach Stubbs. "That's got to be intimidating, having your old coach watch *you* be the coach."

"It is. I keep thinking he's going to give me critique notes or something, but so far he hasn't said a word. In a way, that's kind of worse. I mean, what if he hasn't said anything because he thinks I'm doing it all wrong?" She took the second bowl of stew from him and queued it up for the microwave.

"I'm sure you're doing great." And he meant it. She would be a great track coach.

He leaned against the counter and watched her punch in some numbers and press start to warm up the stew. Since the accident he'd always felt tense when he was in public or around people who weren't family, but that had evaporated with Cami. Their easy camaraderie had returned, like they'd never been apart, and for the first time since he'd woken up in the hospital, he felt normal. But the best part was, there wasn't a trace of pity in her eyes when she talked to him.

He hadn't expected that, but he liked it. A lot.

Two

CAMI KEPT HER BACK TURNED as the microwave warmed the food. She needed to keep herself standing and busy or she'd fall asleep. What a day this had been. One she never wanted to repeat. The nurses had forced her home for some rest, but then she'd realized Lola had gotten out somehow. Everything had gone wrong. But her worry over having to leave Ben in the nurses' care and panic at finding Lola missing were finally wearing off, replaced by memories of Jonah. He'd always been the rock that steadied and grounded her. With everything that had happened to her in the last seventy-two hours, she'd sorely needed his presence and hadn't even recognized it. Being here brought back so many warm memories for her, like sunshine chasing away all her shadows. The reality was, though some things seemed the same, their lives were very different than what they had been. She needed to keep that in mind.

Cami ran a hand through her damp hair and suppressed another shiver. She caught chills easily; that hadn't changed.

Back in the day, no matter what season it was Jonah would be hot and she'd always be cold. He usually had his arm around her to warm her up, though. That was one thing she wished hadn't changed, even if it was just for tonight.

She stole a peek behind her. The military had been good to Jonah. He'd always been athletic and good-looking, but now he was powerful and had a ruggedness to him. His blond hair was cropped, military-style, but the short-sleeved T-shirt he wore that proudly said *Marines* on it pulled across a broad chest and showed off some muscular arms. On the outside, he seemed more like his old self, but every now and then his change in demeanor told her he was struggling with some inner demons. She wasn't sure how to handle that. The Jonah she'd known had been so easy-going about most everything. She'd never seen him withdraw into himself before.

The microwave beeped and she pulled out the bowl and replaced it with the second one. *Turn around and face him; you're not some shy teenager. It's Jonah*, she scolded herself. "So, have you done anything fun since you've gotten home? Been over to the Movie Festival yet? They're showing Christmas classics from the 30s and 40s this year with a live band playing Christmas carols in the lobby."

He watched her with such a serious look on his face, she couldn't help wishing he'd stayed easy to read. "No. I've been getting settled at home."

There it was again. The withdrawal. His voice sounded so flat, like she shouldn't have even suggested he go out. *Maybe I shouldn't have. Maybe it's too hard for him to leave the house.* But he seemed to get around just fine. She shrugged her shoulders. "Well, you probably had a lot of visitors. Once your dad let the cat out of the bag that you were coming home for Christmas, it spread like wildfire."

The microwave dinged and she turned to pull out the last bowl. Pushing one in front of him and taking the other to her stool, she could feel his eyes on her. Nervous flutters started in her belly and she couldn't sit next to him yet. Glancing around, she grabbed the kettle off the stove like it was a lifeline and went to the sink to fill it. "If you have some hot chocolate mix, I can make us both a cup." She put it on to boil and took a breath before she came around the edge of the island to face him.

He was still watching her without saying anything and she couldn't read his expression. *Maybe I should have asked permission first. Maybe he hates hot chocolate now.* "I don't have to make anything, though, we could just eat," she said, turning to take the kettle off. She didn't know what to do anymore, and she was too tired to figure it out.

He reached across the island and held her arm. Even though his touch was light, tingles raced up her shoulder and down her spine. "Hot chocolate would be great, thanks."

Her breath caught as she met his gaze and all her tiredness fled. After all these years he could still affect her like this. He definitely didn't have the same outgoing personality he'd had in high school, though. There was a lot going on behind those blue eyes and he didn't seem in the mood to share. Not that she would ask him to. She could hardly imagine what he'd been through in the last year and her heart ached.

Jonah took a step toward her and sat down. The truth was if she didn't know he'd lost a foot, she wouldn't have guessed it. His limp was hardly noticeable and he moved well. He must have had a fantastic physical therapist. But from his frosty reception when she'd first arrived, she didn't want to bring up any uncomfortable topics.

He seemed to be on the same wavelength. "So, how did

this doggie romance get started?" he asked before he took a bite. She smiled. The dogs were a pretty safe thing to talk about.

"I'm not sure. She's been sneaking out the past few nights and making visits to dogs she's met at the park." Thankfully her neighbors had caught her since Cami had been watching over Ben in the hospital. She touched the bridge of her nose, pushing those thoughts away for the moment. "I can't figure out how she's getting out. I might start calling her Houdini. I can't even tell you how relieved I was she was over here and safe with that storm outside."

They both looked at the dogs, who were sitting at attention and staring at them. Or staring at the stew in their bowls. "Magnus, you know Mom would kill me if I gave you any of her stew," Jonah admonished with a shake of his head. "You have plenty of food in your dish." Magnus gave him a soulful stare. "All right." He got up and moved to the cupboard, taking a box of dog treats out. "Here's a little something for you and your lady friend."

The dogs settled down with their treats and Jonah talked to them the entire time about being good dogs. Cami tore her eyes away from the scene. He was adorable with the animals, like he'd always been, and it made her heart melt. Even something as devastating as losing a limb hadn't taken the sweetness out of him. She rubbed her eyes. Being so tired was making her sentimental. Thankfully the kettle whistled and gave her something to do besides stare at the man next to her.

"The box of hot chocolate packets is in the pantry, first shelf on the left."

"Thanks." She concentrated on getting the hot chocolate ready, worried that it would be lumpy. Somehow hers was always lumpy no matter what she did, but Ben never minded.

She felt the sting of tears and quickly blinked them away. Bending over her task, she hoped Jonah hadn't noticed. Stirring the lumps out of that hot chocolate became her new mission in life until she could get a handle on herself and her emotions. She finally handed him a cup of non-lumpy hot chocolate, a triumphant smile on her face. He gave her a funny look. *Do I look teary?* She made her smile bigger, but that just made him frown. *For Pete's sake, don't scare the man.*

"Thanks."

He was watching her too closely and she backed away. Cami sat down and concentrated on finally taking a bite of her stew. It smelled divine and reminded her that she hadn't had a chance to eat much today. "This is so good." She took several more bites, the warmth of the food taking the edge off the cold.

Jonah raised his eyebrows at her nearly empty bowl. "You were really hungry."

"I didn't have time to eat and I really hate—" She stopped herself. She'd almost said *hospital cafeteria food*. That was a subject she didn't want to broach with him, not if she didn't want to dissolve into tears. Besides, he probably didn't want to talk about hospitals anyway, with what he'd been through in the last year. And all she could think about was Ben being there when he should be home safe with her. She felt the prickle of tears again and forced her thoughts to Jonah and high school. It had been such a happy time for her, filled with so many hopes and big dreams with nothing but smiles for the future she'd planned. But she wasn't that girl anymore and that wasn't her life. Part of her wished it was, though. She couldn't control the little sigh that escaped for what might have been.

"You really hate what?" He leaned forward on his elbows, giving her his full attention.

She pulled her thoughts back to the conversation. "I, uh, really hate it when that happens." She wanted to slap her hand against her forehead. She sounded like an idiot, but she couldn't talk about Ben. Or hospitals. Or anything that would make her cry. She wanted to be the girl he remembered, someone who could handle whatever life threw at her.

Jonah leaned back, giving her a little more space. "I know it's been a while, but I still know you, and something's wrong." He reached for her hand, and she let him take it. "If you want to talk about it, I'm here."

Tears filled her eyes, and she swallowed hard. It had been so long since she'd had someone to lean on and confide in. Six years to be exact. And he was still so perceptive when it came to her and her feelings. She looked down, blinking away her tears. She was not going to cry in front of him if she could help it, and that effort made her throat too tight to talk. Cami squeezed his fingers before she stood and took her bowl to the sink. Taking a second to gather herself, she rinsed it out slowly. Finally, she turned around and found her voice. "It's a long story."

He lifted a hand. "We've got time. And some hot chocolate. I'll even make a fire if you like. Just like old times."

No, it wouldn't be like old times. Back then, they'd sit in front of his fireplace and talk about running strategies and if the team had a chance to go to state. If she sat there with him tonight, she'd have to tell him why she'd never achieved any of her goals. She'd tell him about Ben. Could she really lay her soul bare to Jonah? Could she look into his eyes and see the disappointment that was sure to be there?

As if the universe had heard her thoughts and wanted to help, the lights flickered out. But if anything, her anxiety only grew. How would Jonah feel about her if he knew the truth?

Three

As soon as the lights went out, Jonah grabbed the counter, feeling the dogs brush against his legs. Falling in front of Cami was all he needed. At least it was dark if he did. "Let me get a flashlight." Hopefully his mother still kept them above the fridge. He moved slowly, pushing the dogs out of the way with his good foot. Opening the cupboard and feeling his way inside, he was grateful to touch the shape of a flashlight in the corner. He flipped it on, careful not to shine it in her face. "Good thing we ate before we lost the electricity."

"Too bad about my pants in the dryer, though. I might have to wear yours home." She bit her lip. "Do you think your parents are okay?"

"The staff Christmas party was at the hotel ballroom, so if the storm is too bad, I'm sure they'll just book a room at the hotel for the night. Although knowing my mother, she'll plow through the storm in her heels to make sure I'm not alone."

Cami made a noise of commiseration. "It's hard for her not to baby you, I imagine, but it's only because she loves you."

"I know. I haven't exactly gone easy on her." He thought back to his mom's excited invitation to go with them to the Movie Festival and how her face fell when he said no. He didn't want people gawking at him, but he could have let her down easy. He should have. "I'm lucky to have her."

"Yes, you are," Cami said quietly. "I can only imagine how she feels having you home safe and sound."

He could hear the hitch in her voice. There was definitely something else going on with her, but he didn't push. For now.

Jonah opened the drawer next to him and picked up some matches. "Should we go into the family room? You can get your pants and dry them in there. I really can start a fire."

He offered her the flashlight and she took it. "That sounds great." She got her jeans out of the silent dryer and dragged in a kitchen chair to drape them over next to the fireplace. She walked back and handed him the flashlight when she was done. "I'm definitely ready for that fire."

A sense of satisfaction went through him that she didn't question whether he could do it. The fact was, he hadn't done much for himself since he'd come home and definitely hadn't taken care of anyone for longer than he cared to remember. He grabbed his mug, feeling lucky. Sure, he was walking slowly, but he was balanced and hadn't fallen on his face so far.

She followed behind with her mug and sat in his father's recliner, which was closest to the fireplace. "I just can't get warm."

Jonah knelt down and pulled back the fireplace screen. "Just give me a minute." Before long he had a roaring fire going and he sat back, pleased with himself—until he realized that getting back up on his feet was going to be awkward, especially in front of her. Those old feelings of frustration came rushing back and his fists clenched involuntarily. He didn't want to make a fool of himself or have her see him struggle. So the obvious solution was he'd just sit here on the floor. Watching over the fire was a perfect excuse.

He looked up at her, but she hadn't even noticed his moment of indecision. She was clutching her mug of hot chocolate like it was a lifeline, a little shiver running over her. In the old days, he would have pulled her close against him to warm her up, but that might be awkward now. Jonah reached back and grabbed the blanket off the arm of the couch. "Here. This should help."

"Thanks," she said, sliding to the floor beside him as she took it. "Maybe I'll just get closer to the fire."

He moved back a little to make room for her, and the two dogs joined them, snuggling at Cami's feet as if they knew she needed their body heat. With only the firelight to illuminate the room, her face was shadowed now and the exhaustion lines were back. He really wanted to know what was going on with her, but knew he had to be patient. He'd worked hard in high school to get her to open up about her home life and why her parents never came to their track meets. She was so independent and didn't trust easily back then. Surely she knew he would still keep her secrets. *Maybe this is about her mom again.* Was she in rehab finally? He shifted slightly. That wasn't an easy topic to bring up so he stuck to the dogs, nodding toward their sleeping forms, practically draping themselves across her legs. "Well, if you can't get warm with those two beside you, nothing will help."

Magnus raised his head and gave Jonah a sleepy look.

"Hey," he said to Magnus. "You just going to leave me over here in the cold?" Magnus gave him a "sorry, buddy" look and lay back down with a yawn. "Wow," Jonah said, shaking his head.

Cami laughed. "Those two are pretty inseparable. I hadn't realized it was so serious already."

He liked the sound of her laugh and was glad that hadn't changed. "Magnus didn't even mention he was seeing anyone and here I thought we told each other everything." With the dogs, the fire, and the two of them so close together, it was like there was a little cocoon around them where the world and its pain couldn't enter. He let out a deep breath and relaxed. Picking up his mug, he slowly drank a bit of his hot chocolate. *So smooth*. Whenever he made it from a powder he could never get the lumps out. She obviously had a hot chocolate talent. He watched her, that hollowness back in her eyes, and he had to ask her again. "So, I think you were just going to tell me a long story about what's going on with you."

She fingered the edge of the blanket. "Since we're re-creating old times, let's play our game."

Our game. The words echoed in his head and his stomach tightened. Their game was truth or dare. He'd never turned down her dares before and she'd given him some crazy ones. What if he couldn't do it now? And what if her "truth" questions were about his injury? Everyone had been dancing around it since he'd been hurt. How did it happen? How are you feeling? He hated talking about it. He didn't want to relive the day and he didn't know how he was feeling half the time. Jonah tamped down a sigh. The world just couldn't let him have one moment of peace. But when he looked up at her to see her eyes watching him so intently over the rim of her mug, he knew he'd try. If that was the price of letting her know she could still trust him, he'd pay it. Besides, what else were they going to do until the lights came back on? "Okay."

She laughed again. "You don't sound very sure. I'll go easy on you."

"Promise?" *Can she see that word for the plea it is?* "I'll take truth."

"What did you get your parents for Christmas this year?" She tilted her head. "See? Easy."

But Jonah inwardly jolted at the question. He hadn't gotten his parents anything yet. But since Christmas was a week away, he should have. "I'm still thinking about what they'd like." The excuse rang empty to his ears, but Cami didn't seem to notice.

"At my last dental checkup your dad confessed to me how much he loves *Doctor Who*, so I made him a *Doctor Who* scarf." She gave him a sly grin. "I got your mom the *Pride and Prejudice* with Colin Firth in it so she has something fun to watch, too. Because, you know, Colin Firth."

Jonah watched her, liking how happy she was. This was the girl he remembered, happy, giving, and a little mischievous. Obviously the woman she'd become had some secrets. But that could wait a little longer. The matter at hand was, how did he not know his dad was into *Doctor Who*? "So you're a knitter? That surprises me. How can you sit still for that long?"

She lightly smacked his arm. "You're one to talk."

"Actually, I do a lot of sitting these days." And just like that, the happy mood was gone.

"You don't have to," she said quietly. "Looks to me like you're doing great."

How could he explain what it was like to lose a limb, to

learn to walk again, the pain? He couldn't and didn't want to. But with a year of recovery behind him, he knew she was right. He was doing great and he needed to acknowledge that more. "You're still bossy." But when he looked at her face, so familiar, yet different, he saw a strength around her now. Did she see that when she looked in the mirror?

"I prefer to think of it as helpful."

"Well, maybe I should sit just a little longer so I can at least have a *Doctor Who* marathon and catch up with my dad." He nudged her shoulder. "If that's okay with you."

She quirked up her lips into a half-smile and Jonah smiled with her. The happy mood was back. How long had it been since he'd been this relaxed with another human being? He honestly couldn't remember.

"I don't watch it myself, but almost everyone at work loves it." She took another sip of hot chocolate. "Maybe you could invite me over to your marathon. I'd even bring Lola for Magnus."

"Sounds great." And he meant it. He wouldn't mind spending more time with her. "So, my turn, right?"

"I pick truth."

He let out a breath, glad she hadn't said dare. He didn't want to dare her to do anything because then she'd get him back on her next turn. "What's the best part of your job?"

"The kids." She ran a hand through her hair, making it stand up again. "I love pushing them and seeing them improve. It's a rush."

"So you relate to Coach Stubbs then?" He crossed his legs under him while he waited for her answer.

"Yes and no. I loved Coach, but he pushed too hard sometimes. I work to make sure I don't cross that line."

Jonah nodded. "I always felt like I'd let him down if I didn't place."

"Yeah. Me, too. Which is good and bad for a kid, you know?" She set down her mug and began petting Lola's head. "I want them to do better than they did last time. To keep trying and never give up. That's what I want them to remember when they think of me." She looked over at him, and he could see a flush on her cheeks. "Sorry, I sound like a motivational speaker or something."

"Don't worry, I've heard them all." He leaned closer. "And you're a lot prettier than the ones I had." Her flush deepened, and he grinned. "Do you still run?"

"I get in a few miles a day and there's at least one kid who likes to challenge me at practice," she admitted. "I can hold my own."

Of that Jonah had no doubt. "You were pretty good in high school."

"Pretty good? I seem to recall beating your times more than once." She lifted her chin.

He held his hands up in mock surrender. "All right, you were awesome."

Cami rolled her eyes. "Okay, my turn. With two truths out of the way, you know what it's time for. Dares."

She looked around the room for something to dare him with, and Jonah's heart sank. "There's not much we can do in the dark. What about another truth?" He hoped he didn't sound as anxious as he thought he did.

Her gaze swung back to him, and she raised her eyebrows. "Are you chicken?"

Yes. But he didn't want to admit how scared he really was that he wouldn't be the guy she remembered. That he'd fall or embarrass himself. Or wouldn't be able to do what she asked at all. But the alternative was to chicken out and that was unacceptable. He wasn't scared. He was Jonah Harrison. "Okay, what's your dare?"

She held out her mug and gave him a steady stare. "Get us a refill."

Jonah sighed inwardly. Not a terrible dare, but she didn't know how hard that really was for him. He tried to keep it light. "You just want to sit here warm by the fire while I serve you."

"You got me." Her smile reached all the way to her eyes this time. "Do you accept the dare or not?"

He'd come too far to back down now. "Sure." His voice was nonchalant, but his hands were already starting to sweat. He got on his knees and pushed himself up. With a little hop for balance, he was standing. With two mugs in one hand and a flashlight in the other, he headed for the kitchen. He could feel her eyes on him, but he moved slowly and deliberately. No way was he going to screw this up. Jonah had always given dares his best effort, from eating a rose to giving himself a haircut. He wasn't going to give any less now, prosthetic foot or not.

Four

CAMI COULDN'T SEE JONAH'S FACE, but she could feel his determination as he slowly walked across the room. In the darkness she watched his shadow and could see and hear a small shuffle in between his steps. *Is his prosthetic bothering him?* It was easy to see he didn't want to do it, but she was proud of him for taking the dare. Maybe he was afraid he'd fall in front of her or something. For a second, she thought he might refuse to do it at all, but then he'd clenched his jaw and done it, just as she knew he could. Pride swelled in her heart. Jonah had always been innately sure of himself and what he could do. His injury might have hidden that from him, but it hadn't destroyed it completely. In the brief second after he'd accepted her dare, she'd seen it in his eyes again.

When he drew close to the fire with that little hesitation in his step, she could see how hard he was concentrating on not spilling the hot chocolate. She wanted to say how proud she was, but knew instinctively that wouldn't go over well, so she stayed silent, focusing on the steam coming from the mugs. Gooseflesh prickled on her arms and she rubbed her hands over them. The fire and the dogs hadn't been able to completely ward off the chill she'd gotten looking for Lola in the snowstorm, and she was really looking forward to something hot. "Thanks," she murmured as she took the drink from him. She needed it to warm her from the inside, but wished she could wrap her whole body around the warmth of the mug.

Jonah set his own drink on the fireplace and sank down heavily in front of her. She watched him as he grabbed the poker to stoke the fire. He looked pleased with himself, and a frisson of happiness caught in her chest. *He did it and he's as proud as I am.*

"Are you warming up yet?" He sat back, his hands hanging over his knees, his ever-watchful eyes missing nothing.

"Not really." Even as she said it another shiver raced through her. "Probably just caught a little chill. The hot chocolate will help in a minute."

He tilted his head down and then raised it to look her in the eye. "It's my turn, right?"

Cami nodded, her stomach flipping at the intensity in his face. "Yep." Suddenly the room seemed very small. This dare sounded serious. He'd dared her to do some pretty crazy things in the past, but they'd been kids then. From the tone of his voice, whatever he was going to ask was way above wearing a clown nose to a restaurant or singing Yankee Doodle at the top of her lungs on a street corner.

"Just to be fair, I'm going to ask, truth or dare?" He was holding himself still, but there was an energy zinging between them that made her antsy.

She took a breath. "You know I have to take the dare if we're using our old rules."

His gaze never left hers and he didn't hesitate. "I dare you to let me help warm you up."

Several scenarios from the past raced through her mind. He used to let her warm up by putting his arm around her and holding her close to his side. Was that was he was thinking? Or did he mean get her another blanket? "What did you have in mind?" Her pulse rate picked up as she thought about what she wanted him to say.

He grinned and shook his head slightly, as if he could read her thoughts. Cami flushed and hoped he couldn't see it in the dark.

"Before you go thinking my intentions are anything but honorable, I just thought that sharing body heat could help warm you up faster." He held out his arms. "Just snuggle your back against me and with the blanket over us; you'll be warm in no time."

Her shivering body wouldn't allow her to say no even if she'd wanted to, which she didn't. "Okay." Her heart hammered as she scooted over between his knees, her back against his chest. Curling the blanket around them, she practically melted into him. "How are you always so warm?" she murmured.

He ran his hands up her arms, leaving a trail of heat behind them. "How are you always so cold?" Wrapping his arms around her, he tucked her closer against him.

Cami closed her eyes, her cheek against his chest, breathing in his clean laundry scent. Being in his arms was like coming home after an extended trip. All the fear and anxiety she'd been dealing with were suddenly far away. His heartbeat was in her ear, sure and steady, like him. It would be so easy to fall asleep if her thoughts hadn't turned to how close his mouth was. *What would it be like to kiss him?* She shifted in his arms, moving closer, grateful he couldn't read her thoughts.

He rested his chin on the crown of her head, his hands still moving slowly up and down her arms. "I need to figure out a harder dare next time. I didn't even have to say it twice."

"I know a good thing when I hear it." She didn't want to move as his body heat began to chip away at the ice in her veins. "You ready? It's my turn."

"Well, since we just got comfortable, I pick truth."

Cami looked at the flames crackling next to them. Did she dare ask it? "What's your biggest regret since you came home from Afghanistan?"

His hands stilled and silence followed the question. "I should have picked dare," he muttered.

She backed up quickly, not wanting to spoil what was building between them. "Never mind. You don't have to answer that if you don't want to."

"No, I want to." His arms tightened around her middle. "It's not that easy to explain. The longer I sit here with you, the more regrets I have."

His words pricked her heart. She'd thought things were going so well, that he was okay with her being here. Maybe she'd pushed him too far. Or maybe he had more demons to work through than she thought. Cami shrank back a little. "I'm sorry. I didn't mean—"

"No, no, that came out wrong. I just . . ." his words trailed off. "I look at you knitting a scarf for my dad and getting girl movies for my mom, and if I'm honest with myself, I've been pretty selfish over the past year."

"You went through something life-changing," she said softly, turning in his arms so they could see each other. "You're allowed to be selfish. Sometimes things happen that take us in a completely different direction." Ben popped into her mind. She'd sacrificed so much for him, but she'd do it all over again.

"You sound like you're speaking from experience." He took one of her hands, rubbing his thumb over the back of it. "Care to share?"

"Hey, this is my turn to ask the question. You have to wait." She knew his questions were coming, but didn't mind putting it off a bit longer. "And for future reference, *Pride and Prejudice* isn't just a girl movie, you know."

He gave her a "yeah right" look. "Definitely a girly movie."

"Just because I didn't want to hurt your feelings on the cookie argument, doesn't mean I'll let you get away with that kind of statement. Have you watched it?" His silence confirmed her suspicion. "You do realize the entire movie is about judging someone before you get to know them?"

"I don't need to watch it. Colin Firth is in it." He raised his eyebrow. "You said so yourself."

"That doesn't mean anything. The man is an amazing actor who's been in a lot of movies. If you don't want to see the one with Colin Firth in it, you can see the one with Kiera Knightley in it. I think you'd like that one. And both of them have tons of fantastic dialogue."

Jonah groaned. "Dialogue? Are there any explosions? Swordfights? An awesome bad guy?"

Cami nodded her head. "Mr. Wickham does some terrible things."

He made a face like he'd smelled something terrible. "Okay, he can't be an awesome bad guy with Wickham for a name. It's definitely a girly movie."

"No judgments until you've watched it," she said firmly.

"You're being bossy again, but I'll concede on this one until I've watched the show." He touched her back and started rubbing slow, lazy circles around the center. "So, the answer to your truth or dare question is, I regret being selfish and," he gave a loud sigh, "maybe a little judgmental about *Pride and Prejudice.*"

It was getting harder to breathe, her heart tripping over itself the more his fingers moved over her back, leaving a trail of awareness wherever he touched. "You were dealing with something no one should have to deal with," Cami said finally, leaning back against his chest so he couldn't have access to her back anymore. "No one faults you for being wrapped up in your recovery."

"I know. But I could have been a little more grateful for my parents. A little more upbeat when my buddies called. And a little more welcoming to you." This time he squeezed her in a hug. "I'm sorry."

His touch had started a firestorm inside of her that was warming her up from the inside better than a dozen cups of hot chocolate. "Apology accepted." She looked up at him and he leaned down. Their lips were only millimeters apart. Was he going to kiss her? Did she want him to? "I think it's your turn." Her voice sounded breathless to her ears. "I pick truth."

The corner of his mouth quirked up like he was trying to hold back a grin. Could he read her thoughts? Was she wrong? His thumb ran over her shoulder in a slow circuit that calmed her racing thoughts.

"Okay. Why are you still in Morgan? I thought you wanted to leave and be an Olympic runner." His voice was quiet, but the question was like cold water on her head. She'd known it was coming, but it was still hard. She closed her eyes. Her Olympic dreams had been everything to her once upon a time. How could she explain and see the look on his face? She couldn't bear his disappointment.

"It's a long story." She pulled the blanket closer around her. The fire and their closeness had made her feel safe, but now all the emotions she'd been holding in came rushing to the surface. Anxiety surged over her like a tidal wave.

His hands stilled on her shoulders. "You can trust me, Cam."

"I know." She pushed her hair back behind her ear and fixed her gaze on her sleeping dog, finding it easier to talk if she wasn't looking at Jonah. "I've always trusted you." Gathering her courage, she took his hand. "I want to tell you about Ben."

Five

JONAH'S HEART RATE PICKED UP. Who was Ben? Her husband? Her son? *Is he why she didn't keep in touch with me after high school?* Whoever he was, it was obviously difficult for her to talk about. She'd practically curled into a ball on his lap.

She took a deep breath and let it out before she spoke. "Just after our high school graduation, my little sister found out she was expecting a baby." Jonah remembered Hailey. Really social, not really concerned about classes. The opposite of Cami.

"With no father in the picture and my mom in rehab again for her drug abuse, Hailey had no one to turn to, so I stepped in." The room was so quiet, he couldn't even hear the dogs snoring anymore. He didn't break the silence, just held her hand and waited for her to continue.

"I gave up my track scholarship to Stanford and went to community college so Hailey could get her GED before the baby came, and I don't regret it." Her hands clenched as if she thought he would second-guess her decision.

"Why would you regret it?" He was genuinely confused.

"I don't want you to be disappointed in me." She threw up a hand. "At first, I was so busy helping Hailey that I didn't have time to answer your emails, but then when I heard how well you were doing, I didn't want you to be disappointed with how things turned out for me." Dropping her chin to her chest she said softly, "I told you I was getting out of here, away from my mom and all my family's problems. That I was starting over. But I let it all go in a heartbeat."

Jonah turned her in his arms so she would see him. Hear him. "You said you wouldn't let your mom's addictions hold you back. And you didn't. How could I be disappointed in that? Look at what you've accomplished. You helped your sister become a mother at a really young age and you were hardly older than she was. And yet you got your own degree and have a teaching job doing something you love." A tear rolled down her cheek, and he wiped it away with his thumb. "You've always been so strong. I can't even imagine how hard it was for you. I'm not disappointed; I'm proud."

She sniffed. "I didn't feel strong. The past six years have been hard, but Ben makes it all worth it."

"Tell me about him." He wanted to know everything and wished he would have tried harder to keep in contact with her all those years ago.

Her face lit up as soon as she started talking. "Ben's amazing. He was the most cuddly baby and filled all the empty places in my heart the moment I held him in my arms. He just started kindergarten this year and he's so smart. When he stayed with me for track practice, the kids loved him." She brushed away another tear. "Ben is our world."

Something had happened to Ben. Jonah knew it was coming and part of him didn't want her to say it out loud. She'd already had so much heartache in her life with a single mom addicted to painkillers, and now she'd given up her dreams to help her sister be a single mom. If anyone deserved a break, Cami did. But she needed to get it out and he wanted to be the person to help her get through it. Whatever it was. "You can tell me, Cam."

She closed her eyes. "They were in a car accident three days ago. I've been at their bedside until tonight, when the nurses made me go home to get some rest."

Jonah tightened his arms around her, feeling the tension in her body and wishing he could take some of it away from her. "Are they going to be okay?"

"My sister has a broken pelvis and several broken ribs. Her face is pretty swollen." She turned her face into his chest and he held it there, his hands stroking her hair.

"What about Ben?"

She swallowed hard. "Thankfully he was buckled in his car seat, but even with that, he broke some ribs and his arm. It's the head injury we're all worried about." Her voice was hoarse and uneven. It was obvious she was near her breaking point.

Jonah went very still. "He'll recover, right?"

"They're watching him closely, but the doctor thinks so. It's just going to take some time. Ben was sleeping when I left, but there were so many tubes and machines around him." This time she buried her face in his shirt and let the tears come. "I could have lost them both."

"Shh . . . You didn't. He's going to be fine." Jonah continued stroking her hair to soothe her. When the tears had subsided, he turned her chin so he could see her face. "*You're* going to be fine."

She brushed at his shirt. "I'm sorry I cried all over you."

He pulled her back against him. "I'm not sorry at all." She lay against his chest again, the emotion taking any energy she'd had. They sat there quietly, listening to the storm outside and the fire crackling beside them. Sitting in the dark with her as a teen, usually staring at constellations in the sky, had been a cherished memory for him even after they'd lost contact. But now he'd found her again, and he knew this night was one he'd think about for years to come.

"Cam, I spent a lot of time in the hospital and the holidays were the worst. I can't imagine being a little kid in the hospital at Christmastime. Do you think we could visit Ben together? Maybe bring some Christmas presents?" Jonah asked softly, not wanting to break the peaceful stillness surrounding them. Even the storm outside seemed calmer now. "If you think it's a good idea, of course." He surprised himself with the offer, but it felt right. He didn't know Ben, and he hadn't gone out of his house since he'd gotten home, but he felt a bond with the little guy already. Especially knowing how important he was to Cami.

"That would be great." Cami tilted her head back to look at him. "I know he'd love to hear all about your time in the Marines. He wants to be Captain America when he grows up, and that's pretty close."

It really wasn't, but he wouldn't tell her that. The long, dusty patrols far away in Afghanistan had made him appreciate everything he'd had at home. "I'd like that," he said. "Captain America toys are at the top of our Christmas list for Ben then."

They settled down again, watching the flames in the fireplace. She seemed lighter somehow, as if telling him had relieved her of a heavy burden. He ran a hand up her arm, wishing his presence could always take her troubles away.

Just like she's done for me. He hadn't even thought about his own pain since she'd been in his arms. It was amazing how much less his own foot bothered him when he was talking about her problems and planning a hospital visit. Not that he was pain-free or anything. He was itching to take off his prosthesis. But, for now, just being with her was enough.

He picked up his mug, careful to still keep her close, and finished off the hot chocolate. "Does this mean the game's over?"

She shook her head. "Not when it's my turn."

He groaned. "Just remember I was nice to you last time we did dares." *And nice to myself.* It felt right having her so close.

She laid her hands on his forearms, as if bracing him for what she was about to say. "This one is sort of a truth and a dare."

He tensed. That didn't sound good.

She let the blanket fall to her waist as she met his eyes. "Jonah, I've noticed you've been rubbing your leg and shifting around. If you need to take your prosthetic off, you should do it."

She was perceptive, he'd give her that. And he wasn't as good at hiding his discomfort as he thought he was. "Normally I would have taken it off by now," he confessed.

"Are you afraid to do it because I'm here?" She leaned closer. "I know it must be hard, wondering how people would react, but honestly, it wouldn't bother me."

He reached down and touched her cheek. She was so soft. Graceful. Whole. "It's not pretty, Cami. I don't want you to see what's left of me."

She furrowed her brow. "Aren't we two peas in a pod? I was so worried about what you'd think of me, I let you drift out of my life when you were probably the only steady thing

I had. Now you're worried about what I'll think of your leg." Her hands tightened on him. "It's fine if you want to leave it on, but I wanted you to know you had options."

He blew out a breath. She made it all seem so logical. But could he do it? He'd never let anyone see his stump except his parents and medical personnel. "I just think it might be too much."

She raised her eyebrows and tilted her head. "For me or you?"

He slid his open palm along her jaw, wanting her to understand, wishing he could tell her what he was really afraid of. He ground his teeth together. *Just say it.* "Cami, I'm not the man you remember."

She didn't break his gaze. "No, you're so much more."

Did she mean that? "Do you hear what I'm saying?" he asked, wanting to be sure.

"Yes."

She closed her eyes and his thumb traced her chin. *So silky.* He wanted to kiss her, but is that what she wanted? "Cami."

She let her hands trail up his chest. "Do what you need to do."

Was she still talking about his prosthetic? His stomach tightened at the thought of it, but his leg was ready to breathe for a while. "Okay."

He pulled his leg forward, bent at the knee, but she didn't move and blocked him. "Can I help?"

"If you're sure." She gave him "the look" again. He shrugged and pulled up his sweatpant leg. "Just press that release button there on the side." She did as he asked and the ratchet strap released. The artificial limb loosened, and she gently pulled on it until it was off.

"Is that it?"

"Not quite. I still have my liner on." He bent around her and carefully took off the stump sock until there was just his blue liner. "Are you really sure about this?"

"Stop asking me that." Her bossy tone was back.

His heart sped up as he thought of how wrong this could go, but he took off the liner with the ratchet strap attached. He let out a sigh of relief as soon as it was off. It felt good to let his skin breathe a bit. He hardly dared look to see Cami's reaction.

Cami's hand hovered over his stump, but she didn't touch it. "Does it hurt?"

"Sometimes I get phantom pains at night, but no, it healed well." He looked down at his residual limb. It really was a nice-looking stump as far as stumps went.

"Go ahead and touch it if you want."

She was hesitant at first, but then ran her hand over what was left of his shin. The embarrassment he thought he'd feel never materialized. Instead, her cold hands running over his leg were sending shivers through his body that had nothing to do with the temperature in the room. "Is the prosthetic not fitted properly? Is that why it's bothering you?"

"No, it's not that." He thought for a moment about how he could explain it to her. "I imagine it's like when women have to wear high heels all day. It just feels good to take them off."

She nodded. "That makes sense." Lying back down against him, she was quiet for a moment. "It must have been so hard to get used to."

"It was." He wrapped an arm around her, amazed at how comfortable he felt discussing this with her. "I hated having to relearn how to walk and try to make it look natural. I had great doctors and therapists, though."

"I was thinking that earlier. You hardly even have a limp."

Her praise warmed him. "I've worked hard for that." In that one statement, all the months of sweat and pain were worth it. He let his hands wander through her hair. "Thanks."

"For what?" Her voice was soft and low.

"For tonight. For making me laugh. For making me feel normal again."

"You're welcome."

And he knew she meant it.

Six

She'd never had someone run their hands through her hair like this before and it was wreaking havoc with her senses. It was mesmerizing and tender and yet everywhere he touched ignited a pull of attraction that had her spellbound. She may have helped him feel normal again, but she knew she'd never be normal again after this experience. She wanted more. "Is it your turn or my turn?"

"It's my turn. I took my prosthetic off for you, remember?"

She remembered. It was an experience she'd never forget. "And you haven't fidgeted once since you took it off. I can tell you're so much more comfortable."

"Definitely." His hands kept up their slow torture as they started down her hair, from her scalp to her shoulders. "I want to ask you something, but I don't want it to be a dare. I want it to be your choice, not a challenge."

Her pulse pounded when his hands stopped at her neck, cupping her head. "Ask me what?"

He gently tipped her chin until she looked at him. "I want to kiss you."

The butterflies that had been mildly fluttering in her stomach were suddenly airborne and swooping in so hard she could hardly catch a breath. "What did you say?"

Jonah leaned down until he was a hair's breadth away from her mouth. "I need to kiss you."

He hesitated and their eyes met. Everything was about to change and it seemed right that they both paused to acknowledge it. She reached up and put her arm around his neck, pulling him the last few millimeters to her. His lips were tentative at first, but Cami pushed her hands through his hair, wanting more. He quickly caught up and matched her intensity until a very wet nose came between them.

"Magnus," Jonah ground out.

Cami couldn't help but laugh. "Well, you were worried about being left out in the cold earlier."

"He has terrible timing." But he was smiling and petting the dog. Lola came over to see what all the commotion was about.

"I've been accused of that myself a time or two." She pulled back and allowed the dogs into their small circle.

He resumed stroking her hair. "I've wanted to kiss you for so long."

She turned to him, her eyes wide. "How long?"

"Since the beginning of senior year." He smiled as her mouth dropped open in surprise.

Her hand flew up in the air. "Why didn't you ever say something? I had a crush on you that whole time, but didn't want to ruin our friendship."

"I didn't want to lose you as a friend, either." His voice was low. "I thought maybe you just needed a star-gazing partner or someone to hang out with after the track meets."

"That's what I was thinking about you. We've wasted a lot of time," she murmured.

He leaned forward and gave her a quick kiss on the lips. "Was it worth the wait?" Cami could only nod since both dogs had muscled their way in to give their own kisses. Jonah had to scoot back to make room for them. "Hey, Mag, I'm starting to see a pattern here," he said, giving his most disapproving look to Magnus.

"Me, too." She laughed and patted Lola's head. "Did you guys need some attention?"

Lola took the patting as a signal to climb on Cami's lap. "Oof, you're a little big for a lap dog." Magnus watched Lola on Cami's lap, as if he was waiting to see if she'd stay there or not.

Jonah leaned in close. "Look, Magnus can't decide whether to join Lola on your lap or not."

His breath tickled her ear, making her heart skip a beat. "Like a dog pile, you mean?"

Magnus twitched his ears like he knew they were talking about him. Jonah chuckled. "He's a little more sedate in his attention seeking."

"Like his owner?"

Jonah bent to kiss the spot where her shoulder met her neck. "I'm happy to take any attention you give me. Or give you some attention of your own."

She tilted her head to give him better access and closed her eyes. "You do seem rather good at that." She licked her lips, her throat suddenly dry at his ministrations. "I am so glad Lola came over tonight."

"Me, too." He trailed kisses up her neck to her ear, and she thought her heart might pound out of her chest. He made her feel things she'd never felt before, and she didn't want the evening to end. Here in the dark with Jonah and the dogs, it seemed as if her life was finally coming together. All she needed was Ben and Hailey to make it perfect. For the first time since the accident, she was feeling optimistic about the entire situation, and thinking about Ben didn't send a wave of worry over her. She'd face whatever came in his recovery and she'd have Jonah in her corner to help her. It was a heady feeling. "Jonah, I—"

But her words were drowned out with the lights coming back on and the front door opening simultaneously. "He's probably asleep," Dr. Harrison said from the front hallway.

"I doubt he'd sleep through this storm," his wife retorted.

Cami froze. What would his parents think? Jonah's arms tightened around her middle. "Don't panic." But even with his comforting words, she braced for the look on his parents' faces when they saw them.

His mom and dad walked into the family room and his mom's expression was just as Cami expected. Her eyes wide, her mouth a perfect O. "Hello, Cami," she finally said, obviously needing a moment to find her voice. "I didn't know Jonah was expecting company tonight."

"I wasn't," Jonah said as he reached for his liner and prosthetic.

Cami stood and grabbed the blanket. "My dog got out and ended up over here," she explained while she folded. "The storm was pretty bad so Jonah invited me to wait with him until it broke."

While she'd been talking to his parents, Jonah had finished attaching his prosthetic and stood up next to her. "How was the party?" he asked his dad.

"It was fun. Your mother was worried about you, so we braved the roads. Looks like everything was under control." His father's eyes dipped to the fireplace, where their mugs still sat.

"We'd just eaten dinner when the lights went out, and we had hot chocolate by the fire." She looked down at herself in Jonah's over-sized sweats. "And since my jeans were so wet, Jonah lent me some dry clothes." Cami didn't know why she was babbling. They hadn't done anything wrong, but it was his *parents*.

"I'm just glad you were here." Jonah's mom put her purse down on the kitchen counter and turned to smile at them. A genuine, happy smile. In that moment, the awkwardness disappeared and Cami relaxed. It was okay. "How're Hailey and Ben? I just heard about the accident tonight," Mrs. Harrison said, sympathy lacing her tone.

"The doctors are watching them really close, but it looks like they'll be okay." Her voice hadn't trembled once when she spoke of them and she was proud of herself.

"If you're up to it, I'd love for you to stay a little longer. You can tell me how I can help," Mrs. Harrison said. "And we don't want you to feel like you have to rush off."

"I really can't stay. I have an early start tomorrow, and Lola and I should be going." She felt Jonah's hand tighten on her arm.

"Well, maybe we can all meet at the Movie Festival tomorrow night? After our visit with Ben, and only if you feel okay about leaving him for a while," Jonah said, meeting her eyes. "I know I could use a little more Christmas spirit, if you're up for it."

She nodded and didn't miss the surprised look that passed between Jonah's parents. This was a big deal for him and he was including her. She focused on Jonah and smiled up at him, hoping he could see how much it meant to her that he wanted the closeness they'd shared tonight to continue as much as she did. How had she ever doubted that?

Truth or Dare

He slid his arm around her shoulder and gave it a squeeze. "Just let me get my coat and boots."

"Okay." She watched him head toward his room. Did he have a special prosthetic for his boots? She gathered up her jeans, then started toward the hall. "It was good to see you, Dr. and Mrs. Harrison."

"Nice to see you, too," his mother said, as she came around the kitchen island to hug her. "Thanks for keeping him company. I hope we see you a lot more around here."

"Me, too," Cami said, returning the hug. She called for Lola, who reluctantly came to her side. "You can visit Magnus another day, girl," she chided her dog.

"You both can," Jonah called from the living room. She walked in with both dogs on her heels to see him trying to jam his prosthetic into a boot. "I'll just be a minute." He expertly braced his arm against it and got his artificial foot to slide in. "Let me get your coat."

He grabbed it off the closet doorknob and helped her put it on. He took her hand, but before he opened the door, he stopped. "Oh, look."

Came raised her face to see the mistletoe now hanging above the door. "Was that there all the time?" she asked with a laugh.

"Our little truth or dare game is over, so I don't have to tell." He touched her cheek and gave her a gentle kiss that was just long enough to make her knees turn to water.

"Merry Christmas," she said as they drew apart.

"Now it is." He tucked a piece of her hair behind her ear and Lola jumped up, pressing herself between them. Magnus must have thought it looked like fun so he joined in with a yip and a dance around their legs.

"Do you think the dogs planned this all along?" Cami's lips turned up in an exasperated grin as she tried to stay upright. She was glad Jonah was strong enough to hold them both up or the dogs would have definitely bowled them over.

"Lola does seem to know what she wants." His hands were sliding down her arms, and a shiver rippled through her.

Cami glanced down at the dogs before she pulled him close. "Just like her owner." And then she kissed him again.

ABOUT JULIE COULTER BELLON

JULIE COULTER BELLON is the author of more than a dozen romantic suspense novels. Her book *All Fall Down* won the RONE award for Best Suspense and *Pocket Full of Posies* won a RONE Honorable Mention for Best Suspense.

When she's not writing, Julie loves to travel and her favorite cities she's visited so far are probably Athens, Paris, Ottawa, and London. When she's home, she loves to read, write, teach, watch *Castle* and *Hawaii Five-O*, and eat Canadian chocolate. Not necessarily in that order.

You can find out more about all of Julie's upcoming projects at her website: www.JulieBellon.com

Twitter: @julicbellon

Holiday Bucket List

Sarah M. Eden

OTHER WORKS BY SARAH M. EDEN

Seeking Persephone
Courting Miss Lancaster
The Kiss of a Stranger
Friends and Foes
An Unlikely Match
Drops of Gold
Glimmer of Hope
As You Are
Longing for Home
Hope Springs
For Elise

One

ON THE FIRST DAY OF DECEMBER, Celeste Lagorio finished the last of the Thanksgiving leftovers, had her winter tires installed, and officially gave up on Christmas. After working herself to exhaustion to create twenty-five years' worth of perfect Yuletides for her children, Celeste was ready for a break. Her youngest was away at college and not returning for the holidays. The older two were married, living in different states, and planning to spend Christmas itself with their in-laws.

She would get her shopping done early, then give herself the rest of the month off. Two decades of single motherhood had certainly earned her that much.

The only thing left to decide was what she would do instead.

"A Caribbean cruise," her neighbor Mike Durham suggested when she mentioned her plans to him over the hedge that night. "It would be warm."

"I don't want to travel over Christmas. The airports are crazy." Celeste rubbed her mittened hands together to keep them warm.

"Then what about a big, extravagant Christmas present to yourself? Something you've always wanted but could never justify?"

There was some appeal in that, even if it wasn't realistic. "And how would I justify it now if I couldn't before?"

"You raised three children all by yourself—three children who did not grow up to be deadbeats, criminals, or politicians."

She'd always liked Mike's sense of humor. He'd moved in next door just as her oldest was leaving home. He'd been a burst of much-needed sunshine during a very stressful and overwhelming time in her life.

"I won't argue that I completely deserve a ridiculously expensive gift from myself," Celeste said. "But I'm paying for my daughter to attend a not-inexpensive university. Fancy presents will have to wait a couple more years."

"So no trips and no big presents. You've got to do something for your special Christmas."

She rubbed at her arms. "How did 'I give up on this holiday' turn in to 'This is my special Christmas'?"

He motioned toward his house. "Come in and have some coffee before you freeze."

"I won't say no." She stepped around the hedge and followed him up his front walk.

"Maybe your fancy Christmas present could be a really long extension cord for your electric blanket." Mike held his front door open for her.

She stepped inside, sighing as the warm air hit her face. She pulled off her mittens and knit cap, then laid them on the entryway table. Mike tucked his cap under his arm, reaching up to smooth out his salt-and-pepper hair. She didn't need to wait for him to show her to the kitchen; she'd spent enough time at his house to have a stool at the island designated as her own. She slipped onto it while he started a pot of coffee.

"What did you do the first Christmas you didn't have any children at home?" she asked.

Mike leaned against the counter. "I broke my arm, remember? The back stairs were icy and I slipped."

"I'd forgotten that." He'd only lived there for about a year when that had happened. "Breaking my arm is not exactly what I had in mind for my first-time-alone Christmas. Neither is something flashy and glamorous. The whole point is not to kill myself making the usual preparations. To just enjoy the holidays."

Mike crossed to her side of the kitchen and leaned his forearms on the countertop, facing her. "So which do you want more, low-key or the Christmas of your dreams? Or maybe the Christmas of your dreams *is* low-key."

"I guess I haven't really thought this through. What I did at Christmastime was always about the kids and what would make them happy."

"What about before that? What did you want for Christmas before they were born?"

"Tickets to a Paula Abdul concert."

He laughed out loud, his dark eyes dancing with mirth, and she couldn't help but join in. His laugh was like that. So many times in the years since she'd met him, he'd managed to help her smile through struggles and laugh at even the most difficult moments. She'd never been more grateful for a neighbor, for a *friend*, in her life.

"Well, I don't think you can see Paula Abdul in concert now," he said. "But we might be able to find a concert video. Would that count?"

"What is this, a holiday bucket list?"

"Why not?" He moved back to the coffee maker and pulled out the pot. "You've spent more than half your life raising your kids. I think fulfilling a few of those wishes you set aside in order to focus on them would be a good way to celebrate your first all-by-yourself Christmas."

"I was twenty years old when my first was born. The things someone barely out of her teens wishes for are pretty ridiculous."

He handed her a cup of coffee with just the exact amount of cream and sugar she liked. "Ridiculous, maybe, but probably fun too."

"Fun? Like a fabulous new babydoll-style dress?"

He grinned over the top of his mug. "Before my kids were born I was wearing Hammer pants, so I will not condemn your fashion choices."

"So your Christmas wish would have been for more Hammer pants?"

He nodded solemnly. "And tickets to Depeche Mode."

She shook her head. "You are so old."

"I am only a couple of years older than you are."

"But a crucial couple of years." She set her cup down. "I am still young and spry, and you are falling down your stairs."

"Careful, Celeste. I'll stop inviting you over for coffee if you keep talking like that."

She smiled. "I'm not worried. You like having me over."

"I do," he admitted, his words quieter and less teasing.

Celeste pushed down the surge of uncertainty she always felt when he took on that tone. He was a dear friend—the best she had, in fact. And she had the world's worst dating track record. The few times she'd dated anyone in the last two decades, the experience had ended in disaster, and she never heard from the guys again. Ruining her friendship with Mike was not something she was willing to risk—even if he was handsome and fun and smart and the highlight of her day. Friendship was safer.

"A holiday bucket list." That was a less treacherous topic of conversation. "I kind of like that idea, actually, but under one condition."

He took another sip of his coffee. "What condition is that?"

"That you check things off your list, too. A friendly competition, if you will."

His lips turned up in a smile. "I'm listening."

"We each compile a list of things we would have wanted to do in the years before our kids were born, things that being single parents meant we had to push aside." Few people truly understood the emotional toll of losing a spouse and raising a family alone. Mike knew. He'd lived it just like she had, having lost his wife to cancer when they were both still very young. "The one who can check off the most items wins."

"And what does the winner get?" Mike asked.

She hadn't thought that far yet. They both sat a moment in silence, contemplating.

"I've got it," Mike said. "The loser gives the winner something on his or her *current* Christmas wish list."

"Like that big, extravagant present you suggested I get earlier?" She wasn't sure she wanted to commit herself to spending a lot of money.

He shook his head. "Something on the wish list that doesn't cost anything, or hardly anything. That should probably be a rule for the nostalgia bucket list too."

"Agreed. Neither of us has a fortune to spend. So do we tell the other person now what we want if we win or is that a surprise?"

"I think surprise."

Celeste nodded enthusiastically. "I like it."

"Starting tomorrow?" Mike asked.

"We'll meet at my house tomorrow night to write up our bucket lists."

"I'll be here," he said.

For the first time since her daughter had told her she wouldn't be home for Christmas, Celeste felt excited about the holidays. She had something to look forward to, and a friend to share the season with.

Perhaps there was a reason not to give up on Christmas entirely.

Two

MIKE COULDN'T REMEMBER WHICH of them had come up with the idea for the Holiday Bucket List challenge, but he was glad they had. He would get to spend a lot of time with Celeste, and that, to him, was the definition of a perfect Christmas.

She was amazing. She'd been widowed at twenty-seven, with two elementary-school-aged kids and a newborn. She'd gone back to school to get her law degree, all while raising her kids as a single mother. Rather than take a position in a big, prestigious law firm and earn an impressive paycheck, she'd signed on with a charitable organization where, as she'd once told him, she could know she was doing some good in the world. She had a great sense of humor and an optimistic outlook on life, and she was the best friend he had.

She was also not interested in him as anything other than a friend. At least that was the impression she gave him. Still, sometimes there was something in the way she looked at him that made him wonder if maybe she felt more than she was letting on. He hoped so, because he'd tried over the past seven years to not be madly in love with her. It hadn't worked.

He knocked on her door the next evening, hoping she'd had time to finish dinner. He probably should have waited a little longer, but he never was patient when he knew he'd be seeing her. Pathetic.

The door opened, and there she was, smiling at him. "Hey. Come on in."

He didn't have to be asked twice.

Her house smelled like bacon. If he hadn't loved her already, that might have been enough to convince him.

"How was your day?" he asked.

"Pretty good, except that I came face to face with how old I really am."

He tossed her a questioning look.

"I am realizing just how long ago twenty-five years really is. I can hardly remember any of the things that interested me when I was twenty years old."

"It's twenty-five years for me as well."

Her smile turned taunting. "But your brain is older than mine. I'm impressed you remembered our conversation from yesterday."

"I'm forty-seven, not seventy-four."

Her blue eyes pulled wide and her mouth dropped open. "Forty-seven!"

He had to laugh. She always knew how to pull that from him, even on his hardest days. He'd done his best to return that favor over the years.

She'd set out pens and paper on her dining room table, along with a plate of butter cookies. She took a seat opposite the one he walked to. What would it take to get her to sit next to him, close, maybe even touching?

"I've already written down 'Attend a Paula Abdul concert' and 'Babydoll dress,'" she said. "I admitted to it yesterday, so I figured there was little point denying it."

He pulled a sheet of paper over to him. "So I guess I have to write down 'Hammer pants' and 'Depeche Mode.'"

She reached over and patted his hand. "You remembered."

He pretended that her touch didn't affect him at all. "You should be nicer to me, Celeste. Otherwise I'll require a hand-knitted sweater when I win our little bet, and I know how much you hate to knit."

She grinned. "Then I'll demand you paint my basement, and I know how much you hate painting."

"Does your basement need to be painted?" He tried to help her out when things around the house needed fixing. In return, she had talked him through the minefield of interacting with his new daughter-in-law. He'd raised two boys on his own. He knew next to nothing about women, which was probably a big part of his repeated strike-outs with Celeste.

"It doesn't need it at all," Celeste said, a laugh obvious in her words. "That's why it would be so dastardly."

"What is the third thing on your bucket list?"

"The Christmas before my oldest was born I was going to see *Home Alone* in the theater, but I never did. I don't remember why."

He nodded and pointed at her paper. "Write that down."

"In the theater? We'll never pull that off."

He shrugged. "We may have to make some adjustments, but we'll figure it out."

"What's your number three?"

What were his interests a quarter of a century ago? "An NES gaming console."

"We can look at that antique store on Center."

He set his forearms on the table and leaned toward her. "Are you going to make 'old' jokes throughout this entire thing?"

"Yes. Yes, I am." She raised an eyebrow. "Scared?"

"Bring it."

"I don't think our generation is allowed to say 'bring it.' We need to stick with 'far out' or 'word to your mother.'"

He leaned back in his chair once more. "It's only December 2nd, and we've already resorted to quoting Vanilla Ice. This doesn't bode well."

"Ooh. Vanilla Ice. That needs to be on my list, too." She was already writing it down. "I loved Vanilla Ice, and I remember thinking if I wasn't twenty years old, and married, and supposed to be really grown up, I would get a poster or something."

"Or something? You mean like a notebook or a lunch box?"

A little color touched her cheeks. "I know it's stupid, but . . ."

It was his turn to reach out and take her hand. While he didn't like that he'd embarrassed her, he always loved the feel of her hand in his. "I didn't mean to imply it was stupid. These are all things from when we were young. They're going to seem a little strange to us now, but that's half the fun."

"I got married at nineteen. I don't regret it, and I don't think I was too young, but there were still some things about me that weren't . . ." Her brow pulled as she tried to think of the right word.

"Very grown-up yet?" he suggested.

"I guess. Vanilla Ice was one of them."

"What else was?" He wanted to know her better. These

moments when she talked about her past were like a door being opened, and he had a glimpse of the Celeste he hadn't known, the woman who'd struggled with so many burdens for so long.

"I cried a lot," she said, "and I got frustrated at the world for not functioning the way I thought it should. And I . . . I was so sure that I could simply plan my life and everything would go the way I expected."

He threaded his fingers through hers. "It doesn't work that way, does it?"

She shook her head no.

"You write down Vanilla Ice souvenir, and I'll think of some immature thing that twenty-two year old me wanted. Then we'll be even."

"Deal."

Her phone rang in the next instant. She pulled her hand from his to grab her cell. He immediately missed the contact.

She glanced at the screen. "It's Kristina." She tucked back a strand of her dark brown hair as she raised the phone to her ear. "Hi, hon. What's up?"

Mike should have been concentrating on the next item to add to his list, but Celeste was too big of a distraction. He liked watching her with her kids, even when it was nothing more than a phone call. She lit up when she talked with them. It was little wonder she felt lost not having them around. He'd gone through the same thing when his youngest had left home.

"Talk to the T.A.," Celeste said, still talking on the phone. "That's what he's there for." She listened to whatever her daughter said next. "Mike is here, actually. Okay." She held her phone out to him. "She wants to talk to you."

He took the phone. "Hey. How are you?"

"Okay, so remember that guy I told you about in my Econ class?" Kristina said from the other end.

He leaned back in the dining room chair. Conversations with Kristina could be long. "The one who smiles at you?"

"Yeah. So, I saw him at the student union yesterday and decided to say hi."

Something in her tone didn't bode well. "And?"

"And, even though it was like literally the shortest conversation ever, I totally got this creepy vibe off of him. I don't even know why. Is that crazy? Am I just being all judgmental or paranoid or something?"

Mike had known Kristina since she was twelve. He'd taken on the role of surrogate father, answering endless questions about boys and cars and anything else she thought he might know about. "It's possible you misjudged things, but if the guy's coming off as a creep, there might be a reason."

"He asked me out."

Mike's stomach twisted. "You didn't say yes, did you?"

"I said no, and I was nice about it. But he seemed so disappointed. He kept asking why I wouldn't go out with him. I feel bad."

Man, he wished she was going to school closer. "If he's trying to guilt you in to doing something you don't want to, that might be why he seems like a creep."

She sighed. "Being a grown-up is a pain."

"It sure is." He caught Celeste's eye from across the table. She mouthed a "thank you." He nodded and smiled.

"Can I ask you a huge favor?"

His kids had asked a few favors while they were away at college. Most of the time it involved money. "What is it?"

"Would you hang out with Mom over Christmas? She keeps saying she doesn't care that none of us will be home, but, I don't know, I think she's sadder about it than she's letting on."

"I think you're right." Even then, Mike could see the loneliness in her eyes. If she'd give him half a chance he would happily do what he could to fill that void. "Your mom and I have a Christmas bet going."

Celeste reached out and swatted at him. "Kristina will think I've turned in to a gambler."

"Awesome," Kristina said. "Text me about it. I gotta go."

"Say goodbye to your mom first." He handed the phone across the table once more.

Celeste made a quick goodbye before tapping the end button and setting her phone on the table. "She did turn the creepy guy down, right?"

"Sure did."

Her sigh perfectly matched her daughter's from a moment earlier. "Do you think kids ever realize that their parents never stop worrying about them?"

"Not until they're parents themselves."

She snatched a butter cookie from the plate and snapped part of it off with her teeth. He followed her lead.

"Did you think of something immature to put on your list?" she asked between bites.

"I haven't yet."

"There must be something you wanted or wanted to do but felt too stupid about it at the time."

There were probably a lot of things actually. One jumped immediately to mind. "The Christmas my wife was pregnant with our oldest, the roller rink in our town announced it was closing at the new year. I wanted to go and have one last skate, but Bev was too pregnant and I was too embarrassed to go by myself."

She pointed at his paper. "Write it down."

He shook his head. "There are no roller rinks anywhere near here. I'll never be able to cross that off."

"'We may have to make some adjustments, but we'll figure it out.'" She quoted him word for word. "That's four each, and some of them are going to be tough. What do you think? Are we good?"

Are we good? That was more of a loaded question than she likely knew. Their friendship was good. The idea of "we" was more than good. The fact that she wasn't open to the idea of "we" wasn't good at all.

"Mike?"

He put on his most convincing smile. "I think we need a couple of ground rules. First, no sabotage."

"Where's the fun in that?" She popped another cookie into her mouth.

"C'mon."

"Okay, okay."

"Second," he continued, "the other person has to be present when the bucket list item is checked off. If it's an activity, we have to both be part of it." He'd take any opportunity to spend time with her. "If it's an item, we have to show it to the other person."

"I'll agree to that."

He eyed her closely. "We're really going to do this? Spend the Christmas season together?"

She shrugged a shoulder. "Why not?"

That was exactly the question he'd been silently asking for years: why not?

Three

"He's dedicating his whole Christmas season to this bet of yours?" Celeste's friend and co-worker, Lucy, had been asking her about the holiday bucket list all day. "He is totally in to you, Celeste."

Lucy was more than fifteen years younger than Celeste, which somehow made her both more, and less, authoritative on these things. She leaned on Celeste's desk. "He likes your kids. He's a nice guy. And, I've seen him, Celeste, he's hot—for an old guy."

Celeste tapped her pencil on the desk top. "How do I do this bucket list challenge without giving him the wrong idea?"

"The wrong idea? You mean, that you like him?"

"Right. I don't want to ruin our friendship by making him think I feel more for him than I do." It had, in fact, been a worry of hers for a couple of years, ever since he started looking at her in the way he did.

"He's not blind," Lucy said. "He can probably tell that you like him."

"I don't."

Lucy rolled her eyes and shook her head. "Sure, you don't."

This was getting out of hand. "I didn't bring this up to have you analyze my feelings. I need to know the name of that second-hand shop where you get your vintage clothes."

"Second Time Around. It's on 22nd," Lucy said. "Do you really think your bucket list outfits are going to be in a vintage shop?"

Celeste sighed loudly. "I'm getting old."

Her cell chimed, signaling the arrival of a text. She grabbed it and checked. *Mike.*

"It's him, isn't it?" Lucy asked.

"How did you . . . ?"

"You only smile like that when he calls or texts or comes by." She rolled her eyes again—Lucy was an unapologetic eye-roller—and shook her head. "But, of course, you don't *like* him."

She ignored Lucy and read the text.

Mike: 1, Celeste: 0

What did that mean? Her phone chimed again. A picture text this time. The moment it came up on screen, she laughed out loud. She couldn't help it.

"What?" Lucy asked.

Celeste showed her the photo: Mike holding up a pair of red Hammer pants. "I don't know how he found them already."

"I do," Lucy said. "He's at Second Time Around. That place is amazing."

Celeste looked at the picture again. Mike had always had a nice smile, and he was one of the happiest people she'd ever known. She liked that about him. "I am really going to have to step up my game. He checked something off on the first day."

"I'm surprised he didn't come to your house and model it for you." Lucy walked to Celeste's office door. "Although, maybe that's smart. Those are ugly pants." She left, with a grin, on that parting shot.

Lucy had been teasing, but she'd had a point.

Celeste grabbed her cell again and texted Mike back. *You have to wear it where I can see or it doesn't count.*

Her kids texted shockingly fast. Mike, however, wasn't any faster than she was. She'd set down her phone and taken up her papers again before the next chime sounded.

Humiliation was part of our bet?

She sent back, *Our agreement included specific clauses re: witnessing each item's check-off.* Her kids were always telling her she texted like an old person, too wordy and formal.

Another chime. *I never argue semantics with an attorney.* Mike also texted like an old person.

My place. Tonight. Wear the pants or it doesn't count. That was a little more youthful. Kristina would probably be proud.

Mike answered, *You're killing me.*

She scrolled back up to the picture of him holding those pants. The goofy look on his face brought a smile to hers. Lucy had said Celeste always smiled when Mike was involved. How could she help it?

"I can't believe I'm doing this." Mike was a little too tall for the Hammer pants he was wearing. Rather than looking like a throw-back, he looked like an idiot.

Still, Celeste would laugh with him over it, and the sight of her smiling eyes was worth almost any amount of discomfort. He rang her doorbell and did his best to look like a confident, competent adult who happened to be dressed like a circus clown from the waist down.

For a split second after she opened the door, Celeste's expression was completely normal. Then her eyes pulled wide and her mouth dropped open a bit. The corners of her mouth twitched upward.

"Does this meet the demands of our bet?" Mike asked.

She laughed. "Definitely."

"You don't have to enjoy this so much, you know."

She waved him in. "Come in before you scare someone."

"Too late. I already scared myself."

She closed the door behind him. "I cannot believe you ever desperately wanted a pair of those."

"I wanted a pair that fit." He tugged at one of the signature over-sized front flaps. "You'd think all this extra fabric could have been used to make them longer."

She walked right next to him, her arm swinging beside his. It would be the most natural thing to slip his hand around hers. He never knew, though, how she would respond. Sometimes she threaded her fingers through his and welcomed the connection. Other times, she pulled free so quickly that his hand dropped hard against his side.

"I should tell you that I'm also crossing something off my bucket list tonight," she said.

"Really?" He eyed her T-shirt and jeans—her usual post-work attire.

She shook her head. "Not the clothes. The secondhand shop had one babydoll dress, but it looked the right size for an actual baby doll."

"So what *are* you checking off?" he asked.

They stepped into her living room, and she did a Vanna White style wave of her hand.

"Poster board and markers?" It was the only thing different about the room.

"We're going to a concert," she said.

"What?"

Celeste grinned at him. "'Going' isn't quite the right word. But it will be an epic concert."

"Epic?" He laughed to hear the very word Kristina used so often.

She motioned him over to the sofa. As she sat, she pulled her laptop over. "I made a YouTube playlist of live performances from Paula Abdul and Depeche Mode. We can stream it to the TV."

"Okay. That is pretty epic. Especially since I get to check another thing off my list too."

She smiled. "See how nice I am?"

He nudged the poster board on the coffee table. "What is this for?"

"Fan posters, of course."

Awesome. "So, I'll Depeche Mode mine, and you'll Paula Abdul yours?"

"Exactly."

The smell of markers soon filled the air. They razzed each other about their posters, inquired after each other's kids, and talked about their work, all with complete ease. How could she not see how perfect they were together?

Just as they were putting the finishing touches on their signs, Celeste's phone rang. She glanced at the screen. "It's Kristina. I wonder why she didn't text."

It was unusual but not unheard of.

"Hi, hon." Her expression grew instantly more

concerned. "He is, actually." Another pause as she listened. "I'll put you on speaker."

She set the phone on the coffee table. "She sounds stressed."

Kristina was pretty level-headed. What had happened?

Celeste tapped the screen. "Okay, Kristina. Go ahead."

"Yeah. Go ahead," Mike added.

"So I ran in to that creepy guy from Econ today." Kristina's tone was not one of casual conversation. Mike was immediately on alert. "Like ten times. He just kept showing up. He wasn't pushy or weird, really, and he only talked to me a couple of times but . . . I don't know."

"Your gut says something is off," Mike guessed.

"Exactly."

Celeste clasped her hands and pressed her lips together. Her brow pulled downward.

"Do you feel threatened?" Mike asked.

"No."

He was relieved that she didn't hesitate with that answer. Yet, she was concerned enough to have called to talk to them about it. "You don't usually see him around campus that often, I'd guess," he pressed.

"Until today I only ever saw him in class and that one time at the student union." Kristina sounded calm but a little unnerved. "I don't know for sure that he was following me or anything. It just weirded me out, I guess."

"Have you told anyone?" Celeste asked. "Besides us? Someone *there*?"

"I don't even know who I would talk to," Kristina said. "There's no law against giving off a creepy vibe."

"Well, no," Celeste said, "but it's still a good idea to make sure someone knows about your concerns."

"Like who? My roommates know. Should I tell anyone

else? Someone more official, I guess? And what would I tell them?"

Mike had two sons. Taking on the role of surrogate father to Celeste's daughter had shown him just how different the world was for young women than for young men. He worried about her for entirely different reasons than he had with his boys.

"Kristina, I think you should go to the Office of the Dean of Students tomorrow and find out which department is in charge of student safety." Early in his career, Mike had worked in the IT department at a college. Though he hadn't been directly involved in student services, he'd learned a little about them.

"I don't think I'm actually in danger," Kristina said.

"I know." He leaned a little closer to the phone. "And you can make that clear. Just tell them what you told us and ask what the process is for reporting problems should things escalate. This way you have someone who knows what's going on and there's a paper trail."

"I just feel like I might be making a big deal out of nothing."

"Mike is right, hon. Having someone there who is aware of what's happening is important."

Kristina took an audible breath. "I kind of feel stupid."

"Don't," Mike said. "You're doing what you need to do in order to feel safe. That's smart, not stupid."

"Thanks. You too, Mom."

"Do like Mike suggested," Celeste said. "And then text us tomorrow. Tell us how it went."

"I will."

"Love you, kid," Mike said. "Always have."

It was a familiar exchange between them, one Kristina always finished with, "Always will."

"I love you too, hon," Celeste added. "Don't forget to text."

"Okay."

Celeste didn't say anything for a long moment after the call ended. She steepled her hands and pressed her fingers to her lips. "She is not an over-reactor, Mike."

"She's also not flaky. She'll follow through on this."

Celeste didn't look reassured. "I hate that she's so far away."

He threw caution to the wind and set his arm around her shoulders, pulling her up close to him. "When you talk to her tomorrow, if you're still uneasy, you can call the Dean of Students office yourself."

Celeste leaned her head on his shoulder. "Kristina would kill me."

Mike rubbed her arm with his hand. "Probably, but a parent has to do what a parent has to do."

She slipped her arms around him, something she very seldom did and only, it seemed, when there was a crisis. "Thank you for being a dad to her all of these years. I was more or less enough for the other two, but Kristina needed something more."

"Give yourself more credit, Celeste. Being a single parent isn't simple, and it isn't easy."

"You didn't tell me that it didn't get easier once they'd all left home."

That was the hard truth. "But there is one thing that does get easier," he said.

"What's that?"

"Enjoying a Depeche Mode concert without the kids complaining that the music is old or lame or whatever else they would say."

She sat up straight once more and gave him a look of

teasing disapproval. "This is a *Paula Abdul* concert, with special guests Depeche Mode."

He scooted to the edge of the sofa. "Cue up the concert," he said, standing up. "I'll make you a cup of tea."

She smiled up at him. "You always do know exactly what I need."

"That's because I know you really well." *I know what makes you happy, what you worry about, your wildest dreams and fondest hopes. I know you better than anyone else.* Why, then, did she seem to not know him at all?

He pondered that as he made her tea. They weren't teenagers who were still trying to decide what they wanted in life or needed most in another person. Celeste was not a wishy-washy person who couldn't make up her mind about things.

If she was so dead set against any kind of relationship, maybe it was time he took her at her word and quit hoping for something more.

Four

Mike hadn't been by in days.

He'd sent a few texts, mostly about Kristina, but otherwise Celeste hadn't heard much from him. She didn't know what to think of that. It wasn't that she never went a day without talking to him, it just didn't happen that often, especially in the months since she'd officially become an empty-nester.

I could make Christmas cookies and invite him over. She would enjoy the cookies; she would enjoy his company even more.

Celeste pulled out her phone and sent off a text. *I'm making cookies. Want to come over and have some?*

She pulled on her apron and dropped her phone into the pocket. Mike liked chocolate chip the best, so she gathered up the necessary ingredients. Why had it been so long since she'd baked cookies? She liked baking, and she liked eating. It didn't make any sense to have avoided her own oven.

Holiday Bucket List

Not long after Kristina had left for college, Mike had told Celeste that one of the challenges of suddenly having no kids at home was figuring out which things she'd done primarily for the kids and which things she'd done at least partially for her own sake. Maybe baking was one of those things she'd enjoyed as much as they had.

Her phone chimed. Celeste smiled as she pulled it out of her apron pocket. Mike, just as she'd assumed.

I'm at the annual holiday work party. Give me a rain check on the cookies.

She read it twice just to make sure she hadn't misunderstood. She had gone with him to that party the last couple of years. Everyone else, he'd explained the first year, brought their spouses or significant others. He hadn't wanted to be the only one there alone. Why hadn't he invited her this time?

I hope it's not too miserable, she typed back. She stood at her counter, the cookie ingredients laid out, but nothing actually mixed yet.

Her phone chimed. *Amy from accounting is here alone, too. So, not too bad.*

Amy from accounting? Why would Amy from accounting make his evening so much better? Mike had only ever mentioned her in offhand ways like, "I need to get my expense report in to Amy from accounting before the weekend" or "The last person I would want to watch a fake YouTube concert with is Amy from accounting."

Celeste stared at her phone for a long, drawn-out moment. She didn't know how to respond or if she even should. Interrupting a date was rude—not that Mike was on a date. He and Amy were only at the party together by chance, really. It wasn't like Mike had gone over to accounting and asked Amy to sit with him at the party. Right?

Ask Amy if she knows where to find a vintage babydoll dress. LOL

The moment she sent the text she realized how stupid it probably was. And a little pathetic. She was trying to spend the evening via text with a guy who was already spending the evening in person with someone else. And she'd typed LOL, something she'd always sworn she wouldn't do; it felt too . . . stupid.

In the end, she couldn't say if Mike agreed that the message was pathetic or the acronym stupid. He didn't text back.

A batch of cookies later, he hadn't texted back.

She strung a strand of lights on the front porch. Still no text.

She pulled the tabletop Christmas tree out of the attic and set it up on the end table in the front room. No text.

She even found a babydoll dress in her size on eBay and ordered it. Nothing.

There was nothing to be done but turn on *A Christmas Carol* and have some cookies and hot chocolate. Watching George C. Scott transform into a decent person was usually very cathartic, one of the highlights of the season for her—why had she ever thought that skipping these things would make her happier this year?—but it fell a little short this time.

"I'm Scrooge," she said to the empty room, "no family around, no friends, all alone at Christmas." Except Scrooge had been happy about it, at first anyway. "I was, too. A little bit." She had been looking forward to a very low-key Christmas. Mike had turned that in to an fun scavenger hunt, and she couldn't be satisfied with the quiet any longer.

"That's what friends are for, making a person dissatisfied with the status quo."

Speaking of status quo: why in the world was he at his annual work party with Amy from accounting? He always took Celeste. Always.

She felt like she'd been stood up. Or overlooked. Or something.

Not that the work parties were dates or anything. They were just friends. Friends who were free to date . . . accountants. Except, Mike worked in IT. An accountant didn't seem like the best match for a computer geek. A lawyer would be more likely to offset the geekiness. Not that Mike was super geeky. Or that she was looking to date him.

Then, what was her problem? She was upset about him being out with someone else even though she wasn't looking to be anything but his friend? Was "friend jealousy" a thing? She wasn't jealous of his other friends. She knew most of them; she liked them. She enjoyed hearing about the things Mike did with his other friends.

Just not Amy from accounting.

Mike had never before wished that texting wasn't a thing. But, there he was, making his first attempt at accepting his spot on Celeste's designated friend list, and he'd spent the whole night getting texts from her. *Friend*ly texts, but a lot of them. There wouldn't be any distance between them to make giving up his pursuit any easier.

Amy had been good company that night. Her husband was at home with a sick child, so she'd come alone. They'd spent most of the party talking about childhood illnesses and injuries, and his hope that he'd eventually have grandchildren to spoil.

"Is everything okay?" Amy asked.

"Have you ever tried to break up with someone you weren't actually dating?"

Amy did a double-take. "What?"

"The woman I usually bring to these parties, Celeste. I think I need to break up with her, but we aren't actually dating."

"Then what are you breaking off? Friendship?"

He shook his head. "I guess I'm breaking up with the possibility of being more than friends. I've been hoping for a while, but I'm finally admitting to myself that she isn't interested."

"That stinks." Amy was an enthusiastic listener. She reminded him of his daughter-in-law. She was about the same age and of a very similarly energetic disposition. "And you're sure she's not interested at all?"

"She's my best friend, but every time I even hint at anything more, she—"

"Panics."

He was going to say "rejects me" but "panics" actually seemed like a more accurate description. "She certainly changes the subject fast enough."

"My husband tried for three years to move things from friends to something more. He tried everything from being the friendliest friend in the world to asking me out every chance he got. Neither approach worked."

That sounded horribly familiar. "So what *did* work in the end?"

She held up a finger and dug in to her purse. She pulled out her cellphone. "I think you should ask him."

Mike had only interacted with Amy's husband on rare occasions. He hardly knew the guy. "Are you sure?"

Amy nodded, the phone already to her ear. "Hi, honey. Can you do me a favor?" A quick smile and she continued.

"Mike Durham, from IT, is here at my table and I want you to tell him how much of a disaster our courtship was at first." She laughed. "No, I'm serious. There's this woman he is basically desperately in love with and he can't get himself out of the friend zone." She made a sound of acknowledgement. "So will you?"

This was embarrassing.

Amy held her phone out and smiled as if she was offering him a very welcome gift rather than forcing him to have an awkward conversation with her husband.

"Hi," he said.

"Is this as weird for you as it is for me?" Mr. Amy asked.

"Yes."

Mr. Amy—Mike was having a very personal conversation with someone whose name he didn't even know—laughed in commiseration. "I don't really have any good advice. I got out of 'the friend zone,' as Amy calls it, by getting out of the friendship. I called it quits."

"You gave up the entire thing?" Mike didn't like that suggestion. He'd been backing away a little, giving himself some space to breathe. But ending their friendship entirely was a more drastic step than he was ready to take.

"I told her that I loved her and wanted her to be happy. I told her I respected her decision not to be anything more than friends, but that being her friend would never be enough for me."

"You told her straight out?" Mike had only ever beaten around that bush.

"She wasn't getting the message any other way. I told her to call if she ever needed anything and that I'd see her around. And then I walked out of her life."

Mike couldn't imagine doing that. Just thinking about it turned his stomach to lead. "For good?"

"That was the plan. Not a plan like, 'Hey, if I turn my back on her maybe she'll come crawling back.' I just couldn't do it anymore. The plan was—I don't know how to explain it."

Mike did. "Self-preservation."

"Right. But after a while, she started missing me and realizing there was more between us than just a casual friendship. I'd run into her once in a while and she'd start to realize it more. Then, one day, she came to me and said she'd like to start again. So we did. And now we're married with a kid who likes to throw up on me."

"Every man's dream." Mike liked Mr. Amy.

"Chances are I got lucky that she came back. But, even if she hadn't, I had to get out of there. It was killing me."

Mike knew that feeling. "How soon did you jump to that idea?" Mike had only been trying his methods for seven years, after all. An entire decade wasn't too long to wait. He rolled his eyes at how ridiculous he sounded.

"Not until everything else failed. Pretending I only wanted to be friends was Plan A. Actually asking her out a bunch of times was Plan B."

Mike hadn't moved to Plan B yet. "And walking away was Plan C?"

"More like Plan L or M."

Maybe it was time for Mike to be a little more upfront about his feelings. He could try asking her out, try showing her his interest in her went past hanging out over coffee and YouTube concerts.

And he probably should also formulate a Plan C, D, E...

Five

BY THE NEXT AFTERNOON, MIKE had decided he was never going to attend another work party as long as he lived. Amy had come by his desk three times that day to give him pitying looks and ask if he meant to break things off with Celeste. He must have been crazy to have told her about his problems.

He thought about that on his drive home. He hadn't talked about this with either of his sons; it just wasn't the kind of thing that came up between them. They talked mostly about their jobs, upcoming trips and purchases. He also fielded a lot of questions from them about home repairs. But never his love life. Probably because they knew he didn't have one.

Maybe that's why I can't sort all of this out. I don't know anyone who has any idea how to navigate these waters.

He reached home still trying to convince himself to ask Celeste on an actual date. How clear did he have to be that it was a date? Could he just say, "Do you want to go to dinner?" and hope she figured it out?

No. This was supposed to be him taking the direct approach so she would know where he stood and he could find out what possibilities she was willing to consider.

He pulled his car into the garage and, rather than go in to his own house, went straight to Celeste's. He needed to issue his invitation before she ate and before he ran out of courage.

She opened the door and, before he could even say hi, she started talking. "I was just about to call you. Are you free tonight?"

That depended on how you looked at it. He was free. He was hoping by the end of their initial conversation that he wouldn't be and that she wouldn't be either. "What did you have in mind?"

She grinned as she closed the door behind him. "I can check another thing off my holiday bucket list."

He hadn't thought about their competition in a few days. "Really?"

"Really. And by next week I should be able to check off another."

Ask her. You're going to lose your nerve.

"*Home Alone* in the theater was one of my bucket-list things," Celeste explained, crossing to her living room coffee table. She held up a DVD of *Home Alone*, then pointed to a digital projector on the table as well. "Joey, our IT guy at the office, lent it to me. He said you would know how to connect it to my computer."

"I can do that." *Ask her.* "But I haven't had dinner yet. Maybe we could go have something to eat first." *Not too awkward; good.*

"Sure. What are you in the mood for?"

That was easier than he'd expected. "Just about anything. What about you?"

She grabbed her purse off the counter, her brows pulled low in thought. "What about Curry MacMurray? I haven't been there in ages."

He liked Indian food, and, despite the kind of ridiculous name, Curry MacMurray had great food. "Perfect."

"My car or yours?" Celeste asked.

She did realize this was a date, didn't she? "Everything's on me tonight. The driving, the meal, the complimentary projector set-up."

She laughed lightly and walked with him toward the door. "You are in a very generous mood."

Generous? She really doesn't know this is a date. He needed to clear that up, or what was the point? "My mother always told me that if I was the one doing the asking then I was the one paying for the date."

She didn't look surprised by his use of the word "date." What did that mean? He didn't ask, and she didn't say anything more on the topic. They talked about inconsequential things all the way to Curry MacMurray. He had hoped she wouldn't object to going on an actual date with him, but he hadn't expected it to be this easy.

Over aloo gobi and korma, they updated each other on their work projects and kids. It was exactly like a very laid-back date and precisely like every meal he'd ever had with her. There was never any real discomfort between them, even when the situation could easily have been horribly awkward. And it was a date—a date she realized was a date—and still wasn't uncomfortable.

"So how was your evening with Amy?" Celeste asked as she tore off a piece of naan.

"Evening with—? You mean the work party?"

She nodded. "You said you were there with Amy."

He hadn't been *with* Amy. "Amy and I were just both

there alone. Her husband was home with their sick baby."

Celeste's eyes pulled wide. "She's married? With a baby?"

Why did she sound so happy about that? "I even talked to her husband on the phone for a few minutes. So, I'm pretty sure Amy isn't making it all up."

"I didn't think she was." Celeste seemed to be biting back a smile. "So you weren't there with Amy, you were just both there by yourselves."

He nodded. "I would have taken you, but you said you were swearing off the usual Christmas things. And, while the party isn't specifically a Christmas one, it is an end-of-the-year celebration, which seemed too close to the same thing."

"Ah." Still that barely concealed smile hovered below the surface. "I ended up watching *A Christmas Carol* and putting up a Christmas tree last night, so I think my boycott of the Christmas season is officially over."

"But the bucket list competition lives on?" He hoped she didn't mean to abandon that. He enjoyed spending the time with her.

"Of course."

He took a quick sip of water; the korma was a little spicier than he usually ordered it. "If we include the in-home screening of *Home Alone*, then this date can be dinner *and* a movie. Mom would have wholeheartedly approved of that."

Celeste laughed. "Except I am the one providing the movie part of it. I imagine that would have earned you a tssk or two."

That settled it. Two mentions of a date and she went right along with both of them. This was a date. He kept himself from shooting his fist up in triumph. They were finally on a date!

His phone buzzed in the exact moment Celeste's

chimed. They shot each other quizzical looks as they both pulled their phones out. It was Kristina.

Econ guy is getting weirder. Title IX office & campus police are looking into it. Wish you guys were here.

"The title IX office." Celeste said, her gaze sliding over the screen. "So the school considers this an issue of the safety of women on campus. I'm glad they're taking this seriously."

"She seems calm." Mike read back over the text. "Worried," he amended, "but calm. That's a good sign."

Celeste typed into her phone. A moment later, his phone buzzed as her text came to him as well. *Getting weird in what way?*

Far quicker than either Mike or Celeste could have managed it, Kristina texted back. *Showing up in a lot of places. Asking me out every time he sees me even though I told him to stop. I think he might be stalking me.*

Mike was instantly on full alert. *You told Title XI and the police all this?*

Yup.

"Oh, Mike. I wish we were closer."

"So do I." He typed a response to Kristina. *You aren't going out alone, right?*

My roommates won't let me. Few of the guys in my complex are walking me to campus and back.

Celeste's text popped up next. *Good.*

Then Kristina. *Except they're going home for Christmas in a couple of days. I'm pretty much the only one staying here.*

Was the creepy guy staying as well? Mike didn't like the idea. *Maybe you should come home.*

Celeste looked up at him. "I really hope she does."

Kristina's answer came through in the next moment. *I'll lose my job.*

That was probably true. Kristina worked in retail, where the Christmas season was mandatory.

We could probably find you a job here, Celeste answered.

Feels like creepy stalker guys wins. Kristina was in a tough spot. She didn't want this guy to decide what she did and where she went—he *shouldn't* get to decide that—but she also needed to look out for herself while the authorities tried to get things under control.

But how could those needs be balanced without sacrificing her safety?

"Could you get some time off?" Mike asked Celeste.

She met his eye. "Probably."

"I think we need to go see Kristina," he said. "We can grab a couple of hotel rooms near campus, and have her come stay with us while her roommates and makeshift bodyguards are gone. She won't be alone, and we won't feel so helpless."

She reached across the table and took his hand. "Really?"

"Really." He flagged down the waiter and asked for their check.

A few minutes later, they were in the car driving back home. Celeste was on the phone with Kristina, telling her their plans, which they were figuring out as they went.

Mike had been worried about whether or not Celeste would go on an official date with him. That seemed unimportant now. Kristina was in trouble. He loved her and Celeste both, and he would do whatever he needed to do to help either one of them.

The exact definition of his relationship with Celeste could wait.

Six

"I WANTED THIS CHRISTMAS TO be different," Celeste said, watching the snow-covered scenery fly past the passenger-side window. "This isn't quite what I had in mind."

"You also wanted to go back to Christmases when you were younger. Spending the season near a university campus ought to do that."

She smiled weakly at his attempt at humor. They were both concerned about Kristina. The eight-hour drive to be with her had given them ample opportunity to worry even more.

"She sounded more like herself when I called her from the rest stop a few hours ago." Celeste was reminding herself just as much as she was telling him. "I don't think she's as worried as we are."

Mike nodded, keeping his eyes on the road ahead. "We might get there and find out we are overreacting, but I'd rather know that for sure."

"So would I." She turned in her seat enough to look at

him rather than her window. What would she have done without Mike? He'd been her rock through all of this, just as he had in other difficult times over the past years. He'd even found a hotel with suites: a living room and kitchen with a bedroom on either side. They could comfortably stay there until all was well with Kristina again.

"Thank you again for doing this," she said.

"For protecting my little girl?" He tossed her a smile. "There was never any question."

"But I'm sure you meant to spend some time during the holidays with your boys. They aren't too far from home." Unlike her kids, who all had moved hours and hours away.

"Brad and Connor think of Kristina as a little sister. When I told them why I was going to be gone, they were not only supportive, but offered to come pound the creep themselves."

Celeste adjusted the heating vent so it blew more directly on her. "I hope this turns out to be nothing more than a young man who doesn't understand social cues."

"So do I." His tone was tight, as was his mouth. Mike sounded like he'd enjoy doing a little pounding himself.

"Maybe we can find an Indian food place near the hotel and try our dinner date again." She normally would have objected to his use of the word date, but having spent the night before their trip to Curry MacMurray writhing in jealousy over Amy from accounting—jealousy which turned out to be entirely unwarranted—she'd instead been excited to hear him call their dinner exactly that.

"Date?" He shot her a quick confused glance.

Nervousness clutched her heart. "That's what you called it." Could he hear the uncertainty in her voice? She'd been avoiding anything resembling a relationship with Mike for so long, but now, having crossed that line, even in such a small way, felt like huge a risk.

"Yes, but I also came to your house dressed in Hammer pants, so my judgment is questionable at best. I only questioned the word because I wanted to make certain you thought of it that way too, that I didn't misunderstand."

"Ah."

He glanced at her for the briefest of moments. "Was it? A date, I mean? We've never called any of our time together an actual date."

"Would it be so bad if it was?" She hoped not.

He shook his head. "Not bad at all."

"I should probably warn you," she said. "I have the world's worst dating track record. Every attempt ends in disaster."

He shrugged. "And I have no track record. I can count on one hand the number of dates I've been on in the past twenty years."

"What could possibly go wrong?" she said with a smile.

Mike pulled the car into the parking lot of Kristina's apartment complex. They found only one visitor parking spot; school wouldn't officially be out for a couple of days. The sidewalks had been shoveled but needed to be salted. Celeste walked carefully up toward Kristina's door with Mike close on her heels.

A patch of ice caught her off guard. As her foot slid out from under her, Mike reached out and steadied her. He always did seem to be there when she needed him. That was something a woman didn't always find out about a man until it was too late.

A young woman, probably right around Kristina's age, opened the door when Celeste knocked. "Hey, Kris!" she called back into the apartment. "Your mom and dad are here."

Celeste tried to explain, but the girl had already moved back inside, leaving the door open.

"It's probably simpler just to leave it be," Mike said. "We won't be staying here anyway."

And, when it came down to it, Mike *was* like a father to Kristina.

They stepped inside. Kristina was there in the next instant, her arms around Celeste. "I'm so glad you came."

"So am I, hon."

"But it was so far to drive."

Mike put his arm around Kristina, making something of a sandwich out of the three of them. "Worth every mile, kiddo."

"Have you checked in to your hotel?" Kristina asked.

Celeste held her daughter even more tightly. "Not yet. We wanted to see you first."

"Do you mind if I hang out with you guys tonight?"

"Not at all," Mike said.

Kristina hurried into a bedroom and came back with a duffle bag. She held it up with a shrug. "Mom said there's a living room. I'll crash on the couch."

All the way to the hotel, a full ten minutes, Kristina talked about Econ boy, whose name was Jim, and how she saw him all over campus. He had asked her out repeatedly, growing more insistent each time. Kristina said she'd been very clear in her refusal and had specifically told him to stop asking, but he hadn't. While Celeste couldn't say for certain that it was a dangerous situation, it was clearly a case of harassment, and that warranted addressing.

Mike left them in the car and hopped out to check them in to the hotel.

"How is your holiday bet going?" Kristina asked when they were alone.

"That's not really important right now." Celeste hadn't thought of it since they'd begun planning this last-minute trip the day before. They hadn't bothered with *Home Alone* on the projector, focusing instead on finding hotels and trying to make arrangements for some time off.

"Of course it's important." Kristina sounded annoyed; the dim parking-lot lighting made seeing her expression difficult at best. "You were going to spend Christmas with Mike."

"I always spend Christmas with him."

"I don't mean having him over for coffee and butter cookies, Mom. Hours and hours together. Dates, maybe."

Celeste pushed down the bubble of anticipation that created. "We did have a date last night."

"A real one?" Kristina's tone couldn't have been more enthusiastic.

"We had Indian food, at a restaurant at our own table for two."

"Mom!"

Celeste held her hand up. "Don't get too excited. It wasn't romantic, just friendly."

"You two have always been friendly. When are you going to get on to the kissing part? I've been waiting for years."

Mike was walking back to the car.

"Don't say that when he's here," Celeste said.

"I won't have to. He's been thinking about it for years. I guarantee it."

Celeste hadn't blushed since she was a teenager, but she was almost certain she was blushing right then.

Mike pulled the door open and leaned inside. "We're all checked in, ladies. Let's get our luggage taken up, and then we can go get something to eat."

"I can stay here if you want," Kristina said, "then you two can have another dinner date."

Celeste ought to have known Kristina would jump right on this topic. Any of the kids would have. The only thing they liked more than Mike was giving their mother a hard time.

"Don't sweat it, kid. You interrupted last night's date too." He motioned them out. "Let's get our stuff in."

They stepped out of the car and pulled the luggage from the trunk.

"Do I get to go along as chaperone?" Kristina asked. "Maybe sit between you guys in a booth or something?"

If she hadn't been whole-heartedly relieved to see for herself that Kristina was doing well, Celeste likely would have been very annoyed at her daughter's teasing. She shot Mike a look of mingled apology and amusement, hoping to mask her own embarrassment. "I'm thinking we should order in."

Mike walked with her through the hotel doors. "Chinese?" he suggested. "I know you both like it."

"Sounds good."

Kristina kept up her teasing as they unpacked, while they waited for the delivery guy, and all through dinner. Celeste was actually relieved when Kristina asked if she could use the desk in the bedroom Celeste had claimed as her own to study for her finals the next day.

The moment she and Mike were alone again, she launched into a much-needed apology. "I shouldn't have told her we had a date last night. She probably won't ever let up."

Mike laughed. "I'm just glad to see she's her usual, goofy self. If we'd come here and she was somber and anxious, I would be worrying a whole lot more."

"So would I." She sat on the sofa next to him. "What do we do now?"

"About what? The creepy guy or Kristina's offer to chaperone?"

Celeste dropped her head into her upturned hand. "This could be a long trip."

Mike leaned back, slouching a little. "She's always been a goofball. I love that about her."

"Even when her goofiness is directed at you?"

He gave her a knowing look. "I'm just hoping she never hears about the Hammer pants."

Oh, it felt good to laugh.

Mike put his arm around her shoulders and pulled her close to him. She didn't resist; she didn't want to. Having him nearby during the difficulties of the last few weeks had reminded her what a source of strength he was.

"After we get her down to campus for her finals, I'll go talk to the campus police, see what they've figured out and what they suggest we do." Mike adjusted his position and Celeste found that she fit kind of perfectly beside him. "I'm thinking *you* ought to go talk to the Title IX office, though. Sometimes having an attorney involved, even if that attorney is there as a mother, can get things done faster than anything else."

He was probably right.

"Is it weird that I'm almost hoping we run into this guy tomorrow?" Celeste said. "Part of me wants to come across him so we can beat the snot out of him. Part of me just wants to get a feel for what kind of a creep he is."

"Not weird at all," Mike answered. "I'm hoping the same thing."

She leaned her head on his shoulder. "Thank you again for being here and for caring about us."

"It is my pleasure."

By the end of the next day, Mike was exhausted. He and Celeste had spent the time during Kristina's finals talking with the administration, the campus police, and Kristina's roommates, getting a better idea of what exactly had been happening the last few weeks.

According to the administration, Kristina was not the first woman on campus to report unwanted attention from this Jim guy. The campus police told them that Jim had been cited more than once in the past for loitering outside of other women's apartments—women who had reported his behavior to the police just like Kristina had.

Kristina's roommates said Jim hadn't made any appearances in their complex or at Kristina's work. Mike had silently tacked a "yet" on to the end of that. A guy who had harassed more than one woman, who had been approached by the police for more than one incident of border-line stalking, and who was following that same pattern again was likely to repeat the entire scenario. He hadn't shown up at her apartment or work *yet*.

Still, there was a small sliver of relief along with these discoveries. The administration and police both reported that Jim was in his final semester and was graduating in only four days, and that he was headed to Florida to start a new job. Florida was multiple states away. That was, at least, a little reassuring.

They shared all they'd learned with Kristina as they walked with her from her last final of the day, across campus to the parking lot. She, they discovered, knew a lot of it already.

"I hadn't heard that he was moving to Florida," Kristina said. "That actually makes me feel a lot better. Except, I feel bad for the women of Florida. He'll probably harass a lot of them, too."

"Probably." Celeste's tone was more tired than surprised. "Let's hope the company he'll be working for has a good HR department."

"Let's hope Jim decides to quit being a creep," Mike said.

Kristina took hold of his coat sleeve with her gloved hand. She motioned ahead of them with her head. "That's him."

Mike looked in the direction she'd indicated. A guy about the right age stood a few yards ahead of them. Mike had been picturing a football player, someone enormous. This guy was tall, but slender, the kind of person most other guys probably didn't give a second thought. If not for a little arthritis in his shoulder, Mike wouldn't even wonder if he could physically take on this guy. But of course Kristina would have doubts about her ability to defend herself. Size was, after all, relative.

It was a different world for women in so many ways.

He pulled his car keys from his pocket and handed them to Celeste. "You and Kristina head to the car. I'll meet you there."

"What are you going to do?" she asked.

"I'm just going to talk to the guy." As much as he'd like to pound the kid a little, he suspected it wouldn't actually help. "I think he needs to know she has more allies than he realizes. Allies who are watching him."

Without warning, Kristina gave him a hug. "I love you, Mike."

He hugged her fiercely in return. "And I love you, kiddo. Always have."

"Always will."

He nudged her over toward her mother. "I'll catch up with you in a minute."

He fully expected them to take up the journey to the parking lot once more, but Celeste stepped up to him. She pressed a kiss to his cheek. Before pulling back, she whispered, "We all love you, Mike."

He'd imagined many times hearing her say that she loved him, but that seemed the closest she ever got: a general sentiment about her whole family loving him in a general way. While he appreciated that, he wanted something more personal from her. He wanted *her* to love *him*.

He watched them a moment longer as they walked away, then turned his attention to the matter of Jim. The guy realized once Mike was almost at his side that he was being approached. A look of worry flitted over his features, replaced very quickly by a pointed show of confidence.

"You're Jim?" Mike asked, keeping his tone calm but firm.

"Yeah. Who're you?"

"My name isn't necessary." Mike assumed his most steely glare, the one that had sent any number of would-be bullies running away during his school years and had put a few would-be career saboteurs in their places in more recent years. Mike wasn't the most threatening-looking guy—he knew that about himself—but he also knew how to give people a moment's pause when need be. "You've been making a nuisance of yourself, bothering a young woman who is family to me."

"I don't—"

"Don't play stupid. I know you've been contacted recently regarding this matter, and I know you know exactly who I'm talking about."

Jim didn't make any more objections, so he must have understood.

"You've seen people who've been looking out for her:

her friends and roommates, the police. But you haven't seen me, have you?"

That clearly confused him.

"Think about that. There are people watching you who you don't see." He stepped in the tiniest bit closer and lowered his voice to what he knew was a sinister whisper. "Cause any further trouble for her, and I'll know it. I'll see you, Jim, even though you don't see me." He offered a knowing smile. "Enjoy Florida."

Jim's eyes pulled wide. "How did you know—"

"I always know." Mike left it at that.

He glanced back only once and spotted Jim moving very swiftly in the other direction. The implied threat likely wouldn't be enough in and of itself to send the kid packing for good, but combined with the police's earlier visits, it might make him think twice before continuing to follow Kristina around campus, or anywhere else.

It wasn't a guarantee, but it was something.

Seven

KRISTINA SPENT THE NEXT FOUR nights at the hotel after her shift at the department store, studying for her last remaining finals, taking advantage of free meals, and, though she only admitted it to Mike, enjoying her mother's company. On the fifth day, campus police informed them that Jim had left for Florida. That called for a celebration.

Mike found a few cheap Christmas decorations, a tin of Celeste's favorite butter cookies, and Kristina's favorite: a carton of eggnog.

He also swung by a print shop.

"What is this?" Celeste said when he handed her the rolled-up print, tied with a ribbon.

"A Christmas gift," he said. "For you."

"You're a few days early." It couldn't have been a complaint; she was eagerly untying it.

"What is it?" Kristina asked him while watching her mom.

"Something your mother will appreciate," he answered

quietly. "We've spent a lot of time talking about Christmas wishes."

Kristina tossed him one of her signature grins. "I think you two have enjoyed your holiday, despite having to come up here and sort out my mess."

Mike gave her an affectionate, fatherly hug. He'd told her again and again the past five days that she'd been anything but a nuisance. Eventually she would believe it.

Celeste unrolled the print. She sucked in a quick, sharp breath before bursting with laughter. "Where did you get this?" She managed to formulate the question between laughs.

"I had it made up. I couldn't think of anything you'd want more."

She couldn't seem to stop laughing, which was exactly the response he'd been hoping for.

"What is it?" Kristina stepped around her mom, getting her first look at his offering. After a moment's confusion, she looked up at him. "Is that the 'Ice Ice Baby' guy?"

Mike nodded.

Celeste quickly rolled the print up again and crossed to him. She wrapped her arms around his neck. He swore his pulse jumped straight there as well, pounding hard into his head.

"This has been the best Christmas," she said, smiling at him. "The *best*."

"All this over an Ice-guy poster?" Kristina snatched a cookie from the tin. "Old people get excited about the weirdest things."

Celeste didn't let go, didn't back away. She simply kept watching him with what looked like very real happiness. "You know this means I win, right?"

At the moment, Mike was pretty convinced *he* had won.

She was hugging him, smiling at him, being more affectionate than he ever remembered her being.

"We both agreed to count the *Home Alone* movie viewing even though it was sort of called off. I have my Vanilla Ice souvenir, and I have a babydoll dress at home that I ordered from eBay. Once I show you that, I've checked off my entire Holiday Bucket List. I win."

"Well, then." He settled his arms comfortably around her, fully aware of the fact that she hadn't at all pulled away. "It seems like I owe you something off your Christmas present wish list. What's it to be?"

She didn't hesitate even a moment. "I want you to ask me on another date."

That was not remotely what he'd expected her to say. "Really?"

She nodded. "Our last one started out very promising. I'd like to try again."

"Done." He'd ask her out a hundred more times without question.

"And—"

"And?" He chuckled at the grin that accompanied her tagging-on of another request.

"—I want us to go roller skating and search the thrift stores for an old NES."

"You want me to finish my bucket list?"

"I want to know better the you that you were before I met you. Your Holiday Bucket List is part of that."

This was more than promising. This was downright amazing.

"Again," he said, "done."

"And—" She laughed before he could. "Lastly, I want to know what on your wish list you would have chosen if you'd won."

He must have turned beet red in that moment. He knew exactly what he'd wanted to ask for, but had assumed he wouldn't go through with it even if he'd won their bet.

"What is it?" Celeste's amazed and amused tone told him he had blushed just as embarrassingly deeply as he'd feared.

Her arms *were* still draped around his neck. She *was* still standing close to him, looking at him with something very closely resembling love. Maybe his wish list topper wasn't such a stretch after all.

"The top of my list has looked the same for seven years, Celeste," he said. "It hasn't changed. I just never figured it would ever work out."

He saw her eyes turn a little uncertain. "You didn't think what would ever work out?"

"I've wanted to kiss you."

Rather than running away in horror, something Mike had imagined often over the past seven years, Celeste smiled slowly, coyly. "Kristina might freak out, but I certainly have no objections."

For a moment, he was too shocked to say or do anything. But only for a moment.

He pulled her in ever closer and kissed her with seven years of longing and hoping and loving. He kissed her deeply, and he kissed her well.

"Don't stop on my account." Kristina pulled out her phone. "I'll just be over here pretending to ignore you."

"And we'll be over here," Celeste said, "*actually* ignoring you."

That was invitation enough. He kissed her again. And again.

Until Kristina started giggling. "Sorry," she said. "It's great, you two deciding to give this a go. It's a little weird, too, though."

Mike kept an arm around Celeste as they sat on the sofa. "It's a shame she'll be away at college for all those dates we're going on."

"A real shame." Celeste set her head on his shoulder. "I have warned you about my terrible dating track record, haven't I?"

He nodded. "That track record, my dear, is about to be laid to rest. For good."

Eight

On the first day of December, one year after the holiday-bucket-list Christmas, Celeste picked up a small cake from a local bakery, put on a brand new white dress, and officially gave up on single life.

She and Mike, surrounded by their children, stood before the Justice of the Peace and crossed the first item off of their Happily Ever After bucket list.

ABOUT SARAH M. EDEN

SARAH M. EDEN is the author of multiple historical romances, including the two-time Whitney Award Winner *Longing for Home* and Whitney Award finalists *Seeking Persephone* and *Courting Miss Lancaster*. Combining her obsession with history and affinity for tender love stories, Sarah loves crafting witty characters and heartfelt romances. She has twice served as the Master of Ceremonies for the LDStorymakers Writers Conference and acted as the Writer in Residence at the Northwest Writers Retreat. Sarah is represented by Pam van Hylckama Vlieg at D4EO Literary Agency.

Visit Sarah online:
Twitter: @SarahMEden
Facebook: Author Sarah M. Eden
Website: SarahMEden.com

Christmas Every Day

Heather B. Moore

OTHER WORKS BY HEATHER B. MOORE

Heart of the Ocean
The Fortune Café
The Boardwalk Antiques Shop
The Mariposa Hotel
Timeless Romance Anthologies
The Aliso Creek Series

OTHER WORKS BY H.B. MOORE
Finding Sheba
Lost King
Slave Queen
Beneath (short story)
Eve: In the Beginning
Esther the Queen
The Moses Chronicles

One

Monica's phone buzzed a few minutes before her alarm was supposed to go off. Without opening her eyes, she knew it was David. And she knew he wanted to apologize about the night before—their relationship was that predictable now.

Reluctantly, she reached for her phone and read the text.

Sorry about last night. Didn't mean to blow up. Lunch today?

It was always like that. He'd get mad at something small, and it would escalate into a huge fight that was about everything from the beginning of their relationship up until now. Then she'd finally push back and tell David if he couldn't stand so many things about her, then they should just break up.

Monica turned off her alarm and lay back in bed, closing her eyes for a few minutes. There was no risk of her falling back asleep. Over the past couple of months, she had found herself becoming more and more distant with David. She'd never meet up to his ideal woman, and she should have never gone on that second date with him, especially after he showed her his *list*.

The list had driven a wedge between them from the start. David's list contained twenty attributes his wife needed to have. It didn't bother Monica that he had a list per se, whether written down or just in his head, but it did bother her that he continually brought it up.

Last night over dinner, David had pointed out that he didn't want his wife so dependent on electronics. That he wanted to be able to drop everything and take off camping for a few days. Monica had defended herself, saying she had so many things going on that she had to set her calendar alarms or she'd get off track.

"That's exactly why you should turn your phone off," David had countered. "You wouldn't have so many distractions if you weren't always checking it."

Monica had argued back. She was the assistant manager of the Ungritches' shop, *Christmas Around the World*, and had a lot of responsibility. True to previous arguments, David told her she should go part-time, and Monica countered that she needed the money to help with her mother's care. And if she could afford to only work part-time, then she wanted to go back and finish college.

Monica opened her eyes and puffed out a breath. She was getting worked up again, and the buffer of a night's sleep had disappeared.

She typed a text to David: *I'm swamped today. We'll talk tonight.*

Tonight, she told herself, she'd tell him it was over. *For good.* She loved her job, she loved her routine, and she loved her system of keeping all of her tasks properly juggled. And she wasn't a bad person. Let David take his list and find another woman to patronize.

Monica climbed out of bed. She was a few minutes ahead of schedule thanks to the early morning text from David. She crossed off yesterday's date from the calendar on her wall: *December 20*. It might seem childish, but she was counting down the days until Christmas Eve. This year, she'd play Mrs. Claus to all the young guests at the Ungritches' annual neighborhood Christmas party.

Her bosses, Mr. and Mrs. Ungritch, were getting on in years, and more and more over the past few months they'd given her increased responsibility of their *Christmas Around the World* store. Something David didn't like at all, of course.

In fact, paperwork was being prepared for Monica's purchase of the store right after the New Year. The Ungritches wanted to leave it in good hands. They'd hoped to pass it onto their only son, but there'd been a falling out years ago, and they hadn't spoken to him since.

When Mr. and Mrs. Ungritch first approached Monica with the idea, she had been hesitant. She'd always planned to go back to college and finish her degree. She'd only been about eighteen months into school when her father died and she had to move back home to watch over her mother, who was dealing with dementia.

Monica had found a part-time job at the Christmas shop, and when her mother went to a care center after the dementia progressed to Alzheimer's, Monica worked full-time in order to keep up with all the bills. She ended up having to sell her mother's house and now rented the upstairs apartment above the shop.

The "apartment" had just been a big open space, but now as Monica looked from her wall calendar and scanned the room, she was pleased to see that it had all come together nicely. She had a set of used, but decent couches that sectioned off a living room, an old-fashioned Japanese privacy screen she'd found online that separated her bed and wardrobe, then a refinished kitchen table and mismatched chairs—all adding to the charm of having her own place.

Monica wrapped her arms about herself and gave a happy sigh. December 21. Only four more days until the big party, and only a week after that until she would officially own her own store. The Ungritches had been more than generous and were selling it below market value, and Monica had agreed that they'd be a part of the store for as long as they wanted to. She'd even pay them for their help—although they both refused any pay. Becoming the owner would require a loan from the bank, but she'd already qualified, and the banker had showed her how to set up a salary for herself.

Tonight when she met with David, she'd tell him of her plans to buy the shop. If he wasn't supportive, then that would be her final clue that their relationship had come to a screeching halt.

She couldn't imagine telling the Ungritches that she'd changed her mind on the shop because her boyfriend didn't like the idea. Thinking of the Ungritches' generous hearts always made Monica a bit misty-eyed. The Ungritches had become like her second parents. When she visited her mother at the care center every few days, there was less and less to talk about as her mother slipped farther into an unseen world.

At twenty-four, Monica would make a rather young Mrs. Claus, but she would remedy that with the right makeup. It was early yet, but today the makeup kit she'd ordered online should arrive. Her phone beeped a reminder that it was time to head down the stairs and open the shop.

Monica turned off the reminder, thankful for cell phones and alarms, despite David's abhorrence to electronics. If she didn't set an alarm, then she'd probably forget to eat. Besides, not everyone could spend days camping in the woods like David.

She entered the shop, and, as usual, the scent of cinnamon and pine charmed her. It might be strange for some to be surrounded by Christmas every day of the year, but Monica loved it. She loved to see the customers transformed by the time they left. Whether it was April, June, or September, the painted bulbs, cheery Santa statues, and bins of colorful candies brought a smile to the faces of both the young and the old.

Monica loved spending time browsing through catalogs, finding unique gifts to sell that came from all over the world.

The front door rattled and then opened as Mrs. Ungritch unlocked it.

"You're here early," Monica said, crossing to the woman as she stepped inside. The cold wind caught the door for a moment, and Mrs. Ungritch had to yank it shut.

She turned to face Monica, and Monica knew immediately that something was wrong. The woman's gently lined face now had dark circles beneath her red-rimmed eyes.

"Is everything all right?" Monica asked.

Mrs. Ungritch handed Monica an envelope. "Read it."

She took the envelope and looked at the return address. "Who's Jaxon?" Then she read the last name. "Oh. Your son."

Mrs. Ungritch only nodded and motioned for Monica to open the letter. She felt reluctant to read something that was likely personal. But she couldn't stand for Mrs. Ungritch to be so upset and would do anything to help her.

Dad and Mom,
 I'm coming home Christmas Eve. We have a lot to talk about.
 Jaxon

Monica turned the letter over, but it was blank on the other side. After years of not speaking, Jaxon had written a very short and cryptic note. She met Mrs. Ungritch's watery gaze. "What does this mean?" Monica asked. "Is it good news or bad news?"

"I don't know," Mrs. Ungritch said, placing a trembling hand on Monica's arm. "My husband is furious. No explanation. But I—I can't wait to see him." Her voice cracked, and Monica pulled the woman into her arms.

"Of course you do. Whatever has happened, he's still your son." Monica was more curious than ever as to what had happened between the Ungritches and their son. They were the most loving and generous people she knew.

"Let me make you some tea," Monica said, drawing away from Mrs. Ungritch. "And I got a brand new catalog from London yesterday that will be fun to look through."

Mrs. Ungritch wiped her eyes and gave Monica a tremulous smile. "You're such a dear. I don't know what we would do without you."

Now a lump formed in Monica's throat. She busied herself preparing the tea for Mrs. Ungritch, and when the woman was settled on a stool next to the counter, Monica got the shop ready for opening. She had a couple of deliveries from the day before to unpack and display and then sort out the money for the register. Today they'd be open two extra hours.

"Do you know why Jaxon left?" Mrs. Ungritch said suddenly.

Monica stopped pulling out the bubble wrap from a delivery box. She turned to look at Mrs. Ungritch. "No, but you don't need to tell me."

"I need to tell someone," she said in a soft voice. "It's been about eight years, but it feels like a lifetime."

Monica rose to her feet and crossed the counter to give Mrs. Ungritch her full attention.

"He fell in love," Mrs. Ungritch said.

This, Monica didn't expect.

"He was in his first year at the college, and all along we planned that he'd take over the shop someday." Mrs. Ungritch's eyes welled with tears, and she sniffled. "He was taking business and advertising classes even though we knew he'd just prefer to work with customers and stock things, and then . . . he met *her*."

Monica waited, not interrupting.

"At first we thought it was a fling, but if you know Jaxon, he doesn't have flings. Had a girlfriend for a year in high school, then nothing until Cynthia." She let out a small sigh. "Her father owned a logging company up north. Before we knew it, Jaxon had dropped out in the middle of the semester, moved up north, married Cynthia, and started working for her father."

Monica placed her hand on top of Mrs. Ungritch's.

"Saying it like that seems to make it not sound so bad," Mrs. Ungritch continued. "I mean, our son changed his mind. No big deal, right? But my husband was crushed. He thought Cynthia was manipulative—that her whole family was—she was pregnant, you see. And the baby wasn't Jaxon's. My husband tried to reason with Jaxon, told him to get to know her better before jumping into it all. But Cynthia had a tight grasp on him. We don't even know if the child was a boy or girl, or if Jaxon has any children of his own by now."

Monica was silent for a while. "Maybe he's bringing his children to meet you."

She gave a hopeful smile. "That's what I told my husband. It only made him more upset . . . 'Why now?' he keeps asking. And I don't have an answer. He's still hurt, and so am I, but I'm ready to make amends." She met Monica's gaze. "If that's even possible."

Monica looked at the letter sitting on the counter between them; it certainly didn't give a lot away. "He must want to make amends if he's coming home." Then an awful thought took over. What if Jaxon Ungritch wanted the store? What if he'd heard about his parents retiring and selling it and was coming to stake his claim?

Two

JAXON NEARLY CURSED OUT LOUD, then curbed his tongue just in time. The woman with two small kids standing in line in front of him probably wouldn't appreciate his swearing. His car had broken down the night before, and the repair was going to cost more than the value, so his only recourse to reach his parents' in time was to take the Greyhound. But his knee was already aching like crazy, and he was regretting every minute of this trip in advance.

Jaxon was the first to admit that his life was in shambles, and he dreaded returning to his parents like a dog with its tail between its legs. But there was no other choice right now. The knee surgery had taken every bit of his savings, and his ex-father-in-law had fired him, for good this time. Despite the fact that Jaxon had overlooked his cheating wife's antics for years, reared *her* son, then finally divorced her after the umpteenth betrayal, he continued on as the underpaid foreman . . . It seemed that apparently Jaxon was still the bad guy.

And all because Jaxon had torn his ACL on the job. He'd been denied worker's compensation since his ex-father-in-law claimed that the injury had occurred offsite. There were no witnesses, so it was Jaxon's word against Cynthia's father. And Jaxon's insurance only covered a limited amount. While still recovering in the hospital, Jaxon had received termination papers.

"Next please," a woman's voice sailed through Jaxon's thoughts.

He limped the few steps toward the window. "One ticket to St. Charles."

The woman looked at him over the brim of her reading glasses. "Eighty-five dollars."

Jaxon handed over his credit card, trying not to think how everything had gone on his credit card lately—even groceries. He'd canceled the lease on his apartment, but he had to pay through the end of January regardless.

The woman slid the ticket across the counter, and Jaxon grasped it and shoved it into his jeans pocket. Then he turned and picked up the two black suitcases he'd brought. He'd packed the past eight years into those cases. Everything else was left behind—his handmade furniture, his books, and every picture of Cynthia and her son, Ricky. He was leaving behind good choices and bad choices, good memories and bad.

He only hoped he could swallow his pride enough to tell his father he'd been right all along . . . Jaxon should have waited to marry Cynthia. He should have finished college. He should have taken over the shop for his parents. He should have stayed in St. Charles and built a safe life, one free from heartache, instead of spending the past eight years wallowing in regret.

Once on the bus, Jaxon popped his second-to-last

Lortab and closed his eyes. In six hours he'd be home. In six hours he'd have to face the consequences of being gone for eight years. But for now he just wanted to sleep and to have no pain for a few hours.

The bus took a corner, and then it was heading for the highway. Despite Jaxon's exhaustion and his craving for sleep, he couldn't help but think about the last time he'd taken a bus on this same highway. It had been going the other direction of course, but he'd been sitting hand-in-hand with Cynthia. He thought he'd been in love. But no, infatuation wasn't love.

Love was built on trust and respect. It didn't include cheating and betrayal.

The only thing Jaxon would miss about the last eight years was Ricky, but even that had faded into memories of him as a baby. A year into the marriage, Cynthia cheated on Jaxon for the last time, and he filed for divorce. Spending time with Ricky had slowed to a trickle after that since the boy had become the apple of his grandfather's eye.

Jaxon continued working at the logging company since he felt like he'd burned too many bridges with his parents. He made no demands for a pay raise, time off, or worker's compensation when injured. His years as a loyal employee never amounted to anything more than putting food on his table and continually living in a cloud of regret.

Still, when Jaxon saw Ricky from afar, his heart tugged. And he wished Cynthia could change and somehow things would work out between them. But then it only took seeing Cynthia flirting with another man to harden Jaxon's resolve again.

The sun rose higher in the sky, casting white light on the snowy landscape as the bus sped along the highway. Jaxon put in his ear buds and plugged them into his phone. If he couldn't escape the memories, maybe he could drown them out with music.

But the closer he traveled to St. Charles, the more keyed up his mind became. And by the time the bus arrived, the sun had set, and Jaxon was starving. The granola bars he'd brought were long gone, and he didn't want to show up at his parents' cranky with hunger.

It was about a mile's walk to his parents' house, and if he stayed on Main Street for a bit he could stop at Daisy's Diner. He hoped they still served chicken-fried steak and potatoes. He couldn't remember when he'd last had a decent meal.

By the time he reached the diner, his knee was aching from the effort of carrying the two suitcases. He was actually grateful for the cold air since it seemed to keep him a bit numb. Stepping into the diner was like standing in front of a blasting furnace.

The hostess looked up from the cashier's desk, her thick brows lifted, and Jaxon was grateful it wasn't someone he knew. He wasn't ready to face a series of questions that he didn't yet know the answers to himself. He felt a bit awkward asking for a table for one, but it wasn't something he could help.

The hostess let him stash his suitcases to the side of the podium, then led him through a maze of tables, and Jaxon was glad nothing had changed over the years. Daisy's Diner was still cozy and slightly chaotic. About half of the tables were full, and everything he saw on people's plates looked delicious. The place was decked out for Christmas with twinkling lights spanning the ceiling and holly arrangements on the tables.

When the hostess seated him, he barely had time to open the menu when the waitress arrived.

"Jaxon?"

He stifled a groan before looking up. "Taffy."

Her cheerful Christmas outfit matched her personality perfectly, if Jaxon remembered right. Taffy had been a grade younger than he in school. They'd actually gone on one of those date dances together in a big group.

She popped her gum and grinned. Yep, the same Taffy he remembered.

"It's great to see you," Jaxon pre-empted.

"Oh. My. Gosh. I can't believe it's really you." She leaned down and gave him a light hug. "I mean, I haven't seen you in forever!"

Jaxon nodded. "What's new with you?" he asked, trying to keep questions from pelting him. He glanced at her left hand and saw a ring. "Married? Kids?"

She grinned again. "Yep. Married Grant Lovell, if you can believe it."

"Wow," Jaxon said, not entirely sure he remembered Grant, but he didn't want to get in too deep.

"And Ross just turned two." She looked from side to side then leaned down again, and whispered, "Another bun in the oven."

He shared her smile. "Congratulations." He was happy for her, and relieved, to tell the truth. And perhaps a bit envious to see the unadulterated joy on her face. Her marriage must be filled with trust and respect.

"We haven't told anyone yet," Taffy said. "But I'm so excited that I'm just bursting to tell someone."

"I won't say a word," Jaxon said, making a dramatic show of crossing his heart.

Taffy laughed. "You're just how I remember you. Still handsome, still got those killer green eyes, and still funny."

Funny? Jaxon had never considered himself that.

He closed his menu. "Hey, I already know what I want. Can I get an order of chicken-fried steak and a Coke?"

"Sure thing," Taffy said with an exaggerated wink. "I'll be back soon."

Jaxon handed her the menu, and when she left, he pulled out his phone, checking the weather app. Not that he was planning on traveling again any time soon, but he didn't want to get lost in the memories that were tumbling back after seeing Taffy again.

He'd had a fairly steady girlfriend the last year of high school, but she was married now as well. And according to Facebook, she had a couple of kids. That was probably the story of everyone he'd gone to high school with. It was just as well. He wasn't looking to reconnect with any of his former friends.

"You're kidding me!" a man said a little too loudly a couple of tables over.

Jaxon kept his eyes on his phone until the man's next comment caused him to look up.

"You are seriously crazy," he said, his tone abrasive. "You probably chose this place to eat just so I wouldn't get upset."

Heads were turning now as the man's voice continued to rise. Jaxon's heartrate increased in tandem with the man's temper. Jaxon was definitely watching the couple now. The man looked about Jaxon's age, his hair dark, his eyes even darker as he glared at the woman seated across from him.

Jaxon could only see a bit of the woman's profile. Her hands were clenched tightly together on top of the table, and she was speaking to her date in a low murmur. Jaxon could practically hear the panic growing in her voice, although she was staying pretty quiet.

He looked around for the waitress, or the hostess, or

even someone who might be the manager. Obviously this couple needed to take their personal argument out of the restaurant.

"Dammit, Monica!" The man shot to his feet, his face a deep red. "I've told you a hundred times that working there is ridiculous! It's a *Christmas* store. Freaking selling Santa stuff and lollipop-crap. It's not even a real job."

Jaxon stood, unable to sit and listen to the ranting any longer. The entire diner was dead silent except for the yelling man and the crying woman. Jaxon reached the table just as the man shouted, "And I'm tired of you putting your job before me!" The man slammed his fist into the table, making the plates and glasses jump with a clatter.

It all happened so fast that Jaxon wouldn't be able to explain exactly what did happen, but he grabbed the man's arm, and wrenched it behind him.

"It's time to leave," Jaxon hissed in the man's ear. "I'm escorting you outside, and you'd better not say one more word or you'll lose a few teeth."

"Who the h—" the man started.

Jaxon shoved him forward, and the man cried out, complaining that his arm was going to come out of its socket. Jaxon kept his grip firm, propelling the man toward the door, weaving through the tables, even though the effort made his sore knee burn with pain.

The hostess was waiting, holding the door open, her face pale.

"Thanks," Jaxon said, then shoved the man off the stepdown stoop.

The man whirled as soon as Jaxon let go. But Jaxon folded his arms, knowing that without his jacket, the years spent logging would show in his arms and shoulders.

"Take your best shot," Jaxon said, "because it will be the

only shot you'll get. The next time you open your eyes, you'll see the fluorescent lights on the hospital ceiling."

The man's wrinkled his face into a sneer. "I don't know who you are, but I'm filing a police report for assault."

Jaxon laughed. "You do that. And don't forget to name all the witnesses in the diner."

The man took a step back, then another. Finally he turned and walked away, throwing a few expletives over his shoulder as he went. When the man rounded the corner, Jaxon went back into the diner.

He'd nearly forgotten he'd had an audience, so caught up in his anger toward the jerk, that he was surprised to see more than a dozen pair of eyes staring at him.

"He won't be coming back tonight," Jaxon said. "Enjoy your meals."

To his surprise, everyone started clapping. As Jaxon made his way back to his table, several diners stood and slapped him on the back and thanked him.

He stopped at his table to see a grinning Taffy waiting for him.

"You were brilliant," she said, grasping his hand and squeezing. "That guy is the ultimate jerk. I swear, every time he comes in, he's rude to the waitresses, and he treats his girlfriend like crap. Hopefully she sees him for what he is now."

Involuntarily, Jaxon's gaze slid over to the table where the couple had sat. The woman was still sitting there, staring down at a mug that she was slowly stirring.

"Is she okay?" he asked in a quiet voice.

"Oh, yeah. Or at least she will be. I told her the meal is on the house."

That wasn't quite what Jaxon meant. When Taffy left, he couldn't help but look over at the woman again. At least she hadn't followed after her boyfriend. Maybe they really had broken up, or maybe they had one of those volatile relationships . . . Jaxon was painfully familiar with those.

Then suddenly she turned, catching Jaxon watching her. For a second, he was stunned. The woman was quite pretty; he didn't know why he was surprised. Maybe because he thought with her looks she wouldn't have to settle for a guy with such a rotten personality.

Before Jaxon could think of what to do or say, she rose and crossed to his table, then slipped into the chair opposite him.

"Hey, thanks," she said. Her dark auburn hair tumbled down her back in loose curls, and her pale blue eyes were surprisingly clear and steady, like she hadn't just been crying a few minutes ago.

"Sorry I interfered," Jaxon said. "I wasn't sure if I should." He wanted to say more, to tell her that things wouldn't get better between them, not when her boyfriend treated her like that in public. If anyone knew from personal experience, Jaxon did. Cynthia had been notorious for public demands followed by public humiliation.

"I—I appreciate it, truly," the woman said. "I mean, I wish none of it happened, and maybe David was right. I shouldn't have dropped my career plans on him in public. It should have been done in private. I knew there was a good chance he'd be upset."

Jaxon found himself shaking his head. At one point in his life, he might have let the events unfold without his interference, but he wasn't that man anymore. "I know we're complete strangers, but I also know you deserve more out of a boyfriend. You shouldn't let anyone treat you like that."

She blinked as if she couldn't believe what she was hearing. Then she looked away for a moment. "Thanks again," she murmured, and she was up and out of her chair before he could respond, disappearing almost as quickly as she'd appeared.

Three

IT'S REALLY OVER, MONICA HAD told herself a dozen times in the past forty-eight hours. At first she'd completely ignored David's texts and voice messages. Then finally, she replied, saying there was nothing more to discuss. She was buying the store, and that was her decision. They had broken up, and that was his decision. But this new text had a different tone than the rest. It wasn't confrontational, it was actually . . . agreeable.

Please let's talk in person. You've got to forgive my outburst. I've had time to think about your decision, and it might not be such a bad thing.

Monica released a heavy sigh. It was the end of a long day—Christmas Eve—and although she posted that closing time was 5:00 p.m., it was now well after 6:00, and there was still a shopper in the store. Ironic, since their shop was open all year, but true to form, there were always people who procrastinated. She didn't have much time to get ready for the 7:00 party at the Ungritches. Thankfully, she'd tried on the Mrs. Claus costume the day before and tested out the makeup she'd be using. She could be ready in about twenty minutes.

Monica rang up the last customer, packed the gifts into a sturdy paper bag with the *Christmas Around the World* logo, and sent her on her way. After locking the shop door and turning off most of the lights except for the display window, Monica reread David's text.

A month ago, she might have given in. Allowed him to come over and talk in her apartment. Even a week ago, she might have. But ever since the blow up in Daisy's Diner, something had changed inside of Monica.

She knew it had to do with the man who'd defended her and escorted David outside the restaurant. His words had been echoing in her mind ever since he'd spoken them: *I know we're complete strangers, but I also know you deserve more out of a boyfriend. You shouldn't let anyone treat you like that.*

The thought of a mere stranger seeing the truth of her relationship with David brought shame to her heart. Monica blinked back the burning tears and started to count out the register. The man at the restaurant came to her mind again. He'd been so different than David. Calm, even though he'd been upset with David. And the man had seemed truly concerned for her, yet had given her space.

She had noticed he was good looking, but not in the flashy way of David. The man in the restaurant had green eyes that were kind, yet had depth to them. His light brown hair had touched his collar but seemed well-groomed. He had stubble on his strong jaw, and his tanned skin, even in winter, made it clear he spent a lot of time outdoors. Another fishing and camping enthusiast?

Yet he seemed to exude strength and calmness, unlike David's buzzing energy. For a moment, she wondered what it would be like to have a man like the one in the restaurant in her life. One who didn't shout at her in a restaurant, belittle her in front of others, and try to talk her out of every decision she made.

"I don't even know him," she whispered to herself. His green eyes had seemed to look right into her soul. She'd only spent a few moments with him, but his presence and attention had somehow brought stability to her cracking heart. He'd told her point blank, with no apology, that she deserved better.

Monica *knew* she deserved better, but she didn't always believe it. She'd probably never see the stranger in the restaurant again, but she wouldn't ever forget his help, or his advice.

She typed back a reply to David on her phone: *I hope you have a great Christmas, but please don't contact me again.*

Then she put her phone on silent for the rest of the night.

With every step she took up the stairs to her apartment, she felt her resolve strengthen. She was starting a new chapter in her life. Soon she'd be a business owner, and she was now free of David and his incriminating comments and controlling opinions.

She found herself humming Christmas tunes as she changed into her Mrs. Claus outfit. She wound her hair into a bun, then used the spray-in color to streak it gray and white. Next she used a pale foundation to cover up her freckles and then an eyebrow pencil to draw some lines around her eyes. Finally, she added a pair of gold-rimmed spectacles.

Monica stood back from the mirror. She didn't look exactly like a sweet elderly woman, but who said Mrs. Claus had to be elderly? Just wise in years.

She lifted her cell phone and snapped a couple of selfies. She'd post pictures from the party to the store's Instagram page, but for now, she wanted a couple of her own pictures. She couldn't wait to see the Ungritches' faces. The other night Mrs. Ungritch had called to report on her wayward son. "He says he's come home to apologize, that we were right all along."

Monica could practically hear the woman beaming through the phone.

"The marriage didn't last long, but he felt stuck since he'd been so stubborn with us." Mrs. Ungritch's tone filled with regret. "All those years lost."

"You'll just have to move forward now," Monica had offered.

"You're right, that's all we can do," Mrs. Ungritch had said. "Besides, he's still recovering from knee surgery. Some accident at work. It's good to have my son to take care of for a little while."

At that point in the conversation, Mrs. Ungritch was called by her husband, and they'd hung up after Monica reassured her that she could handle the last couple of days before Christmas in the shop by herself. They had enough going on with their son's return and the Christmas party.

Now Monica grabbed her red wool coat and slipped it on, then shouldered her handbag, making sure she had her keys and phone and the tube of dusty pink lipstick she was sure she'd have to reapply throughout the night.

The final touch was the black boots, on which she'd hot-glued tinsel around the cuffs. "Christmas, here I come," she said to herself as she started down the steps. By the time she pulled up to the Ungritches' home, her silver Mazda was just warming up. She parked on the other side of the street, since the driveway was littered with cars.

The Ungritch home literally glowed with Christmas cheer, making it more beautiful than any postcard. Monica's spirits continued to lift as she approached the house. Laughter and Christmas music seemed to ooze from the bright windows. Monica bypassed the front door and went around the garage to the side door, as suggested by Mrs. Ungritch. That way, Monica could deposit her coat and handbag in the mud room and then show up fully costumed for her part.

She cracked the side door open and slipped inside, immediately consumed by the delicious smells of cinnamon and baked goods. A couple of women were in the kitchen, setting out cookies onto platters. They both smiled as Monica entered.

"Oh, Mrs. Claus, how nice to see you," the woman with a smooth ponytail said, then winked.

Monica laughed. "I heard there's a party here."

"Santa Claus is right through there," the woman said, pointing toward the door.

"Thank you," Monica said, then stepped through the door into the main part of the house.

"It's amazing how the Claus family gets younger every year," the woman's voice chased her, and the second woman in the kitchen laughed.

Monica smiled as heads turned and kids started pointing and tugging on their parents' arms. She was sure she wasn't too hard for the parents to recognize, but the younger kids would remain in happy oblivion. The living room and dining room were filled with guests, from the very young to the elderly. A long table set with platters of

Christmas goodies had been scooted against one of the walls.

The dining table was covered with thick paper, and kids gathered around, making festive crafts that included a lot of glue, glitter, and pompoms. A huge Christmas tree stood in front of the bay window, and dozens of tiny wrapped boxes sat below the boughs. Monica had wrapped most of those boxes and knew they contained an assortment of treats—one box for each guest.

"Santa!" a young voice called out. "Your wife is here!"

The guests near Monica chuckled, and she scanned the crowd, looking for Mr. Ungritch's telltale red Santa suit and naturally white hair. The Santa that came around the corner of the dining room wasn't a stooped, elderly man, but a tall man with broad shoulders, a white-haired wig, and familiar green eyes.

Monica stared, not entirely believing her first instinct. This was the man from the restaurant. And he was wearing a Santa suit at the Ungritches' party. Had they gone and hired an actor?

She barely registered that Mrs. Ungritch had appeared at her side and grasped her hand.

"Isn't it wonderful?" Mrs. Ungritch whispered to Monica. "Jaxon agreed to play Santa."

"Jaxon . . . who is . . . your son."

"Of course," Mrs. Ungritch said, amusement in her voice.

And then Santa—*Jaxon*—was standing before her, an assessing smile on his face.

"This is Monica, I mean, Mrs. Claus," Mrs. Ungritch said. She laughed, then leaned toward Monica. "I need to watch what I say; there are little listening ears around."

Monica smiled. She felt Jaxon's eyes on her . . . did he recognize her? As soon as she thought it, she decided it was impossible. She'd spray-colored her hair gray and white and was wearing spectacles. But when she looked up at him, there was something in his eyes. Amusement? Interest? Remembering?

Four

JAXON KNEW HE HAD THE upper hand here. It was plain that she recognized him despite the Santa getup. His mother had told him about Monica and how she was single and had recently broken up with her boyfriend, David. And how Monica was buying the store. The news had stunned him, and after several carefully placed questions, Jaxon had told his parents that he'd wished he would have known sooner.

Of course that wasn't practical, since they hadn't been communicating. When his father said, "Why would it matter, Jaxon?" he'd been truthful.

"Because I've wanted to come home for some time now, repair my mistakes, and run the store for you so you and Mom can retire."

His parents had stared at him for a long time. Then, finally, his mother had said, "You must meet Monica. She's an angel. I don't know if she'd back out of our agreement though. Perhaps she'll hire you."

It had been like a cold bucket of water dumped over his head. He'd waited too long. It was too late. But when he'd stopped in at the diner again for lunch the day before, Taffy told him how David and "his girlfriend" Monica were always getting into fights. And how eventually they made up, and how Monica would be at his beck and call again.

This tore at Jaxon because he couldn't stand to see a guy like David get away with acting how he did, yet, if Monica did what he wanted, then she wouldn't be buying the store. Then Taffy told him something that swayed him completely toward Monica staying away from David. Apparently David was a huge flirt when Monica wasn't around.

Jaxon's head started to pound immediately at the images that brought to his mind. David was another Cynthia, just gender in reverse. No one deserved that. Not even a woman who was a threat to Jaxon's future.

Jaxon had hoped that tonight he'd be able to find a chance to warn her about her former boyfriend. He might even have to share some of his experiences about his ex-wife.

But for now, his mother seemed thrilled that they were playing the Clauses at her Christmas party. And he was intent on making his mother happy, anything that might make up for the lost years. He'd spent most of the day helping his parents get ready for the party, hanging lights, rearranging furniture, decorating, even hanging mistletoe above the arch between the dining room and living room. He'd probably taken one too many Ibuprofen to ease the pain in his knees, but it was worth it.

His mother grasped each of their arms. "Now the two of you sit up on those chairs from the dining table, and I'll get the line organized so kids can tell you what they want for Christmas." She looked at Monica. "They'll have to sit on Jaxon's right knee, since he had surgery on his left."

Monica flashed a smile and said, "Sure thing."

"Of course," Jaxon added. He let Monica lead the way to the dining chairs. Above all the Christmas scents of cinnamon and pine, he couldn't help notice that she wore a floral-scented perfume. It made him think of the first wildflowers of spring, pushing their way through the cold winter earth.

He sat next to her, and kids started clamoring to be first.

Monica reached for a little girl who was getting pushed back by the bigger kids and gently drew her forward. "What's your name?"

"Elizabeth," the tiny thing said.

"I love your dress, Elizabeth," Monica said. "Can you tell us what you'd like for Christmas?"

Jaxon wasn't even sure he heard half of the kids' requests. Instead, he listened to Monica and paid attention to her sweet nature. He couldn't imagine Cynthia doing this in a million years. She'd be standing in the background, a glass of wine in her hand, while she checked out the men in the room.

The longer Jaxon sat by Monica and watched her with the kids, the more guilty he felt for even wanting her to back out of buying his parents' store.

When all of the kids had had a turn, and some of them were begging for a second turn, Jaxon's father announced, "We'd like to thank Santa Claus and Mrs. Claus for visiting us tonight, but they must be off to help the elves load all the toys into their sleigh."

The kids squealed, and Jaxon rose to his feet, taking Monica by the hand and helping her to her feet too.

"Merry Christmas, everyone!" he called out. "Don't forget to put your stockings out."

Monica called out a "Merry Christmas!" as well and

walked with him to the front door. He led her outside and shut the door behind him.

"Now what?" she said, withdrawing her hand and rubbing her hands together.

Jaxon's breaths puffed out into the cold air. "Did you bring something to change into? We can go back around the house in through the kitchen."

Monica looked down at her red velvet costume. "I didn't. I guess I didn't think past the Santa stunt."

Jaxon tugged the wig from his hair. His hair was probably a mess. His disguise was completely compromised now.

"Are you sure you should be doing that here?" Monica asked. "What if a kid looks out the window?"

"Good point." He moved down the porch steps, scrubbing his fingers through his hair. He turned back to look at her. "Coming?"

"Where?"

"Around the house to the kitchen." He smiled at her, hoping it would encourage her. "It's freezing out here," he added.

"But I don't have a change of clothes."

"I'll get you something of my mom's."

"Uh, she's about a foot shorter than me," Monica said. "I could just run home I suppose."

"Come on," Jaxon said, motioning for her to follow him. "You don't want to miss the party. I can just hurry up to my mom's room."

"Okay," Monica agreed, although she sounded hesitant.

He knew it wasn't her first choice, but going home and changing would probably take longer than she thought. "Oh, wait. What about my gray hair?"

"Beanie?" Jaxon suggested.

She shrugged and followed him around the house. "How's your knee?"

He hadn't even realized he'd been limping, since he was so used to favoring it. "Getting better every day."

"So . . ." she said in a soft voice. "I don't know if you recognize me, but we actually met a few days ago at Daisy's Diner."

He glanced over at her. The red velvety costume, the gray-colored hair, the gold-rimmed spectacles. "I don't know if I would have recognized you right off, but I put it together when my mom told me all about you and your recent breakup." Actually, he probably would have recognized her. Despite her disguise, she was still the pretty young woman from the restaurant with those pale blue eyes that he had found himself thinking about more than once over the past couple of days.

"Oh." She fell silent.

Jaxon rushed to fill in the awkwardness. "Look," he said. "I know what you're going through. I . . ." He stopped just outside the door leading into the kitchen. The night's cold air had left his fingers numb and slowed his words. "Your boyfriend reminds me a lot of my ex-wife."

Monica looked up at him, her eyes glinting silver beneath the moonlight. "Oh." It was a whisper this time. She looked away as if she was embarrassed that he'd said something so personal.

Jaxon wanted to spill out all the warnings that he'd been collecting to tell her ever since his mother told him about Monica's connection to his family. Instead, he simply stood there, watching her as she gazed across the side yard. He'd seen the pain in her eyes, and it was as if he didn't need to say much.

Then he saw that she was trembling. He placed a hand on her shoulder. "Are you all right?"

She nodded, but when she looked at him, he saw tears in her eyes.

"Hey, it'll be okay." He squeezed her shoulder.

"We're broken up for good now, but it's hard, you know?"

"Yeah, I get it."

She sniffed, then stepped toward the door and opened it.

Jaxon followed her into the mud room, wishing he could offer her comfort, but not knowing how.

"I'll be right back," he said. "I'm sneaking up the back stairs and I will change, then bring something down to you."

"All right," Monica said, her smile tentative.

Jaxon had the sudden impulse to pull her into his arms and hug her. Instead, he turned and left her waiting in the mud room. He took the stairs as fast as he could, while favoring his left knee. Once in his old bedroom, he stripped out of the Santa suit, then pulled on a fresh shirt. He stopped to look in the mirror on his way out, surprised that he was caring so much about his appearance.

Once in his mom's room, he searched for something Monica could wear. He finally settled on a blouse and a black skirt. Then he grabbed a pair of black heels from the floor of his mom's closet.

Moments later, he was back in the mud room to find Monica sitting on the bench, scrolling through her phone. She must have washed her face in the adjoining guest bathroom, because the drawn age lines were gone from her face. Her lips were pressed in a thin line as she studied her phone.

He sat beside her. "Something wrong?"

She lifted a shoulder and put her phone away. "I should have left my phone off. David keeps texting. He wants to get together tomorrow—it being Christmas and all. He says he has a gift for me."

"Just tell him you have plans," Jaxon said, trying not to stare at her freshly scrubbed face and silver-blue eyes. She'd put away her spectacles, and her hair was damp—it seemed as if she'd tried to get some of the gray coloring out her dark auburn hair.

"He knows I don't," she said. "My mom's in a care center, and a visit to her will only take a half hour."

Jaxon remembered his mother saying something about Monica's family, but now he couldn't remember what. "Is she sick?"

"Alzheimer's," Monica said in a dejected voice.

"I'm really sorry about that. What time are you planning on visiting her tomorrow?"

"She's always better in the mornings," Monica said. "So I'll take her gift over to her then. She won't remember who gave it to her, but that's okay."

"Come here after," Jaxon said. "My parents would be thrilled."

Monica opened her mouth, then shut it. Jaxon noticed she'd applied some kind of shiny lip gloss, likely something she'd kept in her purse. He really shouldn't be looking at her lips.

"I wouldn't want to impose," she said. "I mean, Christmas is for families, and you haven't spent a Christmas with them in a long—"

"Monica," Jaxon interrupted, grasping her hand. She seemed as surprised at his gesture as he was. "We'd love to have you. My parents would be more than happy for you to spend Christmas with us." He leaned close, keeping her hand in his. "They like you more than me. It's as if you're their own daughter. Please come."

Pink flushed her cheeks, and Monica smiled. "All right. But only because you said *please*."

"Is that all it takes?"

Her face pinked more, and Jaxon gave a quiet laugh.

The sound of a buzzing phone broke the moment—whatever moment it was—and Monica withdrew her hand and reached into her bag.

Jaxon didn't need to see the text to know it was from her boyfriend—a guy he hoped would stay her ex-boyfriend.

Five

MONICA DIDN'T KNOW IF HER heart was racing because she'd just wondered what it would be like to kiss Jaxon Ungritch, or if her heart was racing from increased annoyance with David. Now he was saying he wanted to meet her tonight after the party. He, of course, knew she was at the Ungritches' Christmas party. He probably would have been here with her if they hadn't had that fight. Or broken up.

Jaxon had just left the mud room to join the party again. She'd locked herself into the bathroom and changed into the clothes he'd brought down from his mother's room. They didn't come close to fitting, of course, but they'd do for the last bit of the party. She turned to look at herself in the mirror. The blouse was red—festive, at least—and the skirt black. The low heels were too small and pinched her toes, so maybe she'd find a place to sit and wriggle her feet halfway out of them. The craft table would be the perfect place to hide her feet.

She ran her fingers through her hair again and smoothed it as best as she could. It hadn't been in the bun too long, so there weren't obnoxious bumps in it. She turned to open the door, took a deep breath, and let herself out.

Jaxon had been so attentive to her, listening to everything she said, without interrupting or even pressing for more information. He hadn't asked what David was saying in his texts, and hadn't hesitated to invite her to his house.

She was more than curious about him. What had made him leave; what had made him return? Of course she knew the bare facts as told to her by his mother, but she wanted to know what was in his mind and heart. Jaxon was a confident-looking man, to say the least, and if she didn't know some of his hardships, she would have assumed he had the world in his palm. That he hadn't been through a rocky marriage, hadn't been hurt like she had by someone he cared about.

But she'd seen it in his eyes—the deep pain, the understanding, the empathy. Jaxon knew what it was like to love and lose. To take a risk that backfired.

He was so opposite of David. For Jaxon to humble himself, to return home and to try to reconcile with his family, was something she could never picture David doing. David always thought he was right, no matter what, and if he did realize he was wrong, he'd just spin the situation until it seemed that events had occurred because he had made them happen that way.

Jaxon was . . . genuine.

That was the best word she could use to describe him. It was no wonder—only a good and decent man could come from Mr. and Mrs. Ungritch. Even though he'd been the prodigal son for a while, his basest nature was good. Monica could feel it.

She thought of him choosing the clothing from his mother's closet for her to wear, and she found herself blushing over it. She thought of the way he told her he understood what she was going through with David. She thought of the way he'd grasped her hand, more than once. He wasn't afraid to comfort her.

Monica walked through the kitchen willing her cheeks to stop blushing. She stepped into the living room and stopped.

Jaxon was in the middle of the room, playing some sort of charades game with a bunch of kids. They were jumping around him, trying to guess which Disney character he was. By his exaggerated movements, as he favored his injured knee, Monica knew he was acting like Dumbo the elephant. But maybe that wasn't the latest and greatest hero, so the kids were stumped.

Jaxon turned in her direction, making a sweeping motion with his arm—like it was an elephant's trunk.

"We give up!" the kids called out. "Tell us what you are."

Jaxon's eyes met Monica's, and she smiled. "Let's see if any of the adults can guess."

"All right." Monica crossed toward him, stopped and faced the kids. "Have you guys ever seen the movie *Dumbo*?"

Two of the kids shouted, "Yes!"

Jaxon laughed. "She's right."

"She gets the prize!"

Monica turned to look at Jaxon, arching her brow. "What's the prize?"

"A candy cane!" one kid said while, at the same time, a girl of about ten kid said, "A kiss under the mistletoe."

Monica blinked, then looked up where the girl was pointing. They were standing under the archway that led to the dining room, and there was a sprig of mistletoe hanging from the faux pine bow gracing the arch.

"Oh," Monica said, not sure what to say.

Jaxon shoved his hands in his pockets, his face taking on a red tint. "Either prize works for me."

"A kiss!" Another kid joined in with the girl's suggestion.

If Monica's heart wasn't hammering so hard, she would probably laugh about this. Jaxon was clearly embarrassed, but he was also looking at her with decided interest.

"Candy canes are my favorite candy," Monica told the kids.

"Kiss her," one of the boys called out. "That's the best prize."

She turned to Jaxon, ready to tell him the candy was just fine. But he leaned toward her before she could speak. He kissed her cheek so quickly that Monica wasn't sure she felt anything.

The kids squealed and clapped. One little kid grabbed Monica's hand and said, "Guess what I'm getting for Christmas?"

Monica was sure she was blushing from Jaxon's sudden kiss, but she didn't have time to think about anything before the other kids surrounded her, demanding that she perform a charade for them. It seemed even without their Santa suits, she and Jaxon were the biggest draws of the party.

Another hour passed before parents started to round up their kids and leave the party. Monica couldn't remember a time she'd become so immersed and enjoyed herself so much. And the entire time Jaxon had been with her. They hadn't had any personal conversation except for in the mudroom before they changed their clothes. But Monica was learning plenty about his character as she watched him interact with the kids at the party.

She couldn't imagine David doing this in a million years. Jaxon was patient and genuine with the kids. He listened to them and made them laugh. He made her laugh. She found that she was not only physically aware of him, but she was impressed with him as well. No wonder his mother had missed him so much.

"You've both been wonderful," Mrs. Ungritch said, as if she'd just heard Monica's thoughts. "Thank you for coming, Monica, and playing the part of you know who."

All of the kids had gone home, and only a few adults remained, helping with the cleanup.

"It was a lot of fun," Monica said, meaning it. "I think it was the best one yet."

Mrs. Ungritch smiled and gave Monica a hug. "You are a dear. I'm so glad to see you and Jaxon getting along. He needs a good woman in his life." She had whispered, but it wasn't all that quiet.

Monica drew back. Was Mrs. Ungritch trying to set them up? "I . . ."

Mrs. Ungritch just winked at her and turned away. Jaxon conveniently started to move the furniture back in place, but Monica could tell he'd heard his mother.

She'd give anything to know what was going through his mind. But during the rest of the cleanup, Jaxon stayed busy, always in a different area than she was helping.

When she said goodbye, Mrs. Ungritch said, "Jaxon told me you're coming over tomorrow. That will be wonderful."

Monica nodded, feeling a bit apprehensive. After Jaxon's kiss and after what Mrs. Ungritch hinted at, she hoped she wasn't walking into an awkward situation. "I appreciate the invitation. I'll come after I visit my mother."

She left Mrs. Ungritch and went to the mudroom to gather her coat and handbag. She'd almost forgotten that she wasn't wearing her clothes. She quickly changed in the bathroom again, and when she came out, Jaxon was in the kitchen stacking plates into the dishwasher.

Monica couldn't help but pause and watch him for a few moments. Even when she'd had David over to her apartment for dinner, he'd never made a move to help with anything in the kitchen. Jaxon turned, and Monica felt heat flood her face at being caught watching.

"Thanks for getting me a change of clothes," she said.

His green eyes seemed to hold her in place. "You can just leave them on the bench. I'll take them up to my mom later."

"All right," Monica said, moving toward the door, then depositing the clothes on the bench. "See you tomorrow."

He crossed the room, walking toward her, wiping his hands on a kitchen towel he'd grabbed from the counter. "Sorry about what my mom said."

Monica blinked up at him, wondering if she should act as if she had no idea what he was talking about.

"She's always been like that," Jaxon said, leaning against the wall.

He was a little taller than David, and leaner too, but his shoulders and arms were definitely more sculpted. She remembered now that Mrs. Ungritch had said her son worked for a logging company or something like that.

"It's probably why there were issues over Cynthia in the beginning," Jaxon said. "At least, my stubbornness was in part because I had met her on my own. She wasn't someone my mother had steered in my direction."

"I can see how that would be annoying."

"Yeah," Jaxon said. He scrubbed a hand through his hair. "But I was pretty immature about it. Turns out my parents saw a lot more than I did at the time."

Monica didn't really know what to say to that. They were talking about Jaxon's ex, and the conversation seemed oddly personal for two practical strangers. "How long were you married?" she asked, then wished she hadn't.

"Not even a year," Jaxon said. "She wasn't exactly the type of woman to be faithful. I should have seen it coming, but I was foolish to believe I was different. And that she'd treat me differently. My parents saw it a mile away."

"Parents can be like that," she said, giving him a gentle smile. "Before my mother got dementia, she was full of all kinds of unwelcome advice. She'd probably be disappointed I dropped out of college to come back and take care of her if she understood all that has gone on."

"I'm sure she'd appreciate it and value your sacrifice."

"No," Monica said with a short laugh. "She would have told me to live my life and not change it up for her health problems."

Jaxon studied her for a moment before replying. "I think she'd be proud of you. When it comes to it, titles, degrees, and money don't make much difference in the end. It's your family. And you chose your family."

Monica's eyes burned with emotion, and she blinked rapidly. "You're sweet to say that."

He offered her a half smile. "Just speaking the truth."

Six

"WHAT TIME DID YOU SAY Monica would be here?" Jaxon's mom asked him again.

"We didn't specify a time," he said, finding himself watching out the front window again. "It was just going to be this afternoon."

His mother crossed to stand by him and checked her gold watch. "Well, it's one-thirty. Maybe we should call her."

Just then, the phone rang. "That must be her." His mother hurried over to the living room side table and answered.

By the one-sided conversation Jaxon heard, he knew it was Monica.

"We were just starting to wonder about you," his mother said into the phone. "Jaxon? I suppose so. He's right here." She turned to Jaxon and said, "Monica wants to speak to you."

Jaxon couldn't have been more surprised. As he walked the few steps toward the phone, he sensed the news couldn't be good. Maybe Monica would be spending Christmas with David after all. Maybe they were getting back together. Jaxon was surprised at his disappointed feelings over that matter. He liked Monica, and he agreed with his mother—she was a good woman.

"Hello?" he said into the phone.

Monica's voice was hushed on the other end. "Sorry to bother you, Jaxon, but I need a favor."

He turned away from his mother, who was watching him. Something about her tone of voice told him there was a reason she wanted to speak to him and not his mother.

"I came to the care center to visit with my mother, and when I came out, I saw David's truck in the parking lot. He's been sitting there for thirty minutes." She took a breath. "I know he's waiting for me."

"Are you worried about him . . . confronting you?"

She exhaled again. "I don't know. I just have this bad feeling about it. Last night he texted me in the middle of the night. I didn't see it until this morning, but he's not taking *no* for an answer."

"I'll come pick you up."

"Are you sure?" she asked in a hesitant voice.

"No problem," he said. "I'll borrow my parents' car."

"All right, but don't tell your parents about David," she said. "I don't want them to worry, and I'm probably just being paranoid."

"Got it." Jaxon took out his cell from his pocket. "I'm putting your number into my phone and I'll send you a text so you have it. I'm on my way, but call my cell if anything else happens." She agreed, and he hung up.

Minutes later he was out the door, having told his parents that Monica was having car trouble, and driving along the icy roads. Snow sleeted across the road in front of him, so he took it slow, although all he wanted to do was drive top speed. What if David went into the care center to confront Monica before Jaxon arrived?

But when he pulled into the parking lot, he saw the truck Monica had mentioned. It sat idling, and Jaxon could see David's dark head silhouetted against the window.

Jaxon drove to the drop-off driveway and parked, leaving the car running. He sent her a text that he'd arrived and was coming inside. He found her waiting just inside the lobby, standing behind a tall Ficus tree. She looked pale, and her blue eyes were huge.

"Hey, are you okay?" he asked, crossing to her.

"Thank you for coming," she said in a near whisper.

He grasped her hand and found that she was trembling. This wasn't good. Was there more to her relationship with David than she'd let on? Had he hurt her before? "Come on, let's get out of here." Jaxon guided her to the door, keeping her hand firmly in his. "Don't look over at his truck. I'll let you in the passenger side; lock the door as soon as it shuts."

"Is that necessary?" she asked in a small voice.

"We'll find out." He walked with her through the automatic front doors that whooshed open when they approached. He could feel the tension radiating from Monica, and he sensed that David had noticed them coming out.

He ushered Monica into the car and strode around to the driver's side.

From across the parking lot, David revved his truck engine, then started driving straight toward them.

Jaxon hopped in the car and stomped on the gas pedal, the door barely closing as he jerked the car forward.

The truck veered, and Jaxon barely missed getting hit as he sped his way out of the parking lot. "Call 9-1-1!" he said to Monica. "This guy has lost his mind."

The truck kept coming, barreling out of the parking lot and following them down the street.

Jaxon glanced over at Monica as she spoke to the emergency dispatcher. Her voice was shaking as she talked. He checked the rearview mirror again. David was still following them.

Up ahead the traffic light turned yellow. There was no traffic, so Jaxon sped up and passed through the intersection just as it changed to red. His heart sank when David didn't stop and went right through the red light, continuing to follow them.

"The cops are coming," Monica said to Jaxon. She looked behind them. "Just keep driving."

The fear in her voice was plain, and Jaxon's own pulse was racing. How crazy would David get? As soon as he heard police sirens, relief shot through him, but he knew this was far from over.

Suddenly, David's truck pulled around him and roared past. The police cars came around the corner in front of them and screeched on their brakes. David's truck screamed to a halt. Jaxon slowed as well, letting everything play out in front of them from a safe distance away. As he drew the car to a stop about fifty yards short of where David stopped his truck, Jaxon grasped Monica's hand.

She gripped his hand as they watched the cop get out. David slid out of his truck and raised his hands. The two cops approached him, and after talking to him, one of them started writing up a citation.

David kept looking over at Monica. Although they were too far away to see David's expression, Jaxon sensed the defiance radiating from him.

"Thanks so much for coming," Monica said in a quiet voice. "I didn't know he'd go this far."

Jaxon released her hand and wrapped his arm around her shoulders. She was trembling, which only made him feel more protective. And angry toward David. "Has he ever done something like this before?"

"No," she said. "He gets mad easily and yells, but he hasn't been physically aggressive like this."

She fell quiet as one of the police officers walked toward them. When he reached Monica, he said, "Are you all right, ma'am?"

"I am," she said. "What's going to happen with him?"

"We charged him with as many things as we could, so he'll be spending plenty of time in court." The officer asked for both of their stories, and when they were finished, he told them to let him know if David tried to contact her again.

After the officer left, Monica leaned into Jaxon. "I don't know how to thank you." She released a sigh. "Some Christmas, huh?"

He rubbed her arm. "Let's get you back to my house. My mom is anxious to see you." He walked her to the passenger side of the car and opened the door for her. "How was your mom?"

She took a shaky breath and gave him a faint smile. "She's about the same. Kept calling me Kathleen—I think she was an old friend of my mom's. But she did tell me Merry Christmas."

Jaxon wanted to pull her into his arms and comfort her. But he'd only met this woman yesterday, and she'd just dodged a crazed boyfriend. He could only imagine the emotions tumbling through her. "We'll just have to make sure we do have a Merry Christmas," he said.

Seven

Monica exhaled, letting the breath leave her body in small measurements. Jaxon's car was warmed up now, and the shock of David's actions was fading somewhat. It was still hard to believe, though, that David would go that far. The text from the middle of the night had basically said he was giving her one more chance, and if she blew him off again, he was going to start dating other women.

She knew he was trying to goad her, to hurt her, to get her to reply. If she hadn't already decided they were over, this afternoon's incident had cemented it forever. Jaxon turned the car into his parents' driveway, and she glanced over at him. They'd both been quiet on the drive back, and Monica was grateful to collect her thoughts.

She honestly didn't know what she might have done if she didn't have Jaxon to call. Probably waited who knew how long until David left—but he did know where she lived. She'd never been bothered living by herself above the shop before, but now . . .

"Made it," Jaxon said in that easy tone of his. He seemed to take everything in stride. He hadn't hesitated to help her, and he hadn't seemed cowed by David at all—he'd driven fast, but relatively safely, and she knew Jaxon wasn't afraid to stand up to David.

It was a comforting thought. But it also wasn't realistic to expect Jaxon to be her bodyguard.

"Will you be all right?" Jaxon asked.

Monica realized she'd been staring off into space. Had he asked her anything else? "Yes," she said, turning to look at him. His green eyes were quite incredible—pretty much perfect for a hero. "It's just kind of surreal, you know."

"Yeah, I get it," he said, seeming in no hurry to pry information from her. "When I was with Cynthia and we had a big argument . . . the next day, I'd want to forgive her and to stay together. But after she kept doing what she did over and over, I finally decided I deserved better. Even no relationship was better than one with her. After her son was born, she started to go out with her girlfriends, and one thing led to another." He fell quiet.

"I'm sorry. That must have been awful," Monica said. Even though his voice was even, matter-of-fact, she sensed he still felt pain.

"It was awful, but it's all over now." He gave her a sideways glance. "The longer I'm home, the happier I am that I came. My parents have been more than great, and . . . meeting you has been a nice surprise."

She couldn't help but smile. "Really? You like the damsel in distress thing?"

He smiled back. "I think we all need a little rescuing now and then."

They were quiet for a moment; then Monica said, "Did your parents tell you that I'm buying their store?"

"Yeah." He turned to face her, and she became caught up gazing into his eyes. "I was going to try and talk you out of it so I could take over for them, but I think you're the man for the job."

"You mean the woman?"

He grinned. "Yeah. That too."

"So what will you do? I mean, if you can't change my mind?"

"Is your mind changeable?"

"No," Monica said.

He nodded. "That's what I thought." He chuckled. "I took some business classes, but I'm more of a hands-on guy. Not so much for crunching numbers at a desk."

"Hmmm," Monica said, grateful that he'd admitted as much. "I love to crunch numbers. Spreadsheets and I have a very close relationship."

His eyebrows lifted. "Are you thinking what I'm thinking?"

She narrowed her eyes. "I'm not sure, what *are* you thinking?"

He leaned back and folded his arms as if he had all the time in the world and his mother wasn't most likely watching from the window and wondering why they were sitting in the car for so long. "I'm thinking that since my parents are looking forward to retirement that I could work for you . . . at least for a while until I figure out my next steps."

Monica liked the idea, but she couldn't really match a regular salary he could get somewhere else.

He held up his hand. "I know what you're thinking—why would you hire a grown man when you could hire a high school student for minimum wage?"

"That's part of it, but I also worry that you might not like how I run things."

"My mother trained both of us, and besides, I would never interfere." His voice was soft, and she knew he was referring to David's antics. "Before you turn me down flat, just think about it. I'll volunteer my time anyway. I owe a lot of gratitude to my parents. This will be the beginning of me repaying them."

Monica reached out and touched his arm. He looked down at where her hand rested, then looked up at her, a question in his eyes.

"Just checking to see if you're real," she said, removing her hand.

He gave her a half-smile. "While you're thinking about it, we'd better go inside. My mom's probably wearing a hole in the carpet pacing back and forth."

Jaxon had been right. As soon as they walked in the front door, Mrs. Ungritch was there waiting, her expression a mixture of concern and relief.

"Everything all right with your car?"

"Oh," Monica paused. "Nothing to worry about. Sorry it took a while."

Mrs. Ungritch just smiled and hugged her. "Come on in. Dinner is ready, and Mr. Ungritch is getting grumpy from hunger."

A voice from the kitchen sailed in. "I heard that!"

Mrs. Ungritch rolled her eyes and bustled away.

"Let me help you bring the food out," Monica said, setting off after her. But Jaxon grasped her arm.

"Thanks," he whispered.

"For what? You rescued me," she whispered back.

"For listening to me and for considering my offer."

She knew her cheeks were about to flame red. So she just smiled, then hurried away, taking refuge in the kitchen from those green eyes.

Mr. Ungritch was just coming out when she stepped into the kitchen.

"Great to have you here with us," he said. "How's your mother?"

"She knows it's Christmas, so that's good," Monica said.

Mr. Ungritch patted her shoulder. "You're a good daughter to visit her so faithfully."

"Thank you," Monica said, feeling her chest tighten. She wished she could do so much more. She wished her mother was with her at the Ungritches', about to enjoy a delicious meal.

Mr. Ungritch left the kitchen, and she could hear him talking to his son, although the words were muffled. Monica turned to face Mrs. Ungritch, who was pouring cocktail sauce into a cut-crystal bowl.

"Shrimp?" Monica prompted.

"A tradition," Mrs. Ungritch said. "Do you like seafood?"

"Love it," Monica said, realizing then just how hungry she was. She crossed to the counter and arranged the rolls in a basket, then filled up a pitcher with water and ice.

"I'm so pleased that you and Jaxon are becoming friends," Mrs. Ungritch said. Her tone was more than pleased.

"What makes you think that?" Monica teased.

Mrs. Ungritch laughed. "If I thought it would bother you, I wouldn't tell you what I think. But the good thing about you, Monica, is that I've always been able to confide in you."

Monica's hands stilled at the confession. It meant a lot to her. Mrs. Ungritch had been her employer, yes, but also a mother, and sometimes even like a sister and friend. "I can tell you're just bursting, so tell me what you think."

Mrs. Ungritch's smile grew wider. And Monica realized that behind Mrs. Ungritch's glasses were the green eyes Jaxon had inherited.

"My son likes you."

"All right," Monica said, trying to act nonchalant, when in truth, her heart rate had just increased a notch. "He's a great guy, and of course I like him too. He's your son, after all."

"I mean . . ." Mrs. Ungritch blew out a breath. "I mean, even though he might not admit it, I think he's really drawn to you. *Attracted* to you."

Now Monica's cheeks were heating. She tried to laugh it off. "We just met."

"Stranger things have happened," Mrs. Ungritch said. "Last night when you were playing Santa and Mrs. Claus, he kept trying to sneak in glances your way."

"We're probably the last people who should be dating. I just broke up with David, and Jaxon is going through a lot of changes."

Mrs. Ungritch clapped her hands together. "It couldn't be more perfect. You can help each other through—be there for each other."

"You are thoughtful to think so," Monica started, "but although your son has been really kind, I don't think I can assume to know what he thinks about me."

Mrs. Ungritch lowered her voice. "I'd never push him, you know, but he won't have any argument from me if he decides to ask you out."

And Monica realized she was secretly hoping Jaxon *would* ask her out.

"Need any help?" Jaxon said, coming into the kitchen.

He was a little irresistible.

He flashed her a questioning smile, as if to ask if she was all right. She gave a quick nod.

"You can take in the salad," Mrs. Ungritch told her son.

She bustled out ahead of them, and Jaxon looked over at Monica. "Is she this bossy in the store?"

"Always," Monica said. "Did you hear our conversation just now?"

Jaxon grabbed the salad tongs then picked up the bowl. "No. What was it about?"

Monica was relieved he hadn't heard what his mother said. She slid a glance at him. "It was about how happy she was that you're home."

He narrowed his eyes. "Really? I thought it was about how she wants me to ask you out."

Monica stopped dead. "You heard!"

He only grinned.

She closed her eyes, wondering how red her cheeks were going to get.

"Monica," Jaxon said, his voice causing her to open her eyes. He was standing close to her, close enough that she could practically feel the warmth of his breath, and was staring down at her. "I hope you don't think I'm just taking my mom's advice, because I do want to ask you out."

"You do?" Monica said, unable to look away from him.

"Yes, officially," he said. "If you don't think it's too soon after your breakup with David."

"There you are," Mrs. Ungritch said, coming into the kitchen again. "What's the holdup?"

"Nothing," Monica said, stepping past her and walking into the living room, then the dining room.

Both Jaxon and Mrs. Ungritch remained in the kitchen for a few moments, and it wasn't hard to guess they were probably talking about her. She sat across from Mr. Ungritch and talked to him until Jaxon and his mother reached the table.

Monica was sure that if she made eye contact with Jaxon, she'd blush again. After Mr. Ungritch said grace, the family settled into an easy conversation, mostly Jaxon's parents catching him up on the neighbors' lives. Monica knew most of the people they were talking about, but she found she wasn't paying much attention. She was much too aware of Jaxon's occasional glances.

Her phone buzzed, and her pulse jumped. She slid it out of her pocket without drawing attention to herself, hoping it wasn't David. But Jaxon's name popped on the screen. She'd put in his number when he was on his way to pick her up.

She lifted her eyes to meet his, but he was listening to his father talk. Had the text been sent earlier but been delayed?

She waited a few more seconds, but Jaxon still didn't look at her. So she opened the message.

Do you want to go see a movie tonight or something?

She looked up again and found Jaxon looking at her, a slight smile on his face.

She kept her expression neutral and texted back. *Are you asking me out on a date?*

Monica watched his expression as he surreptitiously read her text. The corner of his mouth turned up, and then he was looking over at his mom as she replied to something his dad said.

Monica's cell vibrated, and she looked down.

I am.

Again, she gave no expression and texted. *It's Christmas. Do people really go to a movie on Christmas Day?*

A moment passed, and his reply came. *I believe they do.*

She felt his gaze on her, unwavering. She looked up, wondering how she could feel such a strong connection to this man already. After delaying her answer by taking several bites of the food on her plate, she finally texted back. *All right.*

Eight

"I don't know why I waited so long to come home," Jaxon told Monica as they were driving back from the movie to the care center to pick up her car.

"You were building a career," Monica suggested.

"That's probably what I told myself." Jaxon *had* told himself that, but after his marriage to Cynthia had broken up, working for her father had been a disaster waiting to happen. He slowed the car and turned into the parking lot. Snow had started to fall, and it muted the light spilling from the lampposts.

"Maybe it was because so much time had passed, that it was hard to turn back," Monica said, her voice contemplative. "I have a hard time remembering what life was like before my mother forgot my name."

"What about your dad?" he asked.

"My dad died a few years ago, right about the time the dementia was overtaking my mom. So I left college and came back home to help out."

He slowed the car, stopping next to where hers was parked, now dusted with snow. "You're an amazing person, Monica. I'm glad you're buying my parents' shop."

She flashed him a smile. "Thanks."

"I'll get the snow off your windows while you warm up the engine," Jaxon said, climbing out.

The night air was cold, but invigorating. Monica climbed into her car and started the engine. He used his coat sleeve to clean off the windshield, then stopped. Someone had spray-painted *bitch* on the glass in red.

Monica must have seen it the same time he had, since she climbed out of the car and came to stand by him, facing the windshield.

He slipped his hand into hers. "Let's call in a report to the police, then follow me in your car to my parents' house. We can get the guest room ready for you."

Monica only whispered, "Okay."

"Are you fine to drive?" he asked. "We can come back tomorrow."

"No, I don't want the care center employees to see this," Monica said. "Although I don't really want to explain to your parents either."

"If anyone can be trusted, it's them." Jaxon wrapped an arm around her shoulder. She leaned into him, and he wrapped his other arm around her so they stood together. "I had to learn it the hard way. Come on. Let's make that call."

They climbed into his car again, and Jaxon dialed the police station and asked to speak with the officer who'd first handled David's reckless driving. When he answered, Jaxon explained the spray paint on Monica's car.

"Thanks for reporting it," the officer said. "We'll go over to his place right now and question him."

Jaxon thanked him and hung up. Then Monica got into her car and followed him back to his parents' house.

On the way, Jaxon's anger grew. He couldn't believe what a jerk David was, but the part that made him the most mad was that Monica had been insulted. And despite the charges against him, David had still taken more action.

Jaxon had Monica pull into the driveway first and parked behind her. They walked to the front of the house together, and Jaxon noticed that only a couple of lights were on in the house. He hadn't realized how late it was; his parents had probably gone to bed.

His cell phone rang just before he reached the front door. "It's the officer calling back," he told Monica.

He answered, and the officer said, "David wasn't at his apartment, and it looked like it was mostly empty when we shone lights into the windows. So we knocked on a neighbor's door and were told he moved out this evening. He left a forwarding address with the neighbor. Two states over. It looks like he left a parting gift for Monica in the form of spray paint."

"So he's gone for sure?" Jaxon asked, his gaze connecting with Monica. He gave her a thumbs up.

"Yes, but we'll still pursue this."

"Thank you, Officer," Jaxon said. When he hung up, he smiled at Monica.

"I can't believe it," she said. "He really left. I'm so relieved."

"Me too," Jaxon said. "But I still think you should stay here tonight. You've been through a lot today."

When she nodded, he opened the front door to the house and found that all was quiet. The Christmas tree was the only light in the living room, making the room glow like scattered stars. Jaxon shrugged off his coat, then took Monica's.

"Looks like they've gone to bed," Jaxon said. "I'll show you the guest room."

"Thanks," Monica said. "I appreciate it." She followed him down the hall, and they both stopped in the doorway of a bedroom.

The mattress had been stripped and propped against a wall. Boxes were stacked three or four high on top of the box spring.

"So . . ." Jaxon began. "Why don't you take my room, and I'll sleep on the living room couch. It could take a while to put this room together."

Monica wrapped her arms about herself. "I can take the couch. I'm so tired, I'll probably fall asleep instantly."

"No, really. I insist that you take my room."

She hesitated, but finally said, "All right. Thank you." Then she gave a soft laugh. "I wonder how many times I've thanked you today."

Jaxon laughed too. "I've lost count. But I hope you know it's no trouble." He grasped her hand and led her up the stairs. He liked the way her hand fit into his, small and warm. They passed his parents' room, then stopped at the end of the hall. Jaxon opened the door and was glad he'd made the bed that morning.

"The bathroom's across the hall," he said. "You can wear one of my T-shirts. Let me know if you need anything else."

"I will," she said, leaning against the door frame as he walked away.

Walking away was hard to do. He wanted to pull her into his arms, to hold her until she stopped worrying about jerks and nasty words on windshields.

Once downstairs, Jaxon found a blanket in a closet, then took off his shoes. He doubted he'd sleep much so he left the Christmas tree lights on as he lay on the couch. He couldn't stop thinking about Monica and how different she was from

Cynthia. Of how his parents loved Monica and trusted her implicitly, and for good reason.

Jaxon might not have known Monica for long, but he'd watched her in several situations already—from being around a lot of hyper kids to dealing with her ex-boyfriend, to seeing how she treated his parents. Jaxon didn't know where things might end up with Monica, but he planned to ask her out again. Tomorrow. It had been years since he felt like he was doing the right thing. But coming home felt right. And being with Monica felt right.

"Jaxon?" Monica said, coming into the room.

He sat up, surprised that she was still awake.

"Sorry to bother you."

"I wasn't asleep," Jaxon said, getting to his feet. "Are you okay?"

She had her arms wrapped around her waist. Her auburn hair tumbled messily about her shoulders, as if she'd been trying to sleep. "I think so," she said, not quite meeting his eyes.

It was endearing that she'd come down to talk to him. To lean on him. It made him feel needed, wanted. He crossed to her and pulled her into his arms. She nestled against him with a sigh. "Sorry," she whispered. "I've been high maintenance from the moment we were in the same room together."

He only pulled her against him tighter. He didn't mind helping her. Not in the least. Hugging her wasn't bad either. "You could take the couch, and I'll grab a sleeping bag for the floor. We'll have an old-fashioned slumber party."

"Your parents would have a heart attack when they woke up."

He drew away and smiled down at her. He loved how her blue eyes met his, trusting, yet amused. "It would be a good heart attack."

"Is there such a thing?" she asked, holding back a smile in an attempt to seem serious.

"We can find out."

She shook her head, and he wanted to touch her hair, to feel its softness.

"I don't think so," she said. "We'd better stick to plan A."

"All right," he said, but neither of them moved. And then he found her looking up, above their heads.

"Mistletoe," she whispered, a smile curving her lips.

"It must be fate." Jaxon moved his hands to her waist and rested his forehead against hers. Closing his eyes, he breathed in her scent. Wild flowers. "Maybe we'll both be able to sleep if we just get it over with."

"Get *what* over with?" her voice was drowsy, husky.

"Kissing each other."

"Hmmm. I don't know if that would put me to sleep," Monica said.

He could hear the smile in her voice. "I guess we should just try it then, to rule it out."

And he did. Monica's hands moved behind his neck, and he drew her against him. With the Christmas lights twinkling beyond them and the snow falling outside, he kissed her gently, taking his time. He didn't want their first kiss to be rushed. Or easily forgotten.

Monica sighed against his lips, her body relaxing until Jaxon felt as if he was suspended in the most delicious dream. She kissed him back, her mouth moving against his in answer to his silent questions.

Yes, she seemed to be saying.

When Jaxon drew away, he was no longer tired, but Monica said, "You're right. I'd better sleep upstairs. Will I see you in the morning?"

"I'll be right here."

She laughed. "Standing under the mistletoe?"

"If that's what it takes to get you to go out with me again."

She placed her hands on his shoulders and rose up on her toes to kiss his cheek. "I think I'm sold, Jaxon. See you in a few hours."

Jaxon watched her leave the room, then crossed over to the couch and sat down. If he didn't sleep tonight, it would be well worth it to know Monica was safe upstairs, that he had reconciled with his parents, that David had left town, and that tomorrow was a new beginning.

He closed his eyes, smelling the scent of wild flowers long after Monica's departure. His cell buzzed with a new text message.

He smiled when he realized it was from Monica.

I've thought about your offer to come and work at the shop. I just wanted to let you know that you're hired.

Jaxon laughed and texted back. *Thank you. I accept.*

As he faded into sleep, he realized he finally felt he had a purpose in his life after years of being adrift, and it centered around his family and the intriguing woman who would be his new boss.

ABOUT HEATHER B. MOORE

HEATHER B. MOORE is a *USA Today* bestselling author. She writes historical thrillers under the pen name H.B. Moore; her latest is *Finding Sheba*. Under Heather B. Moore, she writes romance and women's fiction. She's one of the coauthors of The Newport Ladies Book Club series. Other works include *Heart of the Ocean, The Fortune Café, The Boardwalk Antiques Shop,* the Aliso Creek series, and the bestselling Timeless Romance Anthology series.

For book updates, sign up for Heather's email list: http://hbmoore.com/contact

Website: www.hbmoore.com
Facebook: Fans of H.B. Moore
Blog: MyWritersLair.blogspot.com
Twitter: @HeatherBMoore

First (and Last) Christmas Date

Jennifer Griffith

OTHER WORKS BY JENNIFER GRIFFITH

Big in Japan
The Lost Art
Immersed
Super Daisy
Delicious Conversation
Chocolate and Conversation
Legally in Love Series

One

JULIET LAW TURNED DOWN THE Christmas song on the radio on her desk and reread the e-mail. Her heart had jumped to her throat and lodged there on first reading. The message had to be a prank. Or an overdose of peppermint cocoa.

Hey, Juliet. It's been ten years. Yeah, that last date sucked, but if you're up for it, so am I. I like to keep my promises. –Tag

Tag. Taggart McClintock. The boy next door when she was a kid. Her first date. Her cocoa mug bobbled in her hand and splashed a sip on her paperwork. *Shoot.*

A hot gust of wind threw sand at her Palm Desert office window. Baby, it wasn't cold outside, as the song on the radio insisted. This part of California didn't do ugly Christmas sweater contests. She wound her hair up into a bun, securing it with the pencil she just realized she'd been chewing.

Well, she couldn't exactly say yes. Not considering the

way things were with Newell right now. Throwing a date in with an old friend could rock the boat even further with him.

More than a friend, if she was honest with herself.

Her fingers hovered over the keys while she debated how to answer the e-mail.

Tag McClintock. Whoa. Her heart shot into a wormhole and landed smack dab in Desert Valley high school, circa ten years ago. There'd been so many years of being kids together, throwing rocks, training her dog to do tricks, making that fort, and Tag's promise he'd dangled to take her on her first date. All the build-up, and then—*blammo!* Tag was right. That night, ten years ago, had been the suckiest date of all suckitude. It was off the suckage scale—culminating with the police. And a large dose of Pepto Bismol.

He'd probably needed the full ten years to heal from the PTSD of that night.

Even though Juliet would've gone out with him the very next day, had he asked.

Which he hadn't.

She sipped her drink to combat the dry of her throat and cranked the radio up again. They were playing her favorite version of "First Christmas Date," the duet by Ace Bandage and Sarah Karnes. It kind of described her and Tag, their first Christmas date, young and in love. Well, except the in love part—for him. And how smooth and easy the date went.

Tag. Would he look the same? Like an engineering geek version of James Bond?

Ten years. She could still hear his nervous chuckle as they stood on her doorstep beneath the Christmas lights. "Sorry about tonight, Juje."

To reassure him, she'd filled the chilly air between them with a joke. "Aw, don't worry, Tag. We can try it again in ten years. When we've both had time to recover."

First and Last Christmas Date

He'd looked a little jarred, and he pulled a smirk, twisting a flower off the Christmas cactus on her porch railing and handing it to her. "Yeah." A look of earnest regret crossed his face. She couldn't blame him. Some of it wasn't his fault.

Tag leaned in, placed a soft kiss on her cheek, and didn't ask her out again.

Until now.

Tag was probably only home for the Christmas holidays, needing a little female companionship while his real girlfriend shopped at Bergdorf's or wherever rich big shot businessmen's girlfriends shopped.

Juliet spent most of her salary at Target.

Or maybe he had come home for the holidays, and his parents pressured him into contacting her, the cute little girl who grew up next door.

Frankly, a little part of her wanted to say no. Forget it. Don't call me up after ten years just because you're single and lonely over your vacation and just now remembered I was the best sport ever and the best friend you ever had before you went off to the Ivy League and became some kind of big shot businessman.

Her fingers still floated over the keyboard while she decided how to answer. No matter how tempted she was to type, "Absolutely! Just name the time or place! I'm there in two seconds!" with all the exclamation points, seriously, she should say no. Not because of all her other insecurities about why he might be asking, no. But because he was a ghost from her past. A very potent ghost. No one since even compared to Taggart McClintock.

And after this restitution date, or whatever it was, he would go away, back to his big shot businessman life, wherever he lived now, and she'd be in another decade-long limbo.

She made another cup of cocoa and let the hot liquid slide down into her stomach and burn up the butterflies. She could lie, say she'd gotten married. But next year was their ten-year high school reunion. The truth would out. She could fib and say she was involved with someone. There was Newell—they were "involved." Sort of. Mostly they were involved in a war with management of the prop plane company they both worked for. He was involved with dumping his ex-girlfriend, and Juliet was used as arm candy to make the ex jealous.

At least she got dinner out of it. And when Newell finally did cut loose all those apron strings to his girlfriend, he had real potential for being an awesome boyfriend.

Which sounded pathetic, when she thought about it. But . . . her life was actually something pretty awesome—working as a private pilot for this mom and pop business, but nearly at the point where she could buy her own plane. And Palm Desert was incredible—it was where celebs came to escape L.A. Plus, she had the bonus of living somewhere where she could always, always brag about the weather: it was either the hottest place in the nation and she was a beast for surviving it, or else it had the mildest, most beautiful weather while everyone else suffered through winter. Like today, a week before Christmas, the temperature read sixty-eight. Best of both worlds.

Most of all, it was home.

Her peppermint cocoa had cooled to sixty-eight degrees while she dithered.

Her phone buzzed in a text.

Polly: *Hey, Juliet. Weekend plans? You want to go out with my brother? He's almost divorced and needs a date for his holiday office party.*

Ugh. Polly's brother. He was not Juliet's idea of holiday cheer. Almost divorced was not the same as divorced.

First and Last Christmas Date

Juliet: *Sorry. I have plans.*

Polly: *Plans???? Elaborate, or I'll think you're dissing Vince. And me.*

Juliet debated. Nothing was set with Tag. She still hadn't decided—or answered him. So what if as a teen she'd had a little crush on her neighbor?

Oh, who was she kidding? It had been blinding. She'd thought of nothing and no one else for the rest of high school. Even when he went back to Nadia the cheerleader, Juliet had carried a torch. The only thing that cured it was his leaving for business school back East and her staying home and earning her pilot's license. Okay, maybe it was never cured—just put in a cryogenic containment freezer that she never dared open again.

Tag. Tag McClintock.

And what if she *did* go out with him? Where would they go? He didn't live in Palm Desert. She'd just go out with him, spend a couple of hours, say good-bye, and then live another decade with a gaping ache impossible to fill, even with chocolate.

Her computer chimed a new e-mail.

Come on. Say yes. I mean, there's no *possible way it could be worse than our first date.*

Well, that was true. She bit her knuckle.

Juliet: *Sorry, Polly. I've got a date.*

Two

SIX TIMES. THAT'S HOW OFTEN she changed her clothes while waiting for Tag to knock on her door. Six. Six was too many. Especially since it mashed the beach waves she'd meticulously curled into her long brown hair. Now they were more like lake waves. Or puddle waves. Or, considering the color, mud puddle waves.

Why did she even try?

Then came Tag's text.

Wear something nice. Kind of formal. I have a surprise.

In the entire pile of outfits decorating the chair and floor of her bedroom, not one was "nice" or "kind of formal." It had been a series of jeans and cardigans scented with lingering perfume bursts.

Another text came.

I'll be there in five.

Five! Five *minutes?* Her heart sped. Surely he meant hours. Because it would take her that long to find something kind of formal in this town, let alone in her closet. All she had was . . . the Red Dress. It was a notoriously hot dress. And not the Palm Desert heat meaning. The last time she'd worn it out, was with Polly to her brother's work party, and every single guy at the firm (and even two married guys) had asked for her number.

Yeah, she couldn't wear that with Tag.

The doorbell rang, setting off tremors in her stomach. Tag. He was here.

"Just a sec!" Juliet shrieked but then cleared her throat and called in a calmer tone, "Be right there." She was already in motion. Within thirty seconds she'd yanked the Red Dress off the hanger, tugged it over her curves, slid her feet into the pumps that made her five inches taller, and snagged a breath mint and her keys from atop her dresser.

"Coming!" She chugged across the entryway and threw back the door. And then her blood reversed direction in her arteries. There stood Tag. And no, it wasn't the geeky engineering version of James Bond. Just the James Bond. And he was in a suit—a kind of formal one, black with a white shirt and a narrow black tie. It took her a minute before she could speak. "Tag. It's . . ." That's as far as she got.

He wasn't speaking either, just looking perplexed. Oh, no. She hadn't checked in the mirror. Was her wardrobe malfunctioning? She glanced down in horror, but no. All was fine. Finally he said, "Wow. You look—"

"I know. It's a little much for dinner and a movie, or whatever you have planned." Seeing his face, hearing his voice, sent her into a spin that rivaled those high-powered washers down at the laundromat, the kind for king-sized bedspreads.

"No. Uh . . ." He blinked three times and shook his head. Finally he said, "Hello, Juliet. You look great." Then Tag stepped forward, and Juliet went in for the kiss-hello—

always awkward, and he didn't know quite what to do. Ugh! Why did she do that? She was not the kiss-hello type. He tipped his nose to the right, to the left, and suddenly, he'd kissed her right on the lips.

"Oh!" Juliet gasped, her heart rate kick-starting. Because his lips were hot velvet.

"Sorry. I've never quite mastered that East Coast thing." He shook himself and looked directly into her eyes, and to Juliet, that look was almost tangible, like a cable with a grappling hook shooting from him and snagging deep in her soul. Reflexively, she reached out and touched his hand. He grasped it and led her toward his car. "It's been a long time."

Tag led her down the driveway, and a desert creature, a lizard of some kind, scurried across their path. "They're good luck," he said, pointing to the scaly thing.

"If past is prologue, we need it."

"Oh, I'm not going to let there be a repeat of the past. I have this all planned, down to the last detail." Tag squeezed her hand and flashed her his teeth in a confident grin that sent a flash up her spine.

Tag helped her into his rental car. Nice rental—high end. But when she looked around at the dash and for stickers denoting which rental company, she couldn't find any. Huh. Weird. Where would he borrow it from it if it wasn't rented? Tag's parents didn't seem the type to drive a coupe with a speedometer that cranked into those ranges, so he probably didn't borrow it from them for this trip home. But then again, people could surprise you, like when her clergyman retired and bought a Harley Davidson and a skull-emblazoned helmet.

Had Tag come to stay?

"Merry Christmas," Tag said, extending a hinged box with a satin ribbon. Half his mouth raised in a lopsided grin.

First and Last Christmas Date

"I—oh, thank you. I didn't get you anything." Embarrassment pinged in her. She should've thought of him. Well, not that she'd thought of anything else. But she should have thought *more*. Like what would please him.

"It's okay. I wanted to. I'm glad you wore red." He looked her up and down, letting his eyes loiter on her shape. It made her nervous and pleased her at the same time. *Thank you, water aerobics.* He motioned for her to open it, and inside lay a necklace with flashing red stones set in silver bezels.

"Wow. This is gorgeous. Thank you." She never wore much jewelry, but this? This was incredible. She lifted her hair while he extended it around her neck and fastened the clasp, his hands lingering near the skin of her shoulder a second or two longer. She got goose bumps and shut her eyes. "I've never seen anything like it."

"It's one of a kind." Tag started the car and peeled out of the driveway. So, still the same kind of driving habits—the ones that got them in so much trouble before.

Juliet pulled down the visor to see. She rested her hand on the necklace that came just to her collarbone, its pendant flashing in the last rays of the setting sun. What fire! But even so, it caught her off guard. Jewelry? After ten years of not seeing each other? Her mind swung on the pendulum between best- and worst-case scenarios. Best, he really liked her. Worst, he stole it. No, wait. Worst, it belonged to an ex girlfriend and he wanted it off the top of his dresser.

Geez. She had to stop this erratic mind-reeling and say something normal. "Thank you for thinking of me."

"It's what I do."

What? She cocked her head and looked at him. "Jewelry?"

He peeled onto the freeway, heading west toward L.A., and said, "No. Think of you."

The words hit Juliet like a juggernaut. *Better than best-case scenario.* Her breathing hitched. Sure, she'd never let Tag McClintock out of her heart, but she'd forced him out of her mind—with herculean effort—over the years, especially after they graduated, moved away from living next door to each other where out her window she could see the light around the blinds of his bedroom. Hearing him say this didn't just open her heart's door a crack. It blew it wide open—with a PVC pipe full of C4.

She couldn't respond, but she dialed her knees his direction, and he took the hint and rested his hand on her leg as soon as he'd shifted into fifth gear and they were at cruising speed on the I-10.

"How are your parents?" she asked.

Over the speeding miles, they caught up. But Juliet was surprised how much Tag already understood about her current life. He knew her dad had been sick, that her brother Wyatt got in that wreck, that her mom had been caring for the both of them while Juliet's income supplemented the situation.

But then again, Juliet knew her fair share about Tag's life, too. From her mom Juliet already knew that Tag's younger sister had done a swan dive off the deep end, spent time in rehab, and had come out of it, clean for four months straight.

"That's great for Kenzie."

"Yeah, but . . ."

"But you were worried and came home." Juliet filled in the blank.

He looked out the window. "I just wanted to help them keep an eye on her, you know?"

"She always looked up to you."

"Truth is, I'd always planned to come back. The East

Coast was just temporary, to get my credentials, pay my dues, so I could show up and live back here and not have to do lawn maintenance at the golf courses like half our graduating class."

What he said was true. Most of their class did find jobs in landscaping. But that was never Tag's thing. He was too good with people. And had a brown thumb.

"So, this isn't just a Christmas trip." And this car really wasn't a rental. Or his parents' midlife crisis. This was Tag's. He was here for good. Wow. He must be doing quite well for himself. Or have some kind of wicked-high car payment. Knowing Tag, though, it'd be the former. "And you have a job somewhere."

"It took me six months to find the right job out here. But," he pointed into the distance. "See those?" They were coming up over the pass between the dry part of California and the lush part, where the San Jacinto and San Bernardino mountains caught all the rain and kept it on the west side, leaving Palm Desert a waste of blowing sand. At that junction stood sentinel hundreds of white towers with spinning triple blades. The wind turbines.

"The eyesores of the Golden State?"

"I'm the new director of the project."

Her throat closed. Uh. Whoops. "Oh, jeez, man, I—"

"Don't get me wrong. I know they're eyesores. But they made it so I could relocate. So suddenly they're as charming as the windmills of the Dutch countryside to me."

That being the case, Juliet suddenly saw something whimsical in them as the massive blades spun in the fading winter twilight. "So, Mr. McClintock. What have you planned for tonight?"

Tag jutted his chin in confidence. "You do still like Ace Bandage, right?"

Ace Bandage! Her lifelong favorite singer? "You're not taking me to see Ace Bandage." She let out a squeal. "Are you?"

"There's a Christmas concert at the Pantages Theater."

"And we have tickets?"

"Sweetheart, we have backstage passes."

Juliet sank back against the seat of the car. *Backstage passes!* No way. And what was better—Tag just called her "sweetheart." She let the endearment melt over her like warm caramel sauce.

But then Tag let his foot off the gas. She glanced over, and he was frowning and pulling off the freeway and muttering what might be a curse. Juliet sat up. "What's wrong?"

Tag just shook his head, his mouth forming a tight line as he geared down and pulled into the parking lot of a Mexican restaurant in Covina. Juliet looked around, and then she saw the flashing blue and red lights. Her mouth went dry.

Great. This date appeared to be starting the way their first date had ended. "It's going to be okay, Tag. They're probably just doing random stops." But Juliet knew he'd been close to breaking the sound barrier.

The officer went through the usual, "Do you know how fast you were going, sir?" recitation. When he left with the driver's license, Tag closed his eyes and pounded back against the headrest a few times.

Juliet reached over and rested a hand on his arm. Wow. Tag McClintock, high school band geek, had been working out. Those triceps—hmm.

He looked over at her, clearly frustrated. "This was not in my plan."

"Don't worry. The concert probably doesn't start until

eight. We've got loads of time." Juliet squeezed the triceps (to reassure him, right?).

Tag opened his mouth to say something, but the officer reappeared. "Sir? Will you please step out of the car?"

What? They never asked that. Not unless they had something serious to accuse someone of.

Juliet bated her breath while needles of fear pricked her all over. "Tag? Is everything—?"

Tag gave her a nod of reassurance, but soon he was bent face first over the hood of the car and being handcuffed and then hustled into the back seat of the police cruiser. Juliet stared, eyes wide, kneecaps shaking. She turned down a grating version of "Feliz Navidad" on the radio and then, on second thought, shut off the engine altogether.

An eternal five minutes later, the officer came to the driver's side window and stuck his head in. He started to speak but then seemed to take in Juliet's appearance. He swallowed visibly and said, "I'm sorry for the inconvenience. We'll be taking your husband down to the station."

"He's not my husband," she said without thinking.

The officer's eye softened a little further when they searched out her left ring finger for verification. "Good. Right. Then if you'd like you can follow us there, or you can continue on to your Christmas party without that baggage. Which I'd recommend." The officer cleared his throat. "Or, us guys have plans for drinks at the Tilted Kilt later. If you want to wait and join us."

"You're on duty, sir."

He seemed to recollect himself. "Right."

The cop left, his chest puffed out, and Juliet staggered around to the driver's seat. Try as she might, she couldn't see into the back of the cop car as it pulled away, couldn't make out Tag's face at all. What was going on? Well, she had to follow him. No way was he some criminal with warrants out. No.

The engine purred to life. Just touching the tip of her toe on the gas sent the RPMs revving. Kind of like when Tag had accidentally brushed his lips against Juliet's mouth. Her RPMs had cranked to eight thousand. And they were almost that high now, just recalling it. But she hadn't driven a stick shift in a long time. This could be a disaster. Wincing, she pulled into holiday traffic.

With halting progress, killing the engine twice at every stoplight, incurring three horn-honking incidents, and five bird fingers, she finally made her way to the West Covina police station. Thank goodness for GPS, because that cop car had left her in the dust ages back.

The whole thing at the station took forever. After an hour of sitting on an orange plastic chair, and enduring the lascivious glances of a few obvious drug addicts as they were hauled in, Juliet finally saw the arresting officer again.

"Miss Law?" He knew her name. Tag must have told him. "It will still be a few more minutes. Would you like to post bail?"

"Bail!" Her eyes popped open. "What are the charges?"

The officer smirked. "Just a little joke. Sorry. He's free to go, as soon as the paperwork is done."

She gave him a what-are-you-talking-about wince, and he waved his hand.

"Oh, it was all just a misunderstanding. Different guy used your *friend's* name as an alias, committed a few ATM knockovers in town. But we have video surveillance, and he obviously isn't a match." The officer sniffed. "But the offer still stands for the Tilted Kilt. For you, I mean."

"That's very kind of you. Merry Christmas . . ." Her voice trailed off because at that moment, Tag reappeared, looking slightly rumpled and more handsome than ever.

First and Last Christmas Date

Juliet flew to him. "Are you all right?" She melted against him, hoping the police hadn't roughed him up in any way. They did that sometimes, right? His arms encircled her and pressed her torso to his. Wow, good fit. "If you think we should call it a night and try again some other time, I'm okay with that." Sort of. She was sort of okay with that. But she definitely didn't want to wait another ten years to finish this date. Despite the police, things did seem to be crackling between them. Like the way his hands felt against the small of her back. Something electric popped out of his fingertips and into her stomach cavity.

"No. Absolutely not." He looked down at her. "We are going on our date." Determination pressed around the edges of his eyes, and his jaw set. "We may have missed our dinner reservations, but we can still make it to the Ace concert."

Ace! That was right. She was going to see Ace—up close!

Three

It amazed her that Tag remembered she'd loved Ace Bandage. That, or he'd done recon and asked her mother. Juliet had had one of those withering celebrity crushes on the smoky-voiced tenor all through high school, but she'd never seen him perform live. When his boy band broke up and Ace went solo, Juliet had written him a letter he hadn't responded to—of course. The non-response extinguished her love's flames, but she still lit up for his songs.

Her stomach growled. Snarled, actually.

Tag must have heard, because he looked over. "Dinner is shot. My little rendezvous with justice sealed that." He looked at his watch. "If you're starved, we could skip Ace and find somewhere to eat. Talking over a meal is good."

Juliet would like that too. But saying so might make her seem ungrateful for the effort he'd gone to in order to get the tickets for the show. "Could we grab something afterward? Or drive through somewhere?"

First and Last Christmas Date

Tag drummed his fingers on the steering wheel. "You still a Taco Shack girl?"

"Always and forever." Huh. He remembered her favorite restaurant too. "Give me the cheesy burrito and a pile of *chicharones* and I'm in heaven."

"Remember when I filled your whole locker with *chicharones* right before graduation?"

Wait. Tag was the one who put grease spots on all her textbooks right before she had to turn them in? She about flung this at him, but he was still talking.

"I can't believe you can eat deep fried pork rinds and still be as smoking hot as you are. You must have a killer metabolism."

Double wait. Tag thought she was hot? Her temperature rose a few degrees. Smoking hot? Well, it took one to know one. With his hair all mussed and his necktie askew, he looked like he could spontaneously combust. Or make her do so.

"Here's one." He took the next exit and pulled into a Taco Shack. A huge lineup clogged the drive-through. As soon as they pulled between the tall cement guide curbs, a windowless van snuggled right up behind them. Another minivan with New Mexico plates spewed emissions-violations in front of them while little kids pounded on the back window and made faces at them.

Tag pointed a thumb in their direction. "No changing your mind now." With the tall guide curbs they couldn't even pull out in this low-slung car. "It's tacos tonight!"

When he gave the order at the talking box, it crackled. At the first window, he whipped out a black credit card, and the clerk gazed down at him with a dream on her face for a moment before swiping it, never taking her eyes off Tag. They then inched toward the second window, which looked about an hour away.

"Drive-thru. Why do they have to spell it that way?" Juliet leaned her head against the window.

"This is America. People have a Constitutional right to misspell." Tag inched the car forward. "Doughnut shop, d-o-n-u-t s-h-o-p-p-e. That's a California special. And no one can stop them."

"At least 'shoppe' has a spelling pedigree across the pond. The one that bugs me is light spelled l-i-t-e. Sure, it's more intuitive. But please. It's only one more letter to spell it right. Come on, people."

"People are lazy. We Americans are soft spellers. Our forebears would be so ashamed."

"Down with this weakness!"

The banter they used to share back in the day popped back to life, and she fell into it so comfortably that her thoughts of Newell faded another few steps into the background.

The window rolled down, and her stomach growled at the cumin and garlic and jalapeno of Taco Shack. Cheesy burrito coming through soon.

But the second window woman leaned out, clearly frustrated, yelling at someone inside—probably some poor, put-upon teen working a Friday night instead of going to the school Christmas dance. She handed Tag a too-small paper sack.

"Are you sure—" he started. But then the woman's yelling went louder and included violent gestures toward the poor teen.

Juliet tugged on his shirt. "Whatever's in there will be just fine."

"But you need your cheesy burrito. We are *here* for a cheesy burrito, and you'll have it."

The yelling went louder. "I had a late lunch," Juliet lied

and checked inside the sack. "Oh, look. Vanilla. My favorite." A single vanilla cone lay on its side at the bottom of the bag.

Just then the windowless van behind them started honking, and when Juliet looked back, she gasped.

"Uh, Tag? The dude behind us has some kind of weapon." She whipped back around and sat hard against her seatback, slumping down. In the side view mirror she saw the driver had reached out his window and was brandishing a gun.

"But you need that burrito, Juje. Your stomach is going all hungry lion. We're here, and I'm getting that food." He reached out his window and started pounding on the glass of the drive-thru window.

"Tag! Come on!" Juliet reached across and pressed her hand down hard on his knee, shoving his foot onto the gas.

"Hey, hey. Fine. Okay, we'll go," he shouted over the incessant honking of the van behind him. He put the car in gear and pulled out of the line. "But you can keep your hand on my knee as long as you like." His eye twinkled, and Juliet pulled her hand away, embarrassment flushing her face hot. Uh, touching his leg had not been in her plan.

Back on the freeway, she took the cone out. "Wanna share?" She held it out in front of him, almost in his line of sight, and unsheathed the ice cream. When she pulled it back toward her for a taste, his eyes followed. Mmm. The vanilla coldness was delicious. She might have moaned. "Here, have a taste."

He nodded, obedient, and tasted the proffered food, never taking his eyes off her mouth.

"The road?" Juliet said, and Tag jerked the car back into their lane.

"Whoa. Better not get pulled over a second time. Maybe I'd better not watch you eat that. Getting in a fiery wreck is really the only way this date could be worse than our first." He took the cone from her hand. "In fact—" He rolled down his window and tossed it against the cement barrier in the median. "Better hungry than dead."

"A timeless truth." Juliet's stomach grumped, but a smirk of satisfaction pulled the left side of her slightly sticky mouth. Who'd have thought she could have this kind of effect on Tag McClintock? A tingling decorated the backs of her thighs like strung lights on all the suburban houses they were passing. "I've never been to the The Pantages before."

"Did I tell you?" Traffic hit a sudden snag, and Tag pulled to a slowing semi-halt. "It's stuff from his Christmas album. The old one. And our seats are down front." From his jacket pocket he produced tickets and handed them to her.

"Front row? How did you—?"

Tag lifted a shoulder. Either he had connections or he bought the tickets the second they went on sale—and had been planning this night for months.

Warmth poured through her like her cups of hot cocoa. Wow. He *had* thought of her. She had the sudden urge to kiss him. "Oh, Tag." She leaned over and pressed her lips to where his cheek divided clean skin from stubble. Her bottom lip got the prickles, and her top lip got the smoothness of Tag's face.

His hand slid from the gear shift up across her shoulder and to the back of her head. He pressed her to him while he turned to face her, Juliet's lips scuffing across his cheek and halting when their lips met. "You taste like vanilla."

Juliet's pulse pressed hot blood through her veins. She wasn't sure how long the horns behind them had been honking when they finally came up for air. But Tag hiccupped as he tore his face from hers and eased the car into motion again. Juliet had to catch her breath.

First and Last Christmas Date

"You have no idea . . ." Tag murmured as they resumed speed and the bottleneck opened up.

Oh, yes, she did. She had *every* idea. She knew how long a person could want that kiss. That *very* kiss. The kind that turned every other previous kiss out into the cold night and said don't come back, you're not worthy and never will be. The kind that made her put Newell out to permanent pasture.

Poor Newell. How could she ever kiss that guy again? It just wouldn't be fair to him—since he could never compare, and she'd always be comparing.

Sayonara, Newell. Go back to your girlfriend.

Tag reached over and ran his knuckles down the side of her face just as their exit loomed up. "We'll still make it for the concert if we use valet parking."

Naturally, the main artery of Hollywood Boulevard, which sat a stone's throw from the mansions of Beverly Hills, was jammed with cars and tourists drifting over the stars' names on the Walk of Fame. Tag whizzed around a corner and took a side street, planting them in front of The Pantages with just minutes to spare. He tossed the valet his keys and helped Juliet from the car. They dashed in the front doors.

From their super close seats, Juliet could see the chicken pox scar below Ace's right eye. She'd seen it once before in a rare, un-airbrushed photo of the former boy-band frontman. Even though he'd gone solo and turned from bubble gum pop to R&B years ago, he still had that boyish charm and spiked hair.

There was no opening act, just Ace and his acoustic guitar, Christmas wreaths, and some flickering candles. The Pantages piped in pine scent, kind of like California Adventure did with orange blossom scent on that hang glider ride, and Juliet relaxed against Tag's arm for the nanosecond he waited before reaching around and resting it on her shoulder.

The ghost of their kiss still danced on her lips to the rhythm of Ace's silken voice. She reached up to touch them, in hopes of quelling their reverberations, but the ghost wouldn't be exorcised, as if demanding to be conjured again and again.

Well, the ghost would have to wait. Possibly forever. Because Juliet had no idea whether that car kiss was a fluke or a prelude. Tag's *You have no idea . . .* line might not have meant what she'd assumed—that he'd been waiting a long time to kiss her. It might have meant, *You have no idea how off-base you are in throwing yourself at me. I'm only here to keep my word. Nothing more.*

The ghost of the kiss had been joined by the ghost of her insecurities.

Ace finished a set, told a few stories about growing up in rural Indiana in a family that made Christmas like Disneyland. The audience sighed, charmed. Tag reached over and took Juliet's hand. It fit—and Juliet felt like *she* was six years old and at Disneyland for the first time. Her insecurities lifted a little.

Then Ace looked out into the audience. "If it's all right with y'all, I'd like to do something special with this next song." At this, Ace descended the stairs and walked among the crowd, letting them reach out and touch his outstretched fingers. "A lot of you know, I don't really like to sing alone." His voice went sultry. Women shrieked.

Juliet laughed a little and bent her head toward Tag. "I bet girls shriek when you talk about singing."

Tag shrugged. "I'm sure they would as soon as they heard me sing. But in pain, not—"

Suddenly, a spotlight seared between them, and when

First and Last Christmas Date

Juliet looked up, there stood Ace Bandage, reaching his hand out to her. Juliet stared at it a second, and then she heard what he was saying.

Ace had pulled back his mic and whispered to her, "Do you sing? Even a little?"

She nodded dumbly.

"Do you know the words to 'First Christmas Date?'"

Again, the dumb nod. Yeah, she knew it—better than she'd like to admit. In return he gave her a reassuring nod. "Come on, then. Come sing with me? Will you?"

Juliet's mouth went dry. Sure, she'd had her days of singing—even performed more than her share of solos at school and church functions. But this was in front of strangers, a whole Toys-R-Us holiday truckload of them.

But Ace took her elbow and lifted her to her feet. To her surprise, in the heels she stood an inch taller than he did. She slipped them off, in case he'd be more comfortable that way, and walked up the cold metal steps barefoot behind him.

"What's your name, gorgeous?" He asked in his husky voice. She told him, and he pulled his microphone back to his mouth while a tech crew member in a black T-shirt reading *Rex* hustled out and handed Juliet her own mic. "Ladies and gentlemen, Juliet Law!"

The audience cheered politely. Was it possible applause could be tinged with jealousy? Because if so, this one was more than tinged. It was positively saturation-point-dyed green. But Juliet's embarrassment had stained her face red, and she had on the Red Dress. So, yeah. Red and green. The colors of Christmas. Her stomach clenched. This could be bad. Very, very bad.

Her eyes searched for Tag but were blinded by the spotlight. But then she touched her collarbone and felt the red necklace from Tag. It might not be instant death here.

Then Ace strummed his guitar, and the song poured into her. Every time she'd listened to the Christmas album, which was pretty much a kabillion times, she sang Sarah Karnes's part as closely as she could, picturing herself sitting beside Ace, their foreheads touching as they serenaded each other.

This song was a well-trodden path, but it still might have potholes.

"I took your warm hand." She started a little wobbly—but on key. Yes!

"Our first Christmas date." Ace countered her with perfect rhythm, taking her elbow and giving her a reassuring nod.

"You warmed my cold heart." Her voice steadied more, getting stronger.

"Our first Christmas date." Ace's voice rumbled through the whole theater. He came around and stood in front of Juliet, taking her hand in his. She was glad she'd taken off the heels. Looking up into his face wasn't half bad.

"We skated the ice," she sang, holding the note until he joined her on "Of future dreams." He squeezed her hand and pressed it to his warm chest.

The song's back-and-forth banter progressed. "We meet again now," she sang, and the audience at last warmed to them both. He sang, "I savor your kiss," and pulled Juliet into his lap. He leaned his forehead against hers, running a hand through her long hair and down her arm. At this she laughed a little and missed her "I bask in the holiday glow of your smile" line, but he covered for her, and soon she was back on track, and the audience was eating it up.

When the final combined line of "Last Christmas date, my love" arrived, she hit the harmony just right, and the crowd erupted. Juliet smiled down at where she thought Tag

First and Last Christmas Date

would be sitting, relief swishing away all the heaviness of terror that had accompanied her through most of the notes.

But Ace must have thought the smile was for him. He snaked an arm around her back and leaned in to steal a kiss. Juliet panicked. *No! Not in front of Tag.* She popped her head to the left, dragging the sandpaper of Ace's mouth across to her cheek.

The audience exploded in a volcano of cheers and catcalls.

"Sorry, doll. You were just too delicious not to try." Ace half-shut his eyes and pushed out his lips in a second air-kiss.

Juliet sprang from his lap, waved a trepidatious hand at the crowd, and scuttled down the metal grid stairs and back to her seat beside Tag. His arms were folded over his chest.

"Tell me you didn't plan that." Juliet pressed her mouth toward his shoulder and shouted over the music and crowd shouts.

"Oh, believe me." Tag's arms were still folded. The spotlight flashed past, and she saw his temple bounce in and out from clenching his jaw.

Tag was jealous. Juliet blinked, letting that sink in. Or was he? Could he be? They'd only been together a few hours in the past decade. With a little trepidation, she reached over and rested her hand on top of where his sat on his folded arms. He glanced at her and then relaxed and took her hand back in his.

"You sounded amazing, though. I'd forgotten how your singing makes me feel."

Wow. Juliet preferred that compliment to everything Ace ever said or sang. She nestled against Tag for the duration.

The concert went on for another half hour, and then Ace sang a tender version of "Have Yourself a Merry Little Christmas" and bid the fans good night.

Tag stood and helped Juliet to her feet. A press of the crowd pushed them against one another. He smelled like soap, and she lingered a second longer than the press dictated.

Just then, though, good old Rex the tech bustled up to them. "Mr. McClintock?"

Tag stopped. Juliet knew what this was about.

One hand rested on the round of his belly. "Backstage passes. You two are needed now." He turned to Juliet. "Incredible performance, Miss Law. Best I've ever seen impromptu. I wouldn't be surprised if Ace asks you to come record with him. He really liked you. I mean *really*."

At this, Tag's face darkened into a glower, and Juliet's throat filled with sand.

"Maybe we should skip it. Give our passes to someone else." Juliet had already been much more up close and personal with Ace Bandage than she'd intended to be, and Tag—well, he didn't seem himself. More like a steroid-amped version.

"Oh, no. We are going back there to meet him." 'Roid-raging Tag marched after Rex, almost tugging Juliet, who had to skiff along in her pumps to stay steady. This did not bode well.

Ace's dressing room had a fully decorated Christmas tree. Apple juice mulled with oranges and cloves permeated the air. Wassail, Ace's favorite Christmas drink, she remembered from her *Tiger Beat* reading days.

Did Tag smell it too? She glanced at him, but it looked like all he smelled was blood.

"Mr. Bandage, sir?" Rex cleared his throat to get Ace's attention, for he had his back to them and was on the phone and leaning on one hand against the wall, talking loudly.

"I'm telling you, Sid. She had it all. The voice, the look.

First and Last Christmas Date

The *legs*. I could've dropped to the floor and sunk my teeth into her calf muscles. The audience loved her. I should've just sat down and let her finish the concert. Yeah. Juliet Law. Look her up. See if she has anything recorded already. If not, I'm hiring a P.I. and hunting her down. First I'll take her to bed and not let her out for a month, and then with your help I'll make her a star."

The blood drained from Juliet's face. White—that was a Christmas color too, wasn't it? For the snow? She was a candy cane right now—red dress, white face.

Tag's face, on the other hand, had turned toy-fire-engine-under-the-Christmas-tree red. His fists were pumping, making his biceps bounce beneath Juliet's hand.

Rex volleyed again. "Mr. Bandage? Your backstage pass guests have arrived." This received a pointer finger in the air until Rex said, "It's Mr. Tag McClintock and Miss Juliet Law."

Ace whirled around. "Juliet? She's here? Now?" His eyes lit up, laser focused on her. He jumped forward. "Juliet! My gorgeous—"

But on the second syllable of gorgeous, Ace Bandage's chicken pox scar got a violent, personal introduction to Tag McClintock's closed fist. Juliet staggered backward into Rex, and Ace spun on the heel of his cowboy boot, which Juliet now saw was about four inches high.

"Never speak about a woman like that again. Particularly not about my woman." Tag wiped his knuckles on his suit coat and stalked toward the door.

Juliet's eyebrows scrunched together, and she winced a silent apology at the stricken superstar. Instinct told her to go toward the wounded man, who had crumpled onto the leather sofa and held his cheek. However, the grappling hook that had lodged in her heart from the first moment Taggart

McClintock's eyes met hers tonight cinched tight and yanked her after his departure.

Ace frowned and barked, "Tech guy! Call security." And then to Juliet he muttered, "You and I could've been really good together."

Juliet just shook her head and stumbled after Tag, grabbing his hand. Over her shoulder she heard Rex say something like, "He's leaving. Forget it, boss. You deserved it."

On the chance Ace couldn't be convinced by Rex's logic, Juliet said, "Let's put on some speed."

Four

"What—so you're not going to spend the next month in his filthy bed?" He was still seething. "And then go off and leave Palm Desert, when I just moved back, and, as that jerk said, 'become a star?'"

"That's ridiculous."

They were in the parking lot, and Tag handed a pile of money to the valet stand attendant. "Just give me my keys. I'll get my own car."

Juliet would have stopped to tell him off, but she realized that getting out of there fast wasn't a bad idea. After all, they'd already been in a police station once tonight. The ticketing company had both their names because of the backstage passes. This could still end badly. With assault charges.

Within moments, Tag had shimmied the sports car out of the tight parking spot, and they went weaving through the Hollywood hills, past scores of obscenely expensive mansions with iron gates and So-Cal pink stucco façades.

Soon, Tag's breathing slowed, and the veins on his neck relaxed to their normal size.

However, Juliet had gone from simmer to boil. *How could he?* She tapped the toe of her pumps on the floor mat.

"That was totally not how I saw that concert going." When Tag glanced over and their eyes met, he looked surprised. "Whoa. You're mad?" He let his foot off the gas and reached over to her. His touch grounded her a smidge, but not enough to completely cut the anger. He went on, a little more apologetically. "Okay, so maybe I shouldn't have hit the guy. I know you always liked him. But somebody needed to. He's a jackal." He clenched his fists on the steering wheel.

"That's not what's bothering me." Juliet took a turn folding her arms over her chest. They came to a stoplight on the corner of L.A.'s famous Wilshire Boulevard, and Tag looked over at her, dropping his snark and looking a little confused.

Juliet pushed her chin forward and huffed. "I can't believe you'd assume I'd go to, as you put it, Ace's filthy bed. Come on, Tag. I thought you'd know me better than that. Did you think I'd had an integrity transplant since last time you knew me?"

"No, no. It's not what I meant. I mean, I know *you*." He paused. "I guess it's just been so long. Most of the girls I've met since I left home have been moral vacuums. They would have pressed the turbo button on their engines to get to a rock star's bed."

Disgust rose up in her like bile in the throat. "Please."

Tag looked over at her. "But you. You're a breath of fresh air."

The tension diffused, and she forgave his jealousy-driven comment. It was kind of nice, she had to admit.

First and Last Christmas Date

"Well, thanks for fighting for my honor, anyway."

He smirked and gave her a wink that sent a sparkle back through her.

Juliet leaned her head against the window and watched the steel and glass buildings go by, interspersed with mom and pop stores and relics of old 1960s California. Every window had a Santa or a star or a tree or a menorah. Garlands of evergreen branches stretched between the streetlights. Like the song said, even stoplights blinked a bright red and green. But Juliet was fixated. *Tag held her to a standard?*

If she was honest, she held Taggart McClintock to a standard, too. She let her mind drift back through the years to a potent memory.

They were eleven.

Tag joined the Boy Scouts and needed help learning the creed, the one about loyal, clean, brave, reverent—all of those. He never was good at memorizing.

Juliet let him push her on the tire swing while she quizzed him. For the first time, she'd felt the pressure of his hands on her back. Then when he finally got it, he'd given her a high five. That high five—it was the first time she'd noticed the electric current between her and Tag McClintock. At least on her own part.

Was the current still live? Juliet reached toward where his hand rested on the shifter, and she touched it ever so lightly. Tag twitched at her sudden touch, but he didn't pull away, just looked her direction, his eyes afire.

Wow. Definitely still live. Except now somebody had cranked the amps. And kissing him in traffic earlier? It was like being right at the substation.

Ooh. What would max voltage feel like? She'd better not try to find out tonight.

A text chimed from her phone inside her purse.

Polly: *You are on a date with Tag McClintock? Girl!*

A second one followed fast on its heels.

And you didn't tell me?

How did Polly find out? Because Juliet didn't tell. No way. Polly was notorious for broadcasting things like that through their whole social network of leftover Desert Valley High friends and not-so-friends.

Just didn't want to get my hopes up, Juliet typed and then deleted, tilting her phone out of Tag's sightline. A long moment's thought netted, *It was a last-minute thing.*

Polly shot right back. *Didn't seem like last minute. He had to book early for those backstage passes.*

What in the world? How did she know that?

Don't think something like that *wouldn't hit the interwebs, darling. That and your duet with ACE BANDAGE! Girl, you still got the pipes. Over and out.*

"Uh, Tag?" She wiped the fingerprints off her phone, and the humor of the night suddenly hit her. "I'm sorry to tell you, but you've already gone viral." They were at a stoplight, so she showed him Polly's texts, suppressing a laugh as another text popped in, this time with a picture.

"Polly." He, and everyone else, knew Polly and her voracious appetite for news. "Were those pictures of Ace's trip to the ER? Wow. I guess my right hook is officially famous."

"Former teeny boppers everywhere will hold your name in derision. You'll have to go into hiding. Like that dentist who shot the lion."

"Oh, no. I'll have it easier than that poor bloke. He's ruined. But *this* guy already has the name Ace Bandage. He was asking for it." Tag wheeled his car into a parking lot off Wilshire. "Here we are, Sunset and Camden."

First and Last Christmas Date

Singing in the Rain. Her heart skipped. Any guy who could quote *Singing in the Rain* was okay with Juliet—and even canceled out her annoyance at his suspicions about her virtue being up for grabs by rock stars.

He came around and opened her door. "We should get over to the museum fast, before they put out a BOLO on me." BOLO. Be on the lookout. Right. "I swear, this is not how I saw this night going."

Juliet shrugged a shoulder. "I'm having a great time."

Tag cocked his head at her, but now they crossed the street into a familiar grassy park with buildings dotted around. She'd been here quite a few times as a kid.

"I love how the Los Angeles County Museum of Art is plopped right next to the La Brea Tar Pits." The air smelled of petroleum and sulfur, like one of those oil refineries out on the coast.

"A bold move." Tag took her arm, linking it around his. The suit jacket had great fabric. He was doing very well for himself.

"Is the museum open this late?" It had to be past eleven. They strolled past concrete sculptures of saber-toothed tigers and other creatures exhumed from the pits.

"Tonight only. There's a special midnight appearance of Scrooge's three ghosts. Patrons can speak to any one of them, Past, Present, or Yet to Come, and make a wish."

The words "make a wish" sent a shiver through Juliet's core.

"Kind of like a grown-up version of a kid sitting on Santa's lap?" Magic sparkled in the night air. Juliet's mind pinged from wish to possible wish.

"Let's not mention sitting on anyone's lap. Unless it's mine." Tag stopped and came around in front of her. He stood there, looking all James Bond confident. Desire for him surged in her, and she had to blink a lot to tamp it back down. After all, this could still just be a mercy date.

But he was walking toward her with intent in his eye.

Juliet looked around. Beside them, through the fence, was the biggest, bubbling tar pit, the one where the life-size mammoth family surrounded the pool and anguished over a sinking family member, a total melodrama of the ancient animal kingdom.

Tag steered her backward, until her back rested against the iron bars of the fence around the sticky black lake. She gazed up at him, everything else fading to black as he swooped in and caught her mouth in a kiss so incendiary it could ignite the tar fume filled air around them. Soon his hands were crawling up and down her sides, twining around the back of her neck, twisting in her hair, and his chest pressed against hers. And Juliet gave as good as she got for the half a minute it lasted.

Tag pushed himself back, leaving Juliet's knees a pool of melted cartilage and her lips a little raw. "Whoa," he said. "You'd better take it easy, Juliet. You're playing with explosives."

She gulped and reached up to rest her fingers on her collarbone and gauge her heart rate.

"Oh, no." She patted at her neck in a panic. "No, no, no." Where was it? It had to be there. She felt all over her dress, crouched down on the ground. "The necklace." Frantic fingers flew over the dry, wintered-over Bermuda grass. Tag was on his knees beside her—soiling that perfect dark suit with mud. Oh, if ever there was evidence of devotion, that had to be. "It was on my neck when you accosted me here."

"Accosted, huh?" He pulled out his phone and found the flashlight app. "First it's assault, and now I'm accosting."

"Dude. You're the guy with all the passions."

"Yes, I am."

The necklace didn't glint in the light of his phone—not right away, anyway. Not until he aimed it into the fenced-off area. There! But it lay a good two feet past any hope of reaching. And the holes in the fence were only about three inches square.

Juliet's heart sank. "How did it get so far?"

Tag raised an eyebrow and looked her over, standing up. "Vigorous make-out."

Then they saw it—a stray chipmunk.

The rodent inched toward where he'd clearly already been at work moving the necklace back to his winter lair.

"Shoo!" Juliet stomped her heel. "Shoo, you striped rat." The chipmunk glanced at her in disdain. Her blood boiled. "Can we get some kind of stick?"

"And teach the chipmunk a lesson? Don't forget, we're in California. People don't like that sort of thing."

"I meant to snag the necklace and drag it to us, but still. That dirty rat!" Juliet's insides alternately pinched and ached as she gauged the distance in despair. No way could they snag it. Seriously. It was beyond hope.

The chipmunk scooted toward the necklace again. He was clearly immune to their threats and useless hand-waving.

"It's all right, Juliet. We should just let it go." He rested a hand on her arm, and the warmth of it surged up her shoulder. "It will sink into the tar, become one again with the earth. There's something kind of comforting and cyclical about that, don't you think?"

But it was one of a kind. She couldn't let it sink into tar. "It meant a lot to me."

The words made Tag's head snap upward, and his eyes met Juliet's. "Really?" When she nodded, he began pacing back and forth. "I'll look for a stick." He headed across the sidewalk to the base of a tree and kicked at the grass.

Excitement and relief washed through her. They could do this together. "I'll pelt the little guy with pebbles until you find something."

Unless . . .

"I have an idea. Give me a boost." She slipped off her pumps and hiked up her already short skirt. "I'm going over. If you can boost me, I can get it. I did gymnastics when I was a kid." For six months, and stunk at it.

"But . . . how will you get back?" The voice of reason fell on deaf ears.

"I'll climb." Then she realized she wouldn't. "No. I got it. You're going to call park security and tell them there's an unstable woman who's made her way into the tar pits and is threatening self-destruction. They'll come and open the gate." Juliet made to climb the fence, looking around for security. There was none.

"No. I'll go. I'm taller. I can swing my leg over easier. And there's an outside chance I can get back on my own."

The ground on the other side of the fence was lower by a couple of feet. Juliet rolled her eyes. "They aren't going to be as sympathetic to a man in a $5,000 suit claiming to be wacked. But a crazed woman in a cocktail dress? I can totally make up a story for that. Now, quick. Up with the boosting."

"You are one determined girl, Juliet Law." Faster than she could say "bah, humbug," Juliet tumbled, flailing over the fence, landing partially on her feet with a thud on the mud. The chipmunk chattered and dashed. But the mud was slippery, and before Juliet could get her footing, she lost the tiny remnant of balance she'd retained, double-stepped sideways, and careened toward the lake of bubbling black sludge just a few feet away. Time slowed down.

First and Last Christmas Date

The tar reeled before her, smelling like rubber tires and gasoline and sulfur, and making her eyes sting. No. This dress—she could not get that sludge on it. Not a drop!

"Tag!" She called for him, but it was too late. "Man down. Man down. I mean, woman down." She thudded onto the bank, and her shoulder touched down onto the tar. "Ewww!" Luckily, she'd snapped her head skyward and kept her hair out. At least there was that.

Before she could hoist herself off the muddy bank, a *thud-thud* hit her ears. Tag stood over her, a hand outstretched. She took it, and he lifted her to her feet.

"I see flying comes quite naturally to you."

"It's all the practice I get as a prop plane pilot."

"Someday you'll have to take me up." Tag's eyes sparkled.

Juliet's heels were sinking in the soft, pungent bank of the tar lake, but she didn't care. Tag just said he wanted to do something with her in the future. *Tonight wasn't a one-time date.* Her mouth went dry. Did he really mean it? A little chunk from her continent of fear broke off and sank into the ocean of her soul.

Tag boosted her again, up and over the fence. It was tougher, since the ground was lower, and it took three tries. Three. And then she went all rubbery from laughing, but she finally made it to terra firma on the safe, tar-free side of the fence.

Juliet pressed her face against the bars across from him. He leaned in too, their lips almost meeting. "Looks like you've been behind bars more than once tonight."

He kissed her through the three-inch-square opening in the metal.

"But how will you get out?" Maybe there was a rope lying around. She could lasso him, pull him over. Uh, right.

"Oh, it'd have to be a fifty-foot fence to keep me from finishing this date with you."

He looked around. "This looks as good a place as any." Then he poked his fingers and the tips of his shoes through the grid, and scampered up the metal. At the top he threw his leg over the bar and landed catlike beside her. "And I noticed you forgot something." He held out the necklace.

"After all that—I left it." Great. She lifted her hair to have him put it on again.

But when she glanced down, she saw the Red Dress. It was now a Black Dress. Well, mostly black, with some red still showing. Kind of.

Her heart sank. Tar covered the fabric and her shoes and would be super fun to peel off her legs.

"Oh, man. I'm a disaster." She winced up at Tag. "There's no way we can go to the Three Ghosts and Wishes thingy now." They wouldn't let her in wearing tar. Or, at the very least, shame would prevent her from attending it wearing tar. "Look at this thing, Tag. I'm not—I can't . . ." Surely he'd understand.

"I can fix this." He looked a little panicked, like this might be the last straw. His mouth pressed to the side, like it always used to when he was thinking. It was so cute she momentarily forgot her distress.

"I'm sure it happens all the time. We can still go." She wanted to reassure him.

"Geez, Juliet. I feel like a heel."

"A tar heel? Like from North Carolina?"

"This is so not how I envisioned tonight." He rolled his eyes.

"Not even the kissing part?"

"Well, the kissing part *is* better than I dared plan." He gave her a sly grin, and she held out her hand for him to kiss.

He may have gotten a drip of tar on his lip.

"I guess I'd better figure out a way to fix this." He pulled her toward the museum buildings.

"I can't exactly go in there—not covered in tar." They took a sudden left, up a curving ramp of a sidewalk.

"Don't worry. We've got this." He was so determined, how could she refuse him?

At the top of the ramp loomed LACMA's museum, the Pavilion for Japanese Art. Apparently a late-night event was going on in here as well, because the doors were ajar and both light and happy, almost-Christmasy music poured from them. They dashed in, past all the happy *sake* drinking partiers decked out in Japanese garb.

"I had a hard time deciding between this party and the one next door." Tag was still hustling her along. She saw a clock and noted there were only a few minutes left until their midnight event. No wonder he was in a hurry. "Quick. Take off the dress."

Juliet halted in her tracks and jerked her hand away. "Excuse me?"

"Come on, Juliet. There's no time." They'd stopped at a large counter with racks of odd fabric on hangers behind it. No one was manning it.

"Sorry, pal. If you think I'll be stripping down in front of you, you've got another thing coming."

"Oh, please. I've seen you in your swimsuit a thousand times. We did water polo together in high school, remember?" Exasperation tinged his voice. "You're not the type to go without underwear, so I'm sure you'll be fine."

His logic made sense, but Juliet clutched her dress nevertheless.

Then Tag broke out laughing and pulled one of the wide strips of fabric from the hanger. "Oh, come on. You can't blame a guy for trying. Here." He tossed her the fabric, which turned out to be similar to the garb all the party-goers near the foyer were wearing. "It's a kimono. I'll turn around. Whisk off your dress and wrap it around you. I won't look."

Juliet lifted the robe, eyed it, and then shook her head. She had a hundred names she wanted to call him—not all bad—but she obeyed. And he only peeked once.

"Sorry! I was sure you were finished."

"It's been three seconds."

He laughed, not quite wolfish, but bordering on it.

Soon Juliet had it wrapped around her. Tag rummaged around in the closet and pulled out a long, wide piece of satin fabric. "This keeps it on. Sadly, you'll want to keep it on."

"You know me well."

Tag paused a while. "Actually, I think it do."

Juliet paused, too. Inside her, something cracked. The little pip tooth of the baby chicken of trust had broken through its shell. Tag did know her. And she knew him. Whether it had been ten minutes or ten years, together they were on the same easy terms as always. But this time with a lot more kissing.

"Why didn't you tell me when you came home?"

"I was going to, but I wasn't sure how you'd react." With both his hands, he wrapped the long sash around her a few times.

He wasn't? Juliet looked at the hanging racks of fabric, and her soul tore in two. Half wanted to push him away—to keep herself safe from possible disappointment. Half wanted to clutch him to herself and never let go.

His arms at her waist felt right. So right. As he rested them there, he exhaled against her neck, and a shiver crawled up her skin.

Tag tied the ends of the fabric in the back, but while still

First and Last Christmas Date

standing in front of her, his arms doing the work blindly as their bodies pressed of necessity together.

"There. You're perfect, Juliet. Now, let's go make some wishes."

Five

THE HEELS, WHICH HAD SURVIVED the tar pretty well, and the kimono didn't exactly go together. And Juliet's kimono was the only bathrobe at the whole LACMA event. Well, except for the ghosts' bathrobe-type costumes.

"Come on. Let's pick a line. Which ghost do you want?" Tag handed her a plate of crab puffs. "Unless you want to skip the wishing and the two of us can wipe out all the artichoke dip and Li'l Smokies on the refreshment table over there."

"Tempting." Juliet scarfed down three crab puffs. It was all she could do not to talk with her mouth full, but she did manage to swallow. Ah, food in the gullet at last. "But I have some wishing to do."

"You too?" Tag gave her the smoldering look again. His eyes roamed up and down her kimono. He pressed a kiss to her neck and took a swig of his drink.

"You're incorrigible. So what's the deal here?" About three hundred people milled in the room, and another twenty stood in each line for the ghosts. "Is it like on *A Christmas Story*? You wait in an eternal line, then some maniacal elf says, 'Ho! Ho! Ho! You'll shoot your eye out, kid,' when you ask for the wrong thing?"

Tag choked a little on the combination of his drink and his laugh. "Maybe. What I read is you come with your wish, tell it aloud to the ghost, who will grant it if the spirit wills."

"Which spirit? My spirit? Or the spirit-ghost's spirit?"

Tag shrugged. "It wasn't clear." He smiled. "It *might* not be real, this wish-granting."

Juliet's insides churned with wishes. She ached for some kind of intervention from the Other Side. Because the clock of tonight with Taggart McClintock was about to strike midnight. And she didn't want to be Cinderella at the end of the ball, all her magic expiring, leaving her with nothing but a shoe. Or in her case, a basically stolen kimono (which Tag promised he would return or pay for as soon as humanly possible.)

Worse, she could be like Ebenezer Scrooge, who woke up and found it was all just a series of weird dreams. *But Scrooge was changed forever by that night.*

And so might Juliet be—either for the better, with Tag still at her side after this whole thing, or for the devastated when he (again) never called her for another date after the disasters of this night. He would think she was bad luck.

"Think of your wishes," Tag whispered, his hot breath in her ear as the line inched forward. "I know I am." He ran a hand up and down her back, letting it rest on her hip, just below the satin sash. It left her tingling.

A blizzard of wishes flurried around.

Tag was in her ear again. "You know, at the time that red dress was the hottest thing I'd ever seen. But you in nothing but a robe has me inventing all kinds of things to ask the Ghost of Christmas Yet to Come."

Juliet's heart stutter-stepped. Another hint fell—he wasn't thinking of this as a one-night fling, a duty to check off his list. She swallowed hard, but the lump in her throat lodged—like the question plaguing her mind.

Why hadn't he called after that first date? Why did he leave her dangling on a thread of hope, blown about by every gust of life's wind, longing for him?

Because, compared to Tag, every other man she'd ever known or dated or even talked to for more than a few minutes had left her feeling just as she'd been before: alone.

And if he left her again after tonight . . .

"So you have your wish ready?" The line had thinned, revealing the three ghosts sitting on garland-bedecked thrones in front of them.

Juliet's two minds went to battle: push and pull, open and close, trust and flee.

There was no one left in line behind them. They'd come so late, due to the many, many mitigating (and soon to be litigating) circumstances. They could take their time.

"You have to choose." Tag nudged her.

"Only one?" She thought she could request a wish from each. Disappointment flooded her. "Which ghost are you asking? Can we go together?"

Tag cocked his head to the side. "Well, maybe my wish is kind of private." The grin spread. "Maybe if you hear it, it won't come true. Like birthday candles." He walked toward Christmas Yet to Come, the scariest-looking spirit, the one with the scythe and the whole Grim Reaper thing going on. Juliet had originally planned to pose her wish to the future, but now, seeing him, she balked.

Voices bounced off the tile floors to the high ceilings in the emptying room. Someone flicked off half the lights.

First and Last Christmas Date

Juliet's eyes darted between her two remaining, non-Reaper choices. Should she ask for the Past to change things for her? To make that decade-gone Christmas different—their first date more of a dream than a nightmare, so she could have been with Tag all this time instead of without him? Or the Present—a wish that Tag would fall desperately in love with her? If she knew her magic lore right, it could never be used to alter someone's feelings of love. It was useless, and she didn't want to waste her one chance.

And suddenly, she knew which ghost she needed to see. She stepped forward, armed with, she knew, exactly the right wish.

Six

"So what did you wish for?" Tag handed her another napkin loaded with food. The caterers were cleaning it up already, and they headed out the door. "It took you a bit. I saw you at the Ghost of Christmas Present. Hah. I always think that's a bummer of a name. Like there was really no present for some poor kid under the tree, just a ghost of one."

Juliet popped another jumbo shrimp in her mouth. "Uh-uh. You first."

"Oh, uh. Right. Well." He scratched the back of his neck. "Apparently it's important that you not know too much about your future." He took a shrimp from her pile and ate it. "At least that's what the movies say. And we are in Hollywood."

She shot him a *Seriously?* look, and he relented.

"Fine. Okay. I'm still not going to tell you what I asked. But the ghost did have some surprisingly wise counsel—for a ghost, that is."

"Oh, really?" Juliet's own ghost had said some incisive things. "Go on."

"A lot of it was psychobabble, 'loving yourself' gobbledygook that he probably told everyone, but then he said something that struck me." They exited the building and walked out onto the piazza. Dead center was an art piece Juliet fell in love with instantly—an orderly grouping of dozens, maybe a hundred, iron lampposts, all of varying heights, all lit and glowing in the winter night. *Urban Light,* the placard read. Juliet relaxed as they wandered.

Tag guided her among the posts. "But when he was done with the script, he slid his hood off and looked right in my eyes. He used his normal tone of voice and said, 'Kid, because of Christmas, and what it means, every day is a future yet to come. You can start fresh every single day. That's the real gift of Christmas—hope for a future.'"

He paused a bit, looking up at the night sky, while Juliet watched his chest rise and fall.

"Then he took his robe off and said good night."

"Do you believe that's true?" she whispered.

He looked down at her. "I do."

Tag looked at her a long time, his eyes narrowing and widening alternately, like he was thinking something through or remembering and about to say something more. Juliet watched him, waiting. "But I forgot all the rest of what he said."

She gave his shoulder a little push. "You did not."

He gave hers one back. "Okay, fine. But I'm not going to tell you it tonight. Maybe someday." He kissed the tip of her nose. "You'll be safe if I leave you right here for a minute and go retrieve your red dress where I stashed it?"

She nodded, and he loped off, leaving Juliet alone with her thoughts for the first time in hours. Her conversation with the Ghost of Christmas Present echoed in her mind.

I'm afraid my wish will sound strange.

That is all right, my daughter. Express it anyway. The ghost believed in his character, played the part fully.

It's—I, uh. She hadn't known how to ask it, so she finally just spit it out in imperfect bluntness. *I don't wish for you to give me anything. I wish you could take something away.*

What is it, my child?

He hasn't hurt me, which makes my holding onto mistrust even more wrong.

Speak.

*Can you . . . take away—*she hiccupped—*fear?*

The spirit contemplated, humming an old carol, rocking back and forth. At last he said, *Yes. Your request is far different from the other requests I received on this night. You ask not for possessions or miracles to change circumstances. You ask me to give you a new heart.* He drummed his fingers on his rosy cheek. *I cannot do this for you.*

Juliet moaned a little. *But it's my deepest wish, Spirit.*

My daughter, the thing you seek is the gift of Christmas—of the first Christmas. Consider the Child in His mother's arms. He became a child to show you that you must too. Remember the heart you had as a child. That action will allow you to grant your own wish.

Now, as she stood shivering in this thin robe, her back cold against the stone post, waiting for Tag—always, always waiting for Tag McClintock—she looked up and saw him running toward her, across the brick piazza. All night she'd been drawn to him, drawn in by him. Just like she had as a girl.

The spirit was right. It was time to stop being an adult. To stop withholding portions of herself out of fear.

She would do it.

First and Last Christmas Date

As soon as she asked her most important question.

"Tag—after that first date, why didn't you ever call me again?"

He'd arrived, bearing the dress, and wrapped his arms around her again. Now he pressed his body against hers to warm it.

But after her question, he lost his jaunty smile. He now stared down at her, his face a mask of perplexity. It took too long for him to answer, and finally the anguish of silence overpowered her. She launched into nervous chatter—her default setting.

"I mean, to be honest, I had the best time of my life that night." She was talking too fast. "And I was pretty sure you did too—despite that thing with the snow plow and the storefront window. But then you went right back to Nadia, even though you'd told me she was, how did you put it? More vacuous than outer space?"

She shouldn't ever bring up another woman when she was trying to convince a man to think of only herself. Rookie mistake. Quick, steer it back! "But you and I, we'd been friends. Close, I thought. And you promised me to take me on my first date after my sweet sixteen. And you did! And it was incredible—just like tonight. It was Christmastime, with peppermint cocoa—in spite of the Heimlich maneuver and everything else, when it was over, I was ready for you to be my boyfriend, not just the boy next door."

Tag closed his eyes and furrowed his brow. He didn't loose his arms from around her, but he also still didn't speak.

Great. Terror racked her. She'd ruined it. Botched it by her never ending talking and leaps of logic and relationship assumptions—again. Like always. Worst of all, by asking about his feelings back then, she may very well be jeopardizing any budding feelings he was having right now.

The first date in a decade was hardly the time to do one of these Determine the Relationship talks. Idiot!

She'd have to fix it. Fast.

"But . . ." she backpedaled, her mind racing as her fear resurged and seized dominance of her soul. "But if you just weren't into me, and I misread everything wildly—as I always do; it's my nature—just forget I said anything." The babbling went on, and she wished now that she'd wished for an off-setting for her idiotic spigot.

Tag shook himself. "Wait. You're calling *this* date incredible?" He gulped visibly. "This date *and* our first one?"

"Of course," Juliet breathed—and in an instant, a star twinkled inside her, and her wish was granted. "I'm with you, aren't I?"

Tag loosed his embrace of her and stepped back. He paced in a broad circle around a half dozen pillars, rubbing his palm up and down his cheek. Then he stopped, right in front of Juliet.

"I thought you hated that date. Just like tonight has been a complete disaster from start to finish. To be completely honest, I can't even believe you're still here. Why haven't you called a cab yet?"

Juliet stared at him, almost exasperated. "Don't you know anything about human nature?"

Tag blinked in the night. "Apparently not." He waited for her to go on.

"Tag. Life isn't about doing things perfectly. It's about experiencing stuff. Together. The good times are fine. They're great. But the bad times all go into the mixer of experience and memory, and it polishes them up, like a rock tumbler. They become beautiful." She wasn't sure this analogy was working, but she didn't stop. "When we stop and look back at them, even the bad times are good memories—because of what we learned, or because of who we experienced them with."

Tag squinted. "You're saying I'm not just one big, bad memory to you?"

Juliet punched his shoulder and gave him a smile. "Well, maybe only the snowplow . . ."

"For the record, that thing with the snowplow was not my fault." He stood a foot away from her, slowly shaking his head.

Then his face went serious again. "Going back to your question, I guess I should ask why you said don't call me again for ten years."

Juliet clutched her heart, right over where he'd shot her. She had to grip the cold iron post to keep herself vertical.

"But Tag—it was figurative. I thought my crush on you was blazingly obvious from the time you were a Boy Scout and I was a nerdy girl with a crush."

Tag's mouth twitched. He blinked at her about a dozen times. "Hey, I was a kid. With a return crush, and cement mixer for brains. Deadly combo. I took you literally."

Now Juliet's soul was a cement mixer—all this information churning around and around in a thick slurry. Tag had a return crush? On her? And he only did what she had asked?

He stepped toward her, and she extended her hands. He took both of them in both of his. "If you check your calendar, tonight is ten years *to the very day* from that date. I've been marking time, waiting for tonight."

Juliet's mouth desiccated—because her whole insides had gone up in flames.

But he rubbed his hand up and down on his cheek again. He looked really manly when he was frustrated. "Now, tonight's experience is battling hard for first place in the tournament of worst dates of all time. I'm sorry. Really sorry, Juje. I meant for this to be perfect. Like you."

"Perfect! Not me."

"To me you are. Kind heart, good to your family, strong dose of integrity."

He went on, and the list didn't sound at all like he could be describing *her*. No. "It sounds more like your dossier to me."

Suddenly, she was eleven again. Trustworthy, loyal, brave, thrifty, clean, reverent, et cetera. Tag was reciting his memorized list of Boy Scout traits and giving her an electric high five. But now, here before her, stood successful businessman Tag. Caring for his family in their time of struggle. Keeping his word. Giving her a thoughtful gift. Stealing a kimono for her when she fell in tar. Now *that's* a Scout trait she could write in.

Wide-shouldered, handsome, James Bond but better. Taggart McClintock.

The pride and worry and hesitation drained out of her. She fell into his arms. "I don't know if this will make you feel any better, but all these ten years my heart was pacing back and forth, a tiger in a cage, wondering why you'd dropped me—when we were so obviously right for each other."

He looked down into her eyes. "I know, right?"

"Right?"

And then they were kissing. A lot, and he was lifting her up in his arms and carrying her while their mouths never lost contact. "It's time to take you home, Juliet."

She kissed him some more, and then on a trip up for air, she said, "No."

"No?" He kept kissing her, stumbled a bit but righted himself as they passed the big tar lake and their nemesis chipmunk. "It's so late, though."

First and Last Christmas Date

She pressed her mouth to his cheek, undid the top button of his dress shirt so she could kiss that muscle on the side of his neck. He groaned a little as she said, "I don't want this night to end."

"I'm sorry, but I don't think I can call you again until next Christmas." They'd arrived at his car, and he held the door open for her.

Juliet staggered backward. "What?" What was all this for, then? Her face must have contorted, because he lifted a finger and tweaked her nose.

"Hey, Juje. Remember, next Christmas is only—" he checked his watch, "—about thirty-six hours away."

And he kissed her before she could tell him off, while the cable of the grappling hook that attached Juliet's heart to him got fifty ply stronger.

"Thirty-six hours it is," she said into his ear with her husky voice. "Unless I can't wait and need you to call sooner."

"Deal."

Epilogue

Hot peppermint cocoa left a foam mustache on Juliet's upper lip. Tag, who clearly couldn't help himself, leaned in and licked it off. Then he sat back against the sofa and hit play on his phone's music app.

"Oh, no. Not 'First Christmas Date.' Bad juju there." She waved it away.

"Not for me, it's not." Tag nuzzled her hair and patted her rounding belly. "Without it, I might not be here with my baby, and my baby."

"But I thought you hated that song." Surely it brought back bad memories of when Tag punched a famous singer, got hauled into court for assault, pled his case—to which the judge merely said, *Not guilty on grounds of defending the sanctity of womanhood.* But the ordeal of standing trial still had to sting.

"Nah. It just reminds me of that night."

"Our second first date? I can't believe it's been two years. Two Christmases. Wow." They could mark their lives

First and Last Christmas Date

by Christmases. Their first date, their second first date, their wedding, and now, their baby. He kicked just then, giving her a reminder that he was nearly making his appearance. Being pregnant, with a boy, at Christmas—there was very little in this world that could be more special. "What do you remember most?"

"This." Tag tasted more cocoa off her lip.

"Kissing? I mean, it was pretty fantastic, but—"

"No. This. Us. Together. At Christmas with our own family and future and everything."

"What does it have to do with that night?" Well, other than the obvious, if they hadn't gone on a date, they wouldn't have ended up here. And then she remembered. "You didn't ask the Ghost of Christmas Yet to Come . . . for *this*."

Tag got a sly smile. "I most certainly did." He encircled her with the strength of his arms and hummed the tune of "First Christmas Date" into her ear 'til she could feel it in her toes. "Merry Christmas, baby."

ABOUT JENNIFER GRIFFITH

JENNIFER GRIFFITH and her husband live in Arizona, where they are raising their five kids in the desert where there's never a white Christmas. Sad, right? Because she loves Christmas—even got married at Christmas and had a baby on Christmas Day. But her trusty old SUV also never needs snow tires, so there's a trade-off.

Jennifer loves writing romantic comedy, which she calls cotton candy for the soul. She is the best-selling author of, among others, *Chocolate and Conversation*, *The Lost Art*, *Pandora* (from the Goddesses and Geeks series), and *Big in Japan*, the story of a blond Texan who goes to Japan and accidentally becomes a sumo wrestler, which has been optioned for film.

Visit Jennifer on-line:
Website: AuthorJenniferGriffith.com
Facebook: Jennifer Griffith
Twitter: @GriffithJen

Dear Timeless Romance Anthology Reader,

Thank you for reading *Under the Mistletoe*. We hope you loved the sweet romance novellas! Heather B. Moore, Annette Lyon, and Sarah M. Eden have been indie publishing this series since 2012 through the Mirror Press imprint. For each anthology, we carefully select three guest authors. Our goal is to offer a way for our readers to discover new, favorite authors by reading these romance novellas written exclusively for our anthologies . . . all for one great price.

If you enjoyed this anthology, please consider leaving a review on Goodreads or Amazon or Barnes & Noble or any other e-book store you purchase through. Reviews and word-of-mouth is what helps us continue this fun project. For updates and notifications of sales and giveaways, please sign up for our newsletter on our blog:

TimelessRomanceAnthologies.blogspot.com

Also, if you're interested in becoming a regular reviewer of the anthologies and would like access to advance copies, please email Heather Moore: heather@hbmoore.com

We also post announcements to Facebook as well: https://www.facebook.com/TimelessRomanceAnthologies

Thank you!
The Timeless Romance Authors

MORE TIMELESS ROMANCE ANTHOLOGIES

For the latest updates on our anthologies, visit our blog: TimelessRomanceAnthologies.blogspot.com